Warming Up

Warming Up

A NOVEL

Mary Hutchings Reed

Maureen —

Because you
have kind eyes,

Mary Hutchings Reed

SHE WRITES PRESS

Published 2013
Printed in the United States of America
ISBN: 978-1-938314-05-6
Library of Congress Control Number: 2012920390

For information, address:
She Writes Press
1563 Solano Ave #546
Berkeley, CA 94707

The ideas contained in the novel are solely the author's. All persons and situations portrayed are completely fictional.

For all those who work to make the world a kinder place, whether through art, education, or social services. The author will donate 10 percent of her proceeds to The Night Ministry, which offers housing, healthcare, and human connection to those struggling with homelessness, particularly Chicago's youth.

one

I'm a sucker for kind eyes.

And often, they're a sucker for me. That's why I like to meet my marks face-to-face before I make my first approach. I give them a chance to see I'm just a kid. I am, and I'm basically pretty harmless. I'm not a violent person, not like my dad. I don't mean to hurt anyone.

So, I hang around places where I know people can afford it if I take ten or twenty off them. Fancy restaurants and clubs aren't good—people rush by as if my mere presence on the same block as them could spoil their entire evening. Mostly, I go places where the people are rich enough but more likely to be sympathetic to those "less fortunate," as they like to call us. Places like art museums, the symphony, theaters, certain city churches. Recently I've been working outside Michigan Avenue doctors' and therapists' offices—there's a fair amount of upper middle-class guilt there, and that works to my advantage.

Not that I intend this to be my life's work. It's just what I do right now to get by. To support Charmaigne and the baby. Just until we figure out what's what and what's next.

two

Therapy was making her crazy.

In the lobby of her therapist's building, Cecilia stopped at the newsstand, bought a pack of Marlboros, and tore into it as soon as she stepped outside. She hadn't had a cigarette since the summer after her junior year in high school, when she'd gone to a music camp in Europe and drank wine with the Italian boys, sophisticated and worldly. She tried twice to light one, defeated both times by the wind swirling around the building. On the third time it took, and she inhaled deeply, but the smoke roughened her throat and she immediately coughed. Anyone watching would think her an amateur. She took another hit and her eyes watered. A woman came through the revolving doors behind her and gave her a nasty look, then pointed to a sign, NO SMOKING WITHIN 15 FEET. Cecilia looked back at the door and pointed at the sign herself to indicate that she understood and that she was well within her rights, but the woman had hurried away on her own business.

Late May. Neither summer nor winter; too volatile to be spring. She was enough of a Chicagoan not to believe in spring. She called herself a Chicagoan because, except for school and training and a few gigs at theaters around the Midwest, in all her nearly forty years, it was the only place she'd ever lived. If she belonged anywhere, it was here, but she did not have that feeling of belonging.

A man in a gray security uniform hurried out of the building.

She looked pointedly at the sign, reconfirmed her right to stand and smoke exactly where she was, and then marched toward the street, as if that had always been her intention. She coughed again and when she neared the bus stop, two gray-haired women in wool coats glared at her and moved inside the shelter. She positioned herself twenty steps away and took another drag. A young man, in a grass stained T-shirt and dirty jeans, approached.

"May I trouble you for a light, please?" he asked. His voice was thin, a tenor in need of training.

Wordlessly, she fumbled in her pocket and offered him her pack of matches. He turned his back to her and struck one, then another. She studied his worn bulging backpack, which appeared to be stuffed with clothes. Through a tear she saw plastic and the brown knit of a sweater. An outer pocket was unzipped, revealing a clump of loose white sheets, too many to be a term paper, too few to be a dissertation. He spun and faced her, inhaling deeply and smiling. She noticed then that he was very young, perhaps sixteen. She should've denied the boy the matches. He was too young to smoke. She abhorred smoking.

"Thanks so much," he said again, his manners impeccable. He shouldered the pack, and she noticed he was wearing sandals. A runaway? Living on the street?

"Which way is Union Station?" he asked.

She pointed with her own cigarette, its smoke drifting back at her.

"Walking distance?" he asked.

"Easily," she said.

He nodded, but made no move to leave. He seemed to study her face, with an interest akin to her deaf therapist's. Dr. Richardson probably wasn't deaf, but he kept repeating himself as if he hadn't heard her quite right. "Why" and "Why is that?" and, unapologetically, "How did that make you feel?" He was like a wild dog, scratch, scratch, scratching at dry earth, raising old bones.

"You have kind eyes," the boy said, which startled her, not so much that he would notice—often she'd been told she had nice eyes—but that he would call them kind, and that, at his age, he would voice such a thought to a stranger.

"Thank you," she said. Her purse hung at her side and, without taking her eyes off the young man, she pressed her nonsmoking hand against it. Although she'd lived in the city all her adult life, she'd never had a purse snatched or pick-pocketed, and she attributed that to being alert and having common sense. She didn't put herself at risk. She didn't walk alone at night, even in the nicest neighborhoods; always had her key ready in parking lots; avoided elevators if the only occupants were young men; carried a dollar bill in an easily accessible pocket and a twenty in the other so she could appease those few aggressive homeless men who, though possibly harmless, possibly weren't.

The young man fixed his gaze on her purse, then quickly looked both ways, as if to see whether they'd been noticed.

"West," she said firmly. "About twelve blocks."

He was roughly her height, but skinny, and pale. There was a thin layer of fuzz, reddish-blond, on his upper lip. He smiled, and she saw that his front teeth crossed ever so slightly. He worked his lips, as if deliberating.

"Thanks, again," he said finally. "See ya around."

She watched him walk to the corner, then turn left toward the Art Institute. She thought to call after him to let him know that he should've gone straight to get to Union Station, but as she raised her left arm, she saw the zipper of her purse a quarter of the way open, and was furious. She'd been on guard. How had he done it? She threw the last of her cigarette on the ground and unzipped her purse. Her wallet wasn't on top, and, rummaging around, she couldn't feel it. Damn! There was a bench in the bus stop, and she poured out the contents of her purse, disgusted with herself. Ridiculously, her wallet tumbled out. How could she have missed it? She opened it, saw that her money was there, and was immediately embarrassed that she'd misjudged the boy. He'd said she had kind eyes, and she'd repaid him with suspicion. She looked to the intersection as if to apologize, but he was out of sight.

Ashamed of herself, and further distressed to be distressed over such a meaningless encounter, Cecilia turned toward home, ten long blocks north over the Chicago River and five more east to the lake. She was feeling even crabbier than usual after a session with Dr. R. He'd hardly said anything that she could remember, but she felt almost physically sore from his poking and prodding, his professional snooping.

It was all Tyler's fault. Not long ago, they'd lunched, as they did only twice a year now, and Tyler, her coach and friend since her university days, had let her have it. Complaining about her plight— unemployed but well-off, talented but unknown, functional but depressed—she'd moaned, "I can't stand myself anymore."

"Midlife ennui! You are obviously depressed and have lost all direction and purpose in life," he'd pronounced. "You, my dear, need therapy."

She'd scoffed at his facile solution, insisting she was fine, but he'd ticked off a catalog of ills. "Fine? When's the last time you sang? When's the last time you enjoyed singing? When's the last time you went out—on a date? When's the last time you got any?" She'd squirmed, but he'd not let her off the hook. "Look it, darling, you know I love you. But I can't help you unless you help yourself. Tell me you want your old pep back. Tell me you want to have a life."

Despite herself, her eyes watered, and she'd agreed. The next day Tyler'd called with a name. He'd asked a lawyer friend of his who knew everyone. "Jack says this guy is the best guy for creative people." She'd taken his word for it, called Dr. Richardson, and now visited him weekly, impatiently waiting for the old man to tell her the meaning of life, or at the very least, to save her from her own monotonous, depressed self.

The following week, perched on the right side of Dr. Richardson's mustard-yellow corduroy couch, she found herself chatting with the therapist as if he were holding up his part of the conversation, which of course he wasn't. She was trying to explain to him, perhaps to herself, why she'd stopped singing.

"You go to auditions, people look you over."

Uncharacteristically, Dr. Richardson interrupted her. "What do they see?"

Kind eyes, she thought. The boy last week had said she had kind eyes, but that was not what the casting directors saw. "They don't see you," she said. "They only see whatever they're looking for. They barely hear you sing, a few verses, maybe, and then they decide you don't look right, or they owe a favor to another agent, or whatever. Meanwhile, you've wasted cab fare and God knows how much time and for what? Humiliation. I can't bear it."

"Didn't you have to audition or whatever to win that prize? Or to get the lead in the premiere you told me about?" The man did have a good memory, even if he acted deaf.

Le Prix de la Société de le Public. A minor prize, as classical music prizes go, but nonetheless, she'd won it in an international competition when she was twenty-five. At twenty-nine she'd sung the lead role in *Rumplestilt's Kin,* a world premiere at the Cadillac Theatre. It had been an odd play, a musical take on Rumplestiltskin, from the daughter's point of view, but Cecilia had, in her own estimation, nailed it. Opening night had been a thrill beyond any she could have imagined during her years of understudy, minor, and then supporting roles on city and regional stages. She hadn't told Dr. Richardson about the devastating review that closed the show: "Cecilia Morrison doesn't have the chops for the material this aspires to be, and was in no position Thursday night, struggling just to keep up with George Harris's aggressive accompaniment, to save it from its own shortcomings."

Cecilia's mother hadn't publicly acknowledged the show's closing, as if it were the most shameful thing that could have happened to her, and she simply stopped pushing her daughter toward auditions and prizes. Her father mumbled to her on the phone, "When He shuts one door, He opens another." Cecilia shut herself in her apartment.

"I hate auditioning, but I did it well," she said, trying to sound objective. She'd told Dr. Richardson she couldn't muster the interest in auditioning. She didn't tell him that the thought of singing for a casting director terrified her. "The trick with auditioning is to give the director what he or she wants. I'm pretty malleable. I'm easily transformed."

He raised his eyebrows.

"Transformed," Cecilia chuckled. She wished she could jolly Dr. Richardson along, make him like her so that he could figure out the answer to her question. "I bet you don't think so, or else what would I be doing here?"

She was there, in part, because she'd not sung in public for the past ten years. Even at her own parents' funerals. At the time of her father's death, she'd felt as if her throat had been crushed and her mother, whether out of sympathy or spite, Cecilia never could decide which, hadn't asked her to. Then, when her mother'd died a year ago, her brothers hadn't expected it.

Although she maintained friendships with a couple of people in the business, she never auditioned. Her women friends—also her competitors—didn't encourage her. They played along with the pretense that the press of family business consumed her time. In fact, her two brothers paid her a third of the profits to stay out of it and let them bicker over how best to produce and market industrial fasteners.

Even as she sat in Dr. Richardson's office, she hated herself for having chosen therapy. Her mother would say therapy was for weaklings, people who had no discipline, no control of themselves.

"I can be made to look a lot of different ways. I can take direction. But that's a problem, because most directors, at least the ones I ran into, didn't know what they were doing. You do what they want, and then some critic comes around and says they think you have potential but they don't like the way you were directed. Or they like how you were directed, but . . ."

"I'm sorry, Cecilia, I see our time is up."

Cecilia laughed. He was so serious, such a parody of himself. She wasn't sure why she'd felt so chatty today. Perhaps she was looking forward to her cigarette. She hadn't had one since last week, but she had her pack with her.

Outside, she stopped in roughly the same place, but the wind was from the opposite direction, and she hunched her back against it to strike a second match. When she turned around, the boy from last week was no more than six feet from her. This time she noticed he was blond and had pretty, pale blue eyes.

"Didn't mean to startle you," he said. "Remember me?"

She was momentarily confused. She did remember him, actually, but it would be unseemly to say yes too quickly. She half shook her head, letting her brows knit as if she were trying to recall how they'd met. He seemed to be wearing the same T-shirt as last week, its grass stain on the right chest joined by coffee spills in the middle. It occurred to her he was wearing the same jeans, and she stepped back slightly, breathing through her mouth.

"I bummed a light," he said, as if that were sufficient introduction.

"That's okay," she said. His light blue eyes conveyed complete innocence.

"Um, I don't how to say this. You were so nice to me last week. But I have a problem, and I need to ask someone for help."

She felt her body tense, guilty for her past rush to judgment, but still she squeezed her purse against her side as subtly as she could.

"I. Well. I was robbed. On the El. Last night. Money, cards, everything, my bus ticket home. I reported it and they gave me this." He pulled out a pink tissue carbon of something that looked like a citation.

She barely glanced at his proof, embarrassed to admit she didn't trust him. "Home?"

"To Indiana. My wife and baby are there. I was here to find work, but . . ." She must've looked as if she didn't believe him, because he interrupted himself.

"I know I look young, but I'm not, and they mean everything to me. It's about a hundred dollars round trip—about as far south as you can go and still be in Indiana. One way is fifty-three dollars. I could send you the money when I get home."

Sixty dollars. She had sixty dollars in her purse—three twenties—but it was a lot of money to give to a stranger. Panhandlers asked for a dollar, sometimes two for the El, a mother wanted three once for a gallon of milk for her child. Sixty? The story was so false it had to be true. Didn't it? No panhandler would have the gall to ask for sixty dollars.

Mimicking Dr. Richardson, she looked expectantly into his eyes, and the boy held her gaze without flinching, like someone telling the truth. Unzipping her purse, with one hand she opened her wallet and used her index finger to count three bills. She bit her lip, unsure why she was playing along with so obvious a con.

"You are so kind," he said. "I need your address."

She really didn't want the young man to have her address. She had a little notebook in her purse, and she wrote down, "H. Richardson," and the address of the plaza where they were standing. Cautiously, she held it out. "How old is your baby?" she asked.

The boy grabbed the paper and shoved it in his left pocket. "That's great. Thank you."

He rushed off, not giving her time to change her mind. Halfway down the block, he turned and waved. She noticed that, like the week before, he headed south on Michigan Avenue, not in the direction of the train.

The next day, Cecilia was restless. Although for most of the winter she'd limited her outdoor excursions to a weekly walk to the grocery store, Mass every other Sunday at Holy Name, and the occasional doctor, dentist, or hair appointment, the day after being conned by the boy, she felt imprisoned by her own luxury. Her forty-story building was bright and sunny, and located just off the lake. Built in the 1970s, it was solid, impervious to the noise of busy Lake Shore Drive. A twenty-four hour doorman and a round-the-clock garage man protected its inhabitants from intruders and nonbelongers alike, escorting workmen and delivery boys and announcing visitors. Cecilia's three-bedroom apartment was on the seventeenth floor. Most of the walls were painted a light gray, with bright white crown molding. Over the years, Tyler had selected half a dozen simply-framed splashes of color created by not-yet-famous friends of friends—most of the time these cheered her, though she understood none of them. Her building had its own indoor swimming pool and gym, which she used only at odd hours, usually late in the evening when she could more easily avoid her neighbors. There was also a dry cleaners on the first floor.

There was, in sum, little reason to venture out, but she was antsy, and had the urge to walk down Michigan Avenue to see what was happening. It was midmorning, and a walk would do her good, twenty-five minutes there and twenty-five back. She passed the cat lady and the Flintstones guy. She ignored the woman who camped on the Michigan Avenue Bridge with a pet carrier next to her and begged in a voice that sounded like a goat being hurled into the river below, "Feeeed my caaat, Feeeeed my caaaaat." Her cry for help reminded her of the boy. What was it like to be him? Was there a small home in Indiana where the boy and his young wife tucked their baby good night in a nursery lined in yellow ducklings and proudly displayed the infant's pictures in china frames? She stopped herself. What was she thinking? The boy no doubt slept in the park or on lower Wacker Drive.

The man with the first eight or twelve bars of the theme from the Flintstones was so bad she gave him a dollar just so he would stop playing long enough to say, "God bless you." Some part of her thought that the boy's act, with the gall to ask for sixty dollars, was far superior to these two. As she mulled his performance, reenacting every detail that had prompted her to comply with his outrageous request, it rose to the level of an art form.

"I can't believe I coughed up sixty dollars. I knew I was being taken, and I just let myself. Is that what you call progress, doctor? Does that show that I am less defended now than I used to be? Is that the kind of miraculous transformation I'm supposed to have here?"

"Just to be clear, Cecilia, I never suggested that you would have, or were supposed to have, a miraculous transformation. You came to me, remember, with certain issues, and you thought I could help you deal with them."

She fixed her gaze out the window. You'd think that someone you were paying big bucks to would be a little nicer to you. Dr. Richardson had a real tendency to piss her off. Over the past month or so of their relationship, she got stirred up right before her appointments, almost like she was itching for a fight, and he would neither overtly start one nor defend himself, hugging the goddamn neutral center. She'd been telling him about the boy and the sixty dollars, and he couldn't explain to her why she'd done it. She didn't say that she hadn't stopped thinking about the kid for a week, and that she'd returned to the plaza yesterday and the day before just to see if she might get a glimpse of him on the street.

"You wanted the boy to like you?" Dr. Richardson asked.

He so rarely started a thread of conversation, she wasn't sure she'd heard him right.

She shrugged. "I don't know where you get that."

"I get it from the fact that you did it," Dr. Richardson said evenly. "Why do you think you did it?"

"He needed it," she said, tossing it off.

"How do you know he needed it?"

"Because he asked," she said between clenched teeth. His obvious questions infuriated her, as if she were a child being taunted by a parent, being forced to answer a series of stupid questions that only led to the conclusion that one was stupid: Is the stove hot? What happens when you put your hand in fire? Did you put your hand in fire? Was it hot? Did you burn yourself?

"What would've happened if you hadn't given him the money?" he asked.

"I don't know," she said, and in the face of his silence, she played it out. "He wouldn't have hurt me, if that's what you mean. He just would've gone away; gotten the money from someone else."

She'd given the money because the boy asked. Simple as that. Perhaps another person wouldn't have, but so what? She'd heard a friend talk once about traveling to third world countries in a small sailboat and being asked by total strangers for pencils or gum, or even for her shoes. Her friend had said "no." The cruisers who'd said "yes" found it terribly uncomfortable and said they'd never go back; the ones who'd said "no," that they didn't have gum or pencils to give away and needed their shoes themselves, had actually become friends with the local people. The ones that could be guilted so easily had shown a certain amount of disrespect, and therefore had been disrespected as easy marks. The unapologetic ones, the ones who didn't claim to have so much that they could so easily spare it, had visited as equals; the askers hadn't really anticipated a "yes" and so weren't particularly disappointed. They were no worse off for having made the ask. She'd understood her friend, and it made some sense to her intellectually, but in her gut, she couldn't imagine not giving the gum or the pencils, when she had so much and the person asking had so little. Well, maybe not the shoes. The thought of that was kind of creepy, but it was only a matter of degree, not principle. Sixty dollars was like a pencil to her.

The session ended and Cecilia left feeling unsettled and expectant. She was itching from the confrontation with her young man.

He'd not gone to the train station! He'd not lost a train ticket! He'd taken advantage of her and her need to be loved. How unfair was that?

Everyone needed to be loved, or so the conventional wisdom had it. No, that's not why she'd done it. Even Dr. Richardson hadn't said she was a people pleaser, hadn't said that she desperately needed praise, applause, approval, love. He hadn't said that, and that's not why she'd done it. Not at all.

She finished one cigarette and lit another, angry. The young man was not in sight, would not slip up and show himself, would not return and beg for her mercy or understanding. He would not come home with her, clean himself up, go back to school, be saved. She had no idea where those thoughts came from. She flicked her cigarette, half unsmoked, on the ground and stamped it out. She was about to walk off when a student with a backpack caught her eye. With deliberate, slow dignity, she bent down, picked up the butt, and placed it in the gray plastic receptacle near where, two weeks ago, she'd met the boy.

Cecilia turned north on Michigan Avenue to walk home, irritated at Dr. Richardson for making her out to be so starved for love and attention that she would give a young boy sixty dollars with which he would buy booze and drugs. How dare the boy use the excuse of a wife and baby! And that she would fall for it. At least Dr. Richardson hadn't gone down that path, hadn't made some huge deal out of the fact that she didn't question the existence of the wife and the baby, that she'd so wanted to believe in their existence that she hadn't demanded to see pictures, had instead created her own vision of them, blond and innocent and hungry. Dr. Richardson was a waste of time. They were no closer to solving her immediate problem than they'd been a month ago, and now she was having these totally unrelated thoughts about babies.

The sun was shining and the early June day was promising to be glorious. She couldn't bear the thought of going home, staying inside, playing the piano, or reading. She turned around and headed for Millennium Park, thinking to sit by the flowing stream the landscape architects had thoughtfully built into the plan. She recalled that it had a Zen-like quality, and that no signs outlawed taking off your shoes and cooling your feet in it. On Michigan, she stopped to watch children playing in the granite fountain under the morphing gaze of two glass brick towers, the giant Plensa sculptures on the north and south ends. In between the diverse faces of the city, waterspouts jumped, soaking toddlers while their parents and nannies smiled on from the sidelines. On the opposite side from the street, she saw a blond girl in jeans and a drab T-shirt idly watching the kids while she pushed her own infant back and forth in a simple stroller. She was different from the others: too young to be the mother or a live-in nanny; too engaged to be a sibling. The baby-sitter, Cecilia concluded, and a bit young even for that. How did mothers gather the trust to engage young girls to care for their children? Weren't they afraid of what might happen in the event of an emergency, or, even not an emergency, just a situation that required good judgment? This mother obviously lacked judgment herself. The stroller was old-fashioned, flimsy. Most of the strollers she saw in the parks and on the streets in her neighborhood were like armored cars. In her building, if someone came into the elevator with a gray leather stroller with double wheels and a rucksack on the back, everyone stood aside. This one looked to be canvas, striped pink and white, an awning and a scooped seat, no doubt cheap. Probably second-, if not fourth- or fifthhand. She remembered the young boy saying kids were expensive. He may've been lying, but he wasn't wrong.

An expansive public space. A crowd, even on a weekday. Tourists and conventioneers, and non-English-speaking nannies who resided in the luxurious downtown condos—no place to raise a child—what better place to hide in public, pick a few pockets, search out a new target for a con? There he was, longish blond hair, shoulders rounded, squatting down and poking his finger at the baby's chest, standing up and reaching in his pocket and handing the girl something in a closed fist and then bumping his fist with hers and skipping, literally skipping, south and east, toward the gardens and the river and his next mark. Cecilia stood stunned, uncertain she'd seen what she'd seen. How many young blond couples must there be in a city of almost ten million? How many on Michigan Avenue, on a morning in early June? How many young men so smooth and skilled at the urban sleight of hand: casually in his pocket, quickly in hers, swinging at his side. Skipping off to work the crowds, the young wife confident that he'd return in the evening, bringing home the day's bounty, enough to get them by. There was no point in pursuing him. No use at all.

She was not conscious of a plan, but slowly she strolled the perimeter of the giant fountain, deliberately sidling next to the pink and white stroller. It squeaked softly from its worn tires as the girl idly pushed it back and forth. She used the sound as an excuse to notice the baby.

"May I?" She turned to face the girl, and then, without waiting for an answer, bent down to study the baby's face. She had big round brown eyes.

"Hello there," she cooed, aware that she was cooing, although she never cooed, hated cooing, found cooing condescending. "How old is—," she took a guess, "—she?"

"Five months," the girl replied, her voice weary. Cecilia imagined it had been a long, tiring five months, in and out of shelters, long waits in clinics, long cold walks to stay warm.

"She's darling," Cecilia said, standing up. The girl smiled a tired, lopsided smile. Her eyes were as icy blue as her baby's were brown.

"Live around here?" Cecilia knew immediately she'd pushed too far, too quickly. The girl straightened, stopped rocking the stroller, looked around her as if for the closest exit.

There was an extra beat before she answered. "Close," she said, not inviting further inquiry from a nosey stranger. A better liar, like the boy, would've pointed to the top of one of the indistinguishable green-glass high-rises across the river and said unequivocally, "There."

Cecilia felt her cheeks redden. She had no idea how to continue this conversation. Would Dr. Richardson say she was so self-absorbed that she couldn't think of a routine nicety to say to a young mother on a lovely morning? Or would he think her silence just another fear of public performance? Would he jump to the conclusion that it had something to do with babies?

"Nice day," she said, recovering herself.

The girl nodded, and rocked the stroller, as if getting up the energy to leave.

"Nice to talk to you," Cecilia said. "Maybe we'll see each other here again." She quickly turned, desperate to be the first to leave, not to be left by this scruffy girl and her plain, very ordinary baby.

three

.

Every approach is different. I learned something that first week, when I just lost my courage. You looked so sad, so kind of empty. I could tell by the way you held your cigarette—you don't smoke much, do you? You pinched it so hard you dented the filter. And, your timing was off. You kept looking at it as if you weren't sure when to flick the ash. Real smokers know how long between taps, force of habit.

So I realized after I left you last week that I'd laid the groundwork, so to speak. I figured the plaza had a bunch of doctors' offices and such. It's a high-rise. Downtown, a lot of them have CVS's and Walgreens and Starbucks on the ground floor, then doctors' offices and—I don't know, fertility clinics!—and then expensive apartments on the upper floors. You see a lot of people sitting on the benches and on the edges of the planters, smoking, watching, dabbing their eyes, some writing notes—so I figure there are a bunch of shrinks in there, too. When I was in high school, they sent me to a counselor once a week for a whole semester. I know the drill. It didn't make me want to learn trigonometry, though, or read Shakespeare, so when I was sixteen and a half I left. My folks had four other kids, and I'm not convinced that they missed me all that much. I send my mother a letter once a month, though, just so's I don't add to her worry.

Anyway, I came back the next week because I needed the money. I liked you, liked how you tried not to look alarmed when I approached you, how subtle you were about the purse, which, by the way, was one *quarter unzipped and easy pickin's had I been so inclined. But we needed food, and I've been trying to get us enough to maybe get a place some-where. I was thinking if we moved out to the end of the train line, maybe we could find a small house, and maybe I could work in a restaurant or something. I'm not afraid of work. When I'm eighteen, I suppose it will be easier to get a real job. Even waiting tables, somehow they think you gotta have a high school diploma. I don't know what for.*

I knew you'd give me the sixty. You looked happier that day. I was sweatin', though. I'd never asked anyone for that much. No one had ever given me more than twenty. I remember that time, it was like Christmas. In fact, it was December, and it was cold, and I'm sure the fact that Charmaigne was out to here helped. But I did the asking, and she just stood there, looking pregnant.

Yeah, and the nurses at the ER got together and gave us one hun-dred dollars when we left with our baby. Charmaigne is so pretty, and I guess we looked young, and they were worried about whether we would know how to take care of a baby, but of course we did. We know as much about taking care of babies, more probably, as all those busi-ness people who park their babies with nannies. But it has been pretty expensive, though, more expensive than we realized. We're good about keeping up with clinic visits for the baby, and getting good nutrition for Charmaigne. Charmaigne found a nice shelter for women and stayed there a few weeks during the worst part of the winter. We got our wires crossed and I didn't see her or the baby for four days. I kept going back to our usual places, and waiting where I thought we'd agreed to meet, but it took until the fourth day for us to hook up. Turns out Charmaigne had had a flu bug and the nuns at the place where she was, they wouldn't let her out!

No, a letter to my mom is good enough. If I were to call, there would be too many questions, and I don't have very good answers yet. With my mom, the questions always have right and wrong answers, and I'm not on the right side yet—no job, no GED, no plans to go home.

Oh, the sixty. Long gone! Like I said, it's expensive to have a kid. The pink carbon? I just found it. I knew you wouldn't study it. Don't you wear reading glasses? Most women your age do—I'm sorry, I guess I don't know your age—and besides, if you insist on reading it, I just cut and run. Nothing to lose, and all you've got on me is a pink whatever. Not even my name. You know, you never asked my name.

four

A week later, a friend had an opening of his junkyard sculpture at a trendy gallery on the North Side, and, because it was rush hour, and parking in the area was notoriously unavailable, Cecilia decided to take the Redline train. Not used to the procedures, she purchased a fare card, and then tried it four different ways in the slot at the turnstile, while a line of impatient commuters and baseball fans grew behind her. She felt spatially inept. Even after reading, THIS SIDE FACING YOU, and following the small yellow arrows, the slant of the slot threw her off, and after she successfully gained entrance, the mechanics continued to occupy her thoughts as she trudged down the stairs with the hordes.

Despite the crowd, it was curiously quiet in the concrete tunnel, although many wore Cubs T-shirts and caps, and the fans paced or swayed, anticipating a night game at Wrigley Field. In contrast, stiff, weary regulars on their way home from work stood reading folded newspapers or staring down the tracks, listening for the faint rumble of a coming train. Cecilia walked to the middle of the underground station, and there was surprised to hear the simple chords of a guitar and a man's voice, a light tenor, braving its way through a street musician's classic, "Sitting on the Dock of the Bay." The best of the city's street musicians picked sites like these, pedestrian underpasses, the long corridors at O'Hare, building overhangs, recessed church steps, any place where the structure would provide an acoustic reverb, the sound technician's secret weapon against thin voices or not quite true pitches. This voice was better than that, she sensed, and the echo enriched it even more.

At first she couldn't find the source. Whoever he was, he was not flamboyant. Not like the Naked Cowboy who strummed for a living in Times Square in his jockey shorts and cowboy boots, or like Vincent, the man in the brightly colored suits who waved to the tour boats from the Michigan Avenue Bridge and made it his business to be in the background of almost every on-the-street television shot.

"Thank you, bless you," she heard the voice say, and despite herself, she gasped. She feigned a cough, covering her mouth, and casually turned around, surveying the tunnel. There! Next to a pillar a train car's length away from her. The boy!

"Howard," she heard him say, pointing to the red HOWARD STREET sign behind him indicating the platform for the northbound train. "Call me Howard."

She bit her lip. She doubted he had sixty dollars in his open guitar case, but whatever he had was hers. He owed her. He'd said he was going to Indiana. He hadn't. He'd stayed, and he'd continued to con people and pick their pockets and prey on their kindness, and he'd stayed in her head. Now he was passing himself off as a musician, a performer, someone like her. The nerve! She elbowed her way through the crowd and stood fifteen feet away, hidden in part from his view by a couple of young men dressed in gray T-shirts with large red "C's." She was pretty sure he didn't see her, although she could tell that there were only a few singles in his case, along with some quarters.

"Cupid, pull back your bow," he crooned, choosing another subway standard. He was good. His tones were firm, well-rounded, mellow. No Sam Cooke, but a good rendition, nonetheless. She looked around and wondered what it would be like if the entire station sang along. The image delighted her and she forgot her aggravation. She turned her back to the boy and sang softly to

24

herself, then a little louder, "Right to my lover's heart. . . ." A couple black teens yelped and started laughing, although not, it seemed, at her, then flanked the boy to provide improvised harmony. A mother with a young child in hand joined, and soon there were a dozen people singing along, and, more important, when they finished, she heard the clatter of coins, and a litany of, "Thank you, bless you, thanks so much." The Cubs fans high-fived and a quartet of young men, perhaps loosened by a long lunch, started their own fraternity-style rendition of an off-key, "Take Me Out to the Ballgame," and Howard strummed along and repeated his thank-you's as dollars dropped like manna into his case.

A train barreled in, and the euphoria ended as quickly as it had started. Her side of the landing poured onto the cars, leaving her exposed. The boy was bent over the guitar case, gathering up a fistful of dollar bills, and leaving three. He stashed his money in his front right pocket, then he spotted her. He jerked upright, as if perhaps to flee, but once upright, appeared composed, almost cocky.

"Thanks," he said. "You doubled my take with one song."

She wanted to say that he owed her sixty dollars, but she was curiously touched that he had recognized her voice, muffled though it had been, and before she could respond, he said, "I owe you." He reached for his left pocket and pulled out two fives and a few ones. He held the bills out. "First installment?"

She started to take the money—she'd earned it—when she saw a girl dragging a pink and white striped stroller up the far stairs, an infant strapped to her front. She couldn't tell for sure that it was the girl she'd met at the fountain, but it didn't matter. What if it were the boy's girl and his baby? Surely they needed the cash more than she.

"Another time," she said.

"Okay," he said, without hesitation.

Around them, the station began to fill again, swelling like a bellows about to blow its contents into the coming trains. Do it again?

She realized they were staring at each other, perhaps in the same amazement that they'd stumbled onto a unique phenomenon. Singing commuters! Perhaps the Mayor, who put flowers down the middle of every street and painted cows on corners and sculpture along the lakeshore, would start a campaign for Singing in the Subways. Hilarious!

The boy smiled broadly, as if in agreement with whatever she was thinking, and nodded. There was a large crowd now, and a couple of people standing between her and him. He threw back his head and started with a long "Day-o, Day-ay-ay o," which echoed off the walls and conjured up palm trees and sand amidst the dirt of the tunnel.

"Daylight come and me wan' go home." He finished the first verse and threw it to her, standing just a few feet opposite him as she stood in the "audience."

"Work all night on a drink a' rum," she sang, sweet and clear and startling to the people around her, who, as a group, stepped back, clearing the path for the duet between the two. This time, no one chimed in. The growing crowd—twenty-five? thirty?—stood as if mesmerized, no longer staring blankly at the billboards and their papers, but looking at the performers, as if the subway platform were a stage.

Cecilia and the boy tossed the song back and forth, and she let him lead, filling in backgrounds and harmonies and improvised flourishes, and then a rousing last verse together, ending, "Daylight come and me wan' go home."

There was a sprinkling of applause and a surprising round of generosity, a mother taking her daughter by the hand to let her drop two quarters in the boy's open guitar case, a teenage girl with too much blue eye shadow smiling flirtatiously as she gave him a dollar and scooted back to her group of giggling friends, a kind-looking lawyer-type in a gray suit, perhaps a musician himself, who'd clapped in syncopated time to the island song, dropping five. "You sound professional," the lawyer-type said, leaning close to her ear.

The train roared in, sucking up the crowd, and the boy scooped up his earnings and put them in his right pocket, again leaving a few dollars resting suggestively on the worn red velvet of the guitar case.

"Keep this up, I can pay you back with interest," he said, and strummed a few chords.

Suddenly angry, she shrugged, reached out her hand to stop the doors from closing, and crowded onto the packed train, not looking back. She felt her cheeks burning, conned again! He'd offered her the measly contents of his left pocket, and she'd refused. Something had come over her—no doubt the image of the girl and her baby—and she'd sung, she'd totally embarrassed herself, at least had risked embarrassing herself, to help him out. She'd doubled his take. Twice. And how did he thank her? He'd put his take, like probably all of the day's takes, in his right pocket, leaving the left to plead poverty, like the few remaining bills begging for company in the open guitar case. Anticipating her demand for her money back, he'd made it look like he was willing, but not able.

He'd offered her only a first installment, not the whole of it, and, sorry for him and the girl with the stroller and, even, for the cat lady and the Flintstones guy, she hadn't demanded any of her money back. What was it about the boy that so possessed her? She didn't even know his name, let alone have a relationship with him. All the more reason she needed to figure out this depression or whatever it was. It was making her do crazy things.

The next day, before she could sit down on Dr. Richardson's couch, he handed her a long white business envelope. "I believe this is for you," he said, holding a corner between his thumb and index finger, as if it had germs.

She read the block printing of the address. "H. Richardson."

"It has your name on it," she said.

"It has sixty dollars inside. Three twenties."

She nodded, and he outstretched his palm, indicating she

should sit. Without opening it, she shoved the envelope in her purse. As usual, he waited for her to begin.

"So, how does that make me feel?" she mimicked him. "Toyed with," she answered her own question. "I don't get it. Yesterday, I sang with him. He offered me the money—I'd helped him earn it— but I didn't take it."

"You sang with him?" Dr. Richardson sounded incredulous.

She told him her story, and he retreated. "How did you feel?"

"I just told you, stupid as hell. It's like he's a hypnotist or something. He claps his hands, and I hold out money."

"Yes, it seems that way about the money, although you only gave it to him once. Yesterday was more like a failure to get it back, and today, he made good." He paused, as if he had only recited the facts. "But, I meant about the singing. How did it feel to be standing in a subway singing for a bunch of strangers?"

"Nothing special. What should I have felt?" She used "should" because he'd often said, "There are no 'shoulds,'" and she thought that was ridiculous. Of course there were 'shoulds.' She could hear her mother's voice, refined, but commanding: "You should practice, dear." "You should sing the German song." "You should wear the white gown."

"I'm not saying these are 'shoulds,' but I imagine you could've felt many things: happy, friendly, helpful, nervous, frightened, foolish, criticized, crazy, sucked in. . . ." He spread his hands in a gesture suggesting infinity.

She closed her eyes, trying to picture herself in the subway right before she opened her mouth. It wasn't as if she'd sung in public public. Not a paying public or critic public or any public she cared about. No one in the subway except the boy, and perhaps that lawyer-type, even seemed to notice her singing in particular. His singing had been so very ordinary that the black boys and the frat boys and then a few of the young women, all had felt free to join in, and not one of them probably heard the difference in her trained, practiced, superior voice. "I just wanted to help him. I wasn't thinking about singing."

There were five minutes left in their session, but she didn't want to think about the subway anymore and she let the time expire, thinking to herself how foolish she was to be paying an old man for advice he seemed determined never to give. He hadn't even asked the question that was becoming more important to her than any: Why was she so intrigued with the boy?

She left the building, not stopping for a cigarette, and hurried across the street. She was done with smoking. She wasn't sure, it may have been the damp, stale air of the subway station, but yesterday, singing with the boy, she'd heard a tiny scratch in her voice, perhaps the product of the cigarettes she'd permitted herself these past few weeks. At any rate, smoking didn't help her voice any, and so she entered a coffee shop, ordered a double skim latté, and sat in the window bar, watching her corner. After about an hour, he hadn't appeared.

She spent the afternoon at the Art Institute and at about four-thirty, having wandered from room to room and from century to century, she walked to the Redline subway station on State Street where she'd sung, just yesterday, with the boy. She didn't believe for a minute that his name was Howard, and so, until he told her something more credible, he remained to her "the boy." She reloaded her card and on the second try passed through the turnstile and descended the stairs. She heard a train grumble out. If he was there, he would be fairly easy to spot. All she wanted to do was to say yes, she got the envelope and that he had, in some small way, renewed her faith in people. Maybe she wouldn't say the last part, but she told herself that was why she had to see him one more time.

The station was just beginning to fill. Again, near a post in the middle of the station, next to the red rectangle with the white HOWARD lettering, the boy stood picking at his guitar. He spotted her at once and started toward her, his head cocked to one side to keep an eye on his guitar case.

"Dr. Richardson," he said, with a bow.

"Stop," she said, embarrassed that someone might see. What

would they think? That she was his mother? Technically, it was easily possible, though unimaginable to her. His teacher? His employer, like a modern day Fagin, forcing her kids to sell songs rather than candy bars and magazines? She drew herself up, and folded her hands in front of her, striking a formal pose. "I just wanted to say," she said, recognizing that she'd adopted a slightly British accent, "that I received your envelope. Thank you."

"No, no," he said, "thank you, Dr. Richardson," and he bowed again, holding the position.

"Stop," she said, this time through gritted teeth. She glanced from side to side. "And my name is not Dr. Richardson."

He looked up from his bow with the relish of a court jester, and flailed his arms in a windmill as he bounced up. "Damn! I told Charmaigne you weren't a doctor, but she said you probably were a shrink, and made up a whole story about how your patients drove you crazy and that was why you had to go see your own shrink, because you absorbed all of their problems like a sponge, and you had to go to another doc in the Plaza building to wring them out."

His unbridled energy invaded her irritation, and she found herself amused that they'd been talking about her and delighted to know the boy's wife's name. "How is Charmaigne? And the baby?"

He looked at her quizzically, not sure how she knew, and was about to say something, perhaps to deny it, but another teenager, with a guitar strapped to his back, eyed the boy's open case, and the boy spun and jogged back to the post to protect his turf. She saw the boy reach in his left pocket—the nearly empty one, she recalled—and give the interloper a few bucks.

He started to whistle and then he started to sing, unaccompanied.

> *"Sittin' in the mornin' sun*
> *I'll be sittin' when the evenin' come*
> *Watching the ships roll in*
> *And then I watch 'em roll away again, yeah."*

He added a few chords, sang the second verse, and then looked squarely at Cecelia and sang the third verse:

"I left my home in Georgia
Headed for the 'Frisco bay
'Cause I've had nothing to live for
And look like nothin's gonna come my way."

She sniffed back her tears, ashamed. This boy might be homeless, but a slight tremor in his voice convinced her: He had something to live for—the girl he'd called Charmaigne and his baby girl. And he could sing, not perfectly, but better than most. Where did they sleep at night? On a loading dock? In a doorway? Over a grate? Would a shelter even take a family?

She let him finish his solo, and was happy for him that four or five people dropped some change and dollar bills in the case. He left the money where it lay and struck up another tune, a duet, but he sang both parts of the first verse, then pointed the guitar stem at her. She stood facing him, and remembered Cher's lines:

"They say our love won't pay the rent
Before it's earned, our money's all been spent"

And he answered:

"I guess that's so, we don't have a pot
But at least I'm sure of all the things we got
Babe."

She smiled broadly, laughing at the ridiculousness of it and joining in, "I got you babe. I got you babe."

As before, her voice, pure and rich and so clearly meant for the stage, attracted the attention of the crowd. She was dressed casually, in khakis and a black T-shirt, and while she didn't look as young as the boy, she clearly didn't look like his mother, either. She imagined that others saw her as a victim of the recent downturn in the economy, divorced, overmortgaged, laid-off, perhaps once a school teacher. She was almost them. They responded by filling the boy's case with more dollars than quarters. She was good for his business, and it made her feel good about herself.

"So, do you have enough for the rent for tonight?" she asked him in the lull after the next train stopped, filled and left.

"Depends where Charmaigne wants to stay," he said, adopting his own grand accent. "Don't believe 'twill be the Ritz," he said, as if he were his own man-butler. "But something adequate shall turn up, I suppose. Could you be so kind as to put forth a recommendation?"

She laughed. "Quite good," she said. "Or should I say jolly good?" Their banter reminded her of the banter of actors between acts or at auditions or at parties, posing, pretending, searching for a comfortable persona. Using other people's lines to avoid having to write their own. She understood herself, shy as she was, to have played that game, back when she was living the life.

"Nothing too 'too,' I should say. Comfortable, yes. Ostentatious, quite out of the question."

As they played back and forth, she tried to calculate the cost of living hand-to-mouth for three people, one of them a baby. Even if there were someplace reasonable to stay, what would that be, fifty, sixty, seventy dollars? And food, and diapers, and getting around.

"Where do you stay, usually?" she asked, genuinely curious.

"Around," he said. "Depends on the weather." She understood immediately, and she remembered all the vagrants—that's what her mother had called them—sleeping on park benches and grates and squeezed in the nooks and crannies and behind the pillars of city buildings. "I know a place," she said, dropping the accent. "I. I have an extra room, that you and—Charmaigne, is it?—and the baby, of course, could use. Tonight."

What was she saying? What was she thinking? He could steal her blind! He'd probably bring drugs, or lice, or both. What if the two of them overwhelmed her, stabbed her, tossed her body? How long before they'd be found out? Or what if something happened to one of them? How would she explain it to the police? That she met a boy and brought him home, with a girl—probably not more than sixteen herself, whom he said was his wife, and an underweight infant, probably malnourished and colicky?

It was only one night. She had a doorman who could identify the culprits. They had a baby. The building had security cameras in the garage. The girl didn't seem violent. What could happen in one night?

The boy eyed her. "You don't know my name," he said.

"Howard?" she said, shrugging.

"Why would you do that?" he asked.

"You need a place to stay, don't you?" she said, adopting a matter of fact, business-like tone.

"We do," he said, and his voice cracked. "My name is Kix."

five

Cecilia used one spare bedroom as a study and den, and the other for company. The guest room had a double bed with an old turquoise quilt that one of her aunts had given her for her thirtieth birthday, when the aunt deemed her old enough to appreciate the quality of its hand stitching. In fact she liked the quilt a lot, so much that she displayed it in a room used only for show, like a museum. She had few guests, so the quilt, while old, had aged nicely.

Cecilia'd done all the things to be done for guests. She'd stopped at the convenience store next to her apartment building and bought bacon and eggs, orange juice and two kinds of cereal, Rice Krispies and Corn Flakes, the kind of food she thought guests might expect, even though she herself had been well-trained by her mother to be ever-conscious of her weight and the foods she ate. She bought whole milk rather than skim, thinking Charmaigne might need it for the baby, and she bought some baby food, although she'd had trouble doing that. Standing in front of the shelves of choices labeled as "First," "Second," and "Third," she felt ridiculous, a sad excuse for a woman. Here she was, nearly forty years old, and she had no idea how to buy food for a baby. If it was six months old—and that was only a guess—what stage was it in? How did Charmaigne, at sixteen or seventeen, know? Why didn't Cecilia know? Because you are a depressed, self-centered, crazy spoiled brat, that's why, she said to herself, and chose two Firsts, two Seconds, and a cereal, all organic; applesauce and carrots, and dinners with adult sensibilities, chicken and wild rice, and vegetable turkey and barley.

Now, she double-checked that there were hangers in the closet, put two sets of thick fresh towels on the bed, and took a Waterford vase and sterling brush set from the bureau and stashed them in her own room. She had a safe in her closet, and she put the sterling there, along with her "best" jewels, a three- carat diamond dinner ring that had been her paternal grandmother's, a fine gold chain from her parents when she turned twenty-one, and a strand of thirtieth birthday pearls from her father. She added a few other items she considered "heirlooms," and a couple of pieces, like the hundred-strand liquid silver necklace from a trip to Santa Fe, that weren't particularly valuable except that they were her favorites. She draped a towel over the safe in her closet, just in case, although she told herself Kix wouldn't dare rip her off, and even if he found the safe, he wouldn't know the combination. She assured herself he wasn't the type to torture it out of her.

Nervously, she glanced at her watch. Seven thirty. Kix had said that he was going to go "meet up" with Charmaigne, and then they'd come over. "Charmaigne's really going to dig this," he'd said.

She put a wooden bowl of corn chips and salsa on the coffee table in her living room and poured herself a glass of red wine. She didn't want the boy to see the opened alcohol, so she put it behind the soap box on the shelf above the washer and dryer in the laundry closet. It seemed an unlikely place to look for booze. By eight o'clock she'd finished the first glass, and feeling like an alcoholic, searched the laundry closet to pour herself another.

How would she ever explain this to Dr. Richardson? She decided she wouldn't. First thing in the morning she would call and cancel this week's appointment. By the time she saw him again, the kids would be long gone and it would be none of his business.

At eight thirty, the doorman rang her apartment to say that

Kix Gordon was in the lobby with "a girl and a baby." She said to send them up, finished the last of her wine, and put the glass in the dishwasher.

She opened the door and waited, so they would know which way to turn when they got off the elevator. There were only four apartments per floor, but still, she wanted them to feel comfortable. The pink stroller appeared first, then the girl, and then Kix, carrying two backpacks. He spotted the open door and gave the girl a little encouragement on the shoulder. Charmaigne was indeed the girl Cecilia had met at the Millennium Park Plensa sculptures. She wasn't sure if she should remind Charmaigne of that or just treat Kix's hurried introduction as a first meeting.

"Charmaigne, this is Cecilia, who sang with me in the subway," he said as they approached the door to the apartment.

"We've met," the girl said flatly, neither surprised nor bored. Cecilia sensed that she was not as enthusiastic about her overnight lodgings as Kix had thought she'd be. If living on the street was still a game of sorts to Kix, the girl's failure to meet Cecilia's eyes suggested that the novelty of the challenge, if she'd ever enjoyed it, had become shameful. As a mother, the girl's instincts for nesting and creating a safe home for her baby were no doubt offended by the itinerant nature of her life with Kix. Cecilia noticed that the girl wore an opal ring on her left hand. Charming though Kix could be, Cecilia could not imagine that this was the life the girl had dreamt about.

"I'm so happy to see you again." Cecilia said, closing the door behind them and then bending down to the baby, asleep in the stroller, her bottle by her side.

"She usually stays home while I'm working," Kix said protectively, and Charmaigne shot him a look.

"Come in, come in," Cecilia said. "Let me show you your room." She led them down the hallway, away from the kitchen and living areas. Kix plunked down the backpacks with a thud.

"Where's your guitar?" Cecilia asked.

"Stashed it," he said. "Hey, Char," he said, turning away from her. "Look at this. A quilt just like . . ."

The girl glared at him.

"Like something at the Ritz!"

"Are you hungry?" Cecilia asked. "I have some cheese and crackers. Salsa? A Coke maybe? Something for the baby?"

"Famished," Kix answered. "What about Abby?" he asked the girl.

"I have," she started, and rummaged around in one of the backpacks, as if it were full of nothing but provisions for the baby. After a minute, she took out a single jar and said, "She'll have this."

Seeming more his age in Cecilia's living room than on the street, Kix fidgeted as Charmaigne, sitting stiffly upright, carefully fed the baby, a cloth on her lap. Between spoonfuls, the baby drooled a steady stream. Kix paced around the room, idly plinking a few keys on the baby grand in one corner, inspecting with more interest her state-of-the-art stereo in the other. He took her iPod out of its station and flipped through her lists. Cecilia didn't want to hawk him, but didn't want to create temptation either.

"Afraid I'm not very hip," she said, laughing so awkwardly that she felt even less than hip. "'Hip' probably isn't even the right word anymore," she hurried.

Kix flung around and shot her a look that swept from fury to apology in a split second. Cecilia's heart pounded. She hadn't meant to offend him, but he was known to be a con and a pickpocket. What did he expect? As if reading her thoughts, Kix nodded and returned the iPod to the station, and then stood for a while before the south-facing windows. The view was one of the things that had attracted Cecilia to the building: the lakefront stretched from Monroe harbor, with its hundreds of moored boats, south as far as Gary, Indiana, where, on certain days, the atmosphere created the illusion that the city's factories and smoke stacks rose three times their height, shimmering a rosy gold.

"Where are you from, Charmaigne?" Cecilia thought to ask.

"Wisconsin," the girl answered, and Cecilia felt rebuffed.

Perhaps sensing that Charmaigne's answer bordered on rude, Kix turned from the view and plopped himself on the wrap-around gray leather couch, at the opposite end from Charmaigne. "I'm from Normal, Illinois!" he said, laughing. "Isn't that perfect?"

"Not perfect, dummy," Charmaigne said. "Normal." The girl seemed to enjoy the word play. Her baby had fallen asleep in her arms, and she leaned back on the couch, relaxing. Cecilia could understand how the girl, probably from a small farm town just over the Illinois border, might at first feel overwhelmed by her good fortune to have landed in such an elegant place, and she was glad Charmaigne was finally comfortable.

"How big is Normal?" Cecilia asked, eager to keep a conversation going.

"I dunno," Kix said. "Bigger during the school year. My dad teaches physics there."

Never having been to Normal, Cecilia pictured a college town in central Illinois, a place where, she imagined, everyone knew everyone and kids rode bikes all over town and played outdoors in their back yards, safe and unthreatened. "Can I ask why you left home?" she ventured.

Charmaigne raised her chin, shot Kix a look, and twisted away from Cecilia to look out the window, where the lights were coming on in the buildings along the lakefront. Kix caught Charmaigne's signal, and stood up. "We're really tired. Can we go to sleep now?"

"Sure," Cecilia said, springing to her feet with forced energy. She shrugged. "I didn't mean to pry."

"Come on, Char," the boy said. "Get up."

Cecilia turned off the lights in the living room and kitchen and guided her guests back to their room. "I'm usually up early," she said. "Sleep well."

She was about to close the door to her own room when she heard Kix behind her. She turned and he was not even an arm's length away. "Thank you," he said. "This is really great."

"Good," she said, exhaling. She tried not to recognize the queasy feeling of relief, as if she knew she was inviting danger, but didn't want to acknowledge it. What was the worst that could happen? She couldn't bring herself to think about it.

She closed her bedroom door and turned the lock. She'd never locked a bedroom door before; had thought it odd when she'd moved in that such a lock was standard. Tonight, though, despite her good intentions and her desire to trust others, she gave the door a little tug to make certain she'd done it right. Luckily, the wine had made her drowsy, and she fell asleep within an hour.

Cecilia woke with a start in the middle of the night, her heart pounding so hard she could hear it in her ears. A clatter, a shattering of glass. As if there was someone in the apartment. A burglar? Impossible to get past the doorman. An inside job?

Guests! The kids! She sat up, fully awake now. She lit the lamp on her bed stand, and grabbed her robe from its hook in her bathroom. She put her ear to her bedroom door, and, hearing no further noises, turned the knob slowly, then stepped out into the hall and switched on the hall light. A figure at the end of the hall shielded his face with his forearm. "What?" the boy cried.

"What?" she shot back.

"I'm sorry," he said, calmed. "I went to make a sandwich," he said. "Peanut butter and jelly. Wanna bite?"

"No," she said. "It's 2 a.m.."

"And do you know where your children are?" he mimicked a public service announcement. "In the kitchen. Eating you out of house and home."

"Is that what your folks said?" she asked, thinking she'd stumbled on an insight. "'Is that why you left home?'"

"Only at the end of the month," he said, and Cecilia wasn't sure whether or not she was being conned. His father taught physics. There had to be enough money. How many brothers and sisters did he say he had?

"Seriously?" she asked.

"Nah. Just fooling with ya."

"Then why did you leave?" she asked.

"We had to," he said, and turned, clearly not about to say more.

Again, she knew she'd overstepped, but part of her felt that if she knew their story, she wouldn't think herself so crazy, would feel better about how she'd gotten sucked in.

"Anything beats juvey."

She checked a gasp. Perhaps it was better not to know—what if there was a warrant for his arrest? Would they put her in a jail for harboring a juvenile delinquent? What had he done to get himself arrested? Probably just a con, not a violent crime, she calmed herself. "Well, good night, then," she said, as gamely as she could muster.

"Good night," he said, looking over his shoulder. "Oh, sorry about the glass. I was pouring some milk. I cleaned it up. But don't walk around there barefoot, if you know what I mean."

She awoke to muffled sounds in the kitchen and the sharp odor of bacon. She brushed her hair and her teeth, skipped her ritual gargle, and pulled on black jeans and a black T-shirt.

"How do you like your eggs?" Kix greeted her. He'd tucked a white tea towel into his jeans, and, looking more a short-order cook than a juvenile delinquent, rubbed his hands enthusiastically. Charmaigne sat at the table in the kitchen nook, lazily feeding the baby something from a jar. She hardly looked up. Whether the girl was embarrassed or sullen, Cecilia couldn't say. Clearly, between the two of them, Kix was the extrovert, the life of the party, and Charmaigne, the serious young mother, perhaps the strong and silent one, the one who grounded him, proving again that opposites attract.

"Over easy," she said tentatively. She'd meant to be up first, to offer them breakfast and send them on their way, but the sight of Kix prodding bacon and popping wheat bread into the toaster chilled her. They looked as if they'd plugged themselves in, like a trailer at a campsite or a boat at dock, settled in for an indefinite stay. Of course, she thought to herself. How could she have expected anything else? Who'd want to go back to a tunnel or a box or even a shelter after a stay at the Ritz? She'd invited them. How was she going to dis-invite them? Dr. Richardson would think her such a desperate fool. All she'd wanted to do was to help. A little. To help a little. To offer a pencil, not her shoes.

Unlike a typical teenager, Kix was obviously a morning person, a bundle of energy, darting from icebox to stove to cabinet. He held up a bag from the donut store at the end of her block. "And with our protein, a treat," he said. "Cruller?"

He'd picked her favorite. Although the temptation was close, rarely did she indulge herself. Sometimes an "everything" bagel with light cream cheese; the delicate, accordion-plaited deep fried cruller dough, maybe once a year. Why not? After the risk she'd already taken, how could a little trans-fat hurt?

"Yum!" she said, with genuine enthusiasm. She deserved it.

Cruller in hand, she sat opposite Charmaigne in the breakfast nook, thereby ceding control of the kitchen to Kix. Charmaigne was not a morning sort. She didn't speak, and her whole body seemed asleep as she gently fed Abby spoonfuls of something like applesauce, lazily wiped her drool, and periodically yawned. Cecilia decided not to push the girl. Soon enough, Kix would bounce over with plates heaped with food, and while she and he would feel their spirits rise as cheery as the yolks of their over-easy eggs, it was clear that Charmaigne would be more inclined to pick at her food, chop the egg in small bits, and try to pass it off to the baby. She was the kind of person for whom breakfast was a meal that shouldn't be served before noon, much like the feeling of Cecilia's own mother, whose nights were spent crawling the charitable-cultural-social scene—and not infrequently imbibing at least one glass too many.

"We'll get out of your hair as soon as we do the dishes," Kix said. Charmaigne gave Cecilia a shy smile.

"That's okay," she said. "I'll just put them in the dishwasher."

"Yeah. Right. I can do that," he said. "I like to pay my own way, even when I'm not paying."

"All right, then," she said, surprised their leaving would be so easy and so quick. "What are you doing today?"

It was a risky question. What plans could they have? And if they had none, then she'd feel compelled to let them stay, and if they stayed longer, then the afternoon would become the evening, and there would again be the question, "Where are you going to stay?"

"I thought we'd conquer the world," Kix said with a bravado that made Charmaigne look up and smile. Turning toward Charmaigne, he punched softly at the air, as if warming up.

"Of course," Cecilia said gamely. "But where will you start?"

Kix shrugged. "Depends on the weather, who's in town, what's happening."

She guessed she wasn't going to get more information from Kix this morning. "How about a sandwich for the road?"

He hesitated, and Charmaigne studied her baby. "Nothing fancy," she said, and dropped her plate in the sink for him while she pondered the contents of her refrigerator. She made four sandwiches of ham and low-fat cheese on wheat bread while Charmaigne and Kix packed their things in their room. They came out together, Kix with both packs, and the girl with the baby in the stroller. She handed them a paper sack with the sandwiches, two little bags of carrots, and two apples, and gave Kix half an index card on which she'd written her name and phone number and email address.

"Take care of yourselves," she said to them as they waited for the elevator. "Call me every now and then and let me know how you're doing." She felt a little sad, like the letdown after the final curtain of a successful run.

"Will do, Miss M," Kix said, with a little bow. "Thank you for your hospitality. Come sing with me sometime," he said. "You know where to find me."

The girl mumbled a thank-you and they stepped into the elevator. Cecilia stood for a moment, staring at the closed doors, and then returned to her apartment, where she double-locked the door and leaned against it, sobbing.

The kids didn't seem unhappy to be leaving. Even if it was the Ritz to them, they didn't seem sad to be leaving it behind. Was it because they were uncomfortable in the midst of so much? Were they intimidated by her easy life? Were they really juvenile delinquents, escapees from whatever prison they put children in, hardened to the kindness of others? Did Cecilia's condo remind Charmaigne of home, and make her sad? Had she come across as a knee-jerk liberal do-gooder, and they rejected her condescending kind of good? She'd let him earn his keep. He'd supplied the donuts and done the cleanup. She'd tried to make it even. Why had she even bothered? Why were they leaving her?

She cried because she didn't understand herself. Couldn't decide what to do with her life, couldn't make a simple decision to go to an audition, couldn't contemplate performing onstage again. She couldn't imagine waiting for the reviews, as if for her execution, yet she could bring home a teenage boy and a teenage mother and the mess they've made so soon of their young lives, and her fear could come and go, and her heart open out to them and close tight as a fist, and she felt whipsawed by emotions that she didn't understand and certainly couldn't explain to Dr. Richardson.

"You wanted to cancel today?" Dr. Richardson repeated her explanation for being a few minutes late. She'd meant to cancel, thought she had, then remembered she hadn't.

"I had guests," she said.

"I see," he said. "Should you be with them now?" he asked, as if he were genuinely sorry to be taking up her time with this foolishness.

"I thought there weren't any 'shoulds,'" she said, wanting to tweak him.

He raised his right eyebrow quizzically and waited for her to say more. There was something about the silence that felt confessional. Silence abhors a vacuum, she thought, that's why humans rush to fill it with music and theater and films and television and radio. That's why restaurants don't mind the clatter and bustle—complete silence would be so much like death. She heard herself talking to fill the void, to confirm that she was alive and feeling and had a life worthy of reporting, and feelings worthy of being acknowledged, and more feelings for which she did not as yet have words.

"You'll never guess what I did last night," she said, edging forward on the couch to tell her secret. "I had the kids over."

Dr. Richardson remained passive. What would it take to make this man crack? When would his expression betray the slightest trace of surprise or dismay, approval or scorn? The graying mustache, thick and neatly trimmed, protected his lips from involuntary disclosure. His blue eyes were ever steady, almost meditative, but benignly curious. She wasn't sure how he did it. Nor was she sure why it worked to cause her to talk in ways she hadn't talked to others in a long time, maybe since freshman year in the dorms, maybe ever. "You can always feel safe here," he'd said to her the first day. Mentally, she'd pooh-poohed the safety bit. After what she'd been through, auditioning, performing, being publicly dissected, microscoped, analyzed, and critiqued, she doubted that there was anything in talking privately not to feel safe about. She would control the conversation. She could be "safe." What could he say? "Sticks and stones," she'd repeated to herself at the time, even though the truth was, she was sitting in a therapist's office because words had hurt her, had, in fact, sent her to her room, quivering. If his words were "safe," it was because they were privileged and private, not public fodder. Perhaps that's what Dr. Richardson had meant.

"I ran into the boy—his name is Kix—in the subway again, and thanked him for the money, and then, I don't know, I felt like I wanted to let him know that I trusted him."

"Even though you hadn't before he returned the money."

"Yeah. You know. It seemed like that good behavior should be rewarded, and I have no idea where they would've stayed otherwise."

It hit her like a ton of bricks when Dr. Richardson asked, with as much curiosity as he ever showed, "Just one night?"

She flopped back on the couch and crossed her legs. "They left," she said, trying not to display the emotion that had overcome her at the door. "I didn't ask them to move in," she said. How dumb did he think she was?

He smiled broadly, but she couldn't parse it. What was funny? Was he relieved? What if they did move in with her, and she was able to help them get back on their feet? Wouldn't that be something? Something meaningful?

"I thought it was some progress," she said, trying to rehabilitate herself from the unspoken accusation. "I know it was risky, but I hid my really good stuff and I locked my doors, and I have a full time doorman, so . . . . He had a baby with him," she said.

"I see," Dr. Richardson said. He rose. She'd been late, and their time was up.

six

Haverill Richardson stretched, touched his toes, and looked out the floor-to-ceiling window to the plaza below. A few weeks ago, he'd been mildly shocked to see Cecilia light a cigarette; intrigued when a young man approached her and eyed her purse; relieved when he took the light she offered and skipped away. Cecilia smoking? Of course, many clients took a little while to come down from therapy. All that adrenaline pumping up the defensive mechanisms, receding like an ebbing tide, filling the coffee shops with customers on stools staring out at sidewalks, notebooks open idly in front of them. He'd watched alcoholics leave his office and enter the Italian restaurant across the street, probably not for a cappuccino; watched bankrupt spendthrifts drop a bill in a beggar's paper cup; watched married men strike up conversations with young, short-skirted women. It was some form of self-destructive stubbornness that would make Cecilia taunt her talent with a cigarette. He was glad to see now that she was past that phase.

But a new phase, this thing with the boy, could be far more dangerous. He wanted to trust Cecilia's judgment, but sometimes, at the beginning, especially, clients—both exuberant and defiant—weren't so trustworthy. He hoped she knew what she was doing. Or that, having reached out to these adolescents, she might be more willing to let more people into her life. He found himself wishing she'd brought home instead an eligible fellow her own age, and quickly dismissed that thought.

Cecilia's case frustrated him: open-ended, nonurgent, self-indulgent. He had to acknowledge these frustrations so that they wouldn't interfere with his treatment, but in an odd way, Cecilia angered him. Hers was a high-class problem. She had too much talent, too little ambition. Her degree of discomfort with her inability to publicly perform was mild, perhaps below the threshold necessary for motivation to change. She thought she should want to perform. It wasn't clear to him that she actually wanted to. She said she wanted to find meaning in her life, but more than likely she expected him to tell her what it was. As if he knew. It would be slow going in talking therapy to cause her enough discomfort to want to change, and it would be touch and go whether she would tolerate the discomfort long enough for the motivation to develop. It was an intellectual challenge, but a slow, slow trudge. In his long career, he'd worked both with the psychotic, who required drug therapies, and with the merely neurotic, and had found in each the unique satisfactions that had drawn him to psychiatry in the first place, but he'd always preferred, in a way, the psychotic, the way they demonstrated, over and over, that the human spirit was indomitable. Howling at the moon, maniacally bursting with spontaneous creativity and compulsive productivity, almost always, if they stayed, the psychotic were grateful to the doctor who shooed the voices away. The merely neurotic, who undoubtedly also suffered, could tend toward the whiny, resentful of the time and money needed to change even slightly.

Cecilia wasn't making as much progress as he might have hoped. She had yet to express any real desire to go back to the stage. Her ambivalence made him wonder if she had as much talent as she claimed. She said she was looking for meaning. When someone has so much creative talent, isn't their creative activity what gives their life meaning? It's not as if she had to clean house for a living. She could sing, act, entertain, teach. There were ways to make money at her profession. And, she didn't have to make money. Money was neither a roadblock nor a motivating force.

Her parents, now both gone, no longer were the prodding hand. That she had defied her mother and quit during her thirties suggested that she had issues with her mother, that she was getting back at the woman by not performing. If she could identify those issues, then perhaps she would be freed to sing. If singing was the meaning she was looking for. He had to remind himself not to force that upon her. That was, he was aware, the mirror image of what he wanted for himself: The talent to match his own artistic desires. He wished he had confidence that what he might someday create would in some sense be satisfactory; meet artistic standards, or win modest critical acclaim, even a blue ribbon at a local juried art fair. Something. As it was, he had his sculpture studio on the fourth floor as well as an area on the roof of their building. He had, sadly, the time now to devote to sculpting. Yet, night after night, weekend after weekend, he had an extra cup of coffee, reread the sports pages, deadheaded the potted geraniums his wife had wintered over in their kitchen, prepared his tools, sketched, molded, paced. But he had yet to chisel even a corner of the block of ivory-colored marble that stood waiting in his studio.

The blinking light on his office phone claimed Haverill's attention. "I'm fine," he told his adult daughter, herself a therapist, who lived down in New Orleans and worked with Katrina victims. Since Rosalyn Richardson had died a year ago, Maddie called every Tuesday, just about this time, during a break in their respective client schedules. He assured her he was wearing his aids, confirmed that his hair was brushed discreetly over his ears "except when I'm on the phone with you," and repeated that he was keeping himself busy enough.

Although he wasn't his daughter's supervisor, she kept him abreast of her patients' progress and he was flattered. He'd been pleased when she told him she was following in his footsteps, quite convinced that he had not unduly interfered in any way with her choice. He'd not asked her to join his practice, and she'd moved out East, then moved south. It was best that way, he thought. Adults should be adults, independent and autonomous.

"Trudy is pregnant," she informed him.

Dear God, no, he thought, but was too good a therapist to voice that negative reaction.

"She's pleased?" he ventured, thinking that he would himself be pleased to hear his daughter had found a man, married, was having his grandchild.

"She's undecided," his daughter said.

"Ambivalence can be telling," he ventured.

"It'll keep her coming back a few more sessions," she laughed. His daughter had a more cynical view of their profession than he did, perhaps because he'd started back when therapy wasn't micro-managed by the employee assistance programs and the insurance companies, when people came because they knew they needed to change, not because they thought they should or were told by a court they must.

"That's it for now, Dad," his daughter said. "You take care of yourself like you would a patient, okay?"

He hadn't had a chance to tell her Cecilia's news, but she sounded busy. "Okay," he said, but his eyes watered. He missed his wife terribly. Being slightly deaf, he was used to the quiet of his home at night. Now, what he missed most was her physicality—her warmth stretched out next to him in bed, her busyness in the kitchen, baking something unexpected, if not for him, for the church or the woman's club or the garden club, her hand as she helped him from his chair after the ten o'clock news.

Friday nights in particular had become troublesome to him. Rosalyn had died silently in the wee hours of a Tuesday morning of a brain aneurism and the memorial service had been on a Friday afternoon, followed by a buffet at a small hotel. It wasn't until the service that he understood how much she'd sacrificed for him. As speaker after speaker spoke of her charm, her theatrical talent, her humility, her generosity of spirit, he became aware of her unrealized potential. After his medical school, they'd chosen Chicago in part because of its vibrant theater community, but then she'd gotten pregnant right away and they'd moved to the suburbs and he'd objected to her commuting in the dark and being away the nights that a theater career demanded. She'd kept her hand in with anonymous voice-over work, which was recorded during the day, and involved a minimal amount of time.

So that she could make a new stab at her acting career, Rosalyn had finally convinced him, a year before she'd died, to move to the city, to a brownstone in the affluent and trendy Lincoln park neighborhood on the north side, steps from the convenience of public transportation and from upscale restaurants, theaters and boutiques. At fifty-five, she hoped to be a fresh face. At sixty, he ought, she said, to begin to slow down. She'd dedicated the rooftop to a garden with room for the sculpture he planned to create and the fourth floor to his studio.

He'd tinkered a little while Rosalyn was alive. She'd shoo him upstairs several evenings a week, with instructions to go "play." He'd molded some clay, made a few sketches, but had failed to produce a work that would demonstrate to Rosalyn how much he appreciated her encouragement. When she asked, he said true art took time. Once, frustrated, he'd even suggested that creating something from scratch was far more difficult than reading someone else's words onstage. She'd agreed that the creative acts were different—she preferred, she said, the cooperative, collective nature of the theatrical endeavor and the challenges of bringing to life another person's vision. Not as focused on the self as the work of a solo artist. He'd heard "selfish," and had refused to go to his studio for a month. Then, for what turned out to be their last wedding anniversary, she'd bought him a two-foot-high cube of Colorado Yule Marble from the quarries near Aspen, and then, at fifty-seven, she'd died.

When he contemplated the marble these days, he felt the guilt of not using or displaying an expensive gift so enthusiastically given, yet, like the good crystal, he feared using it. He was not satisfied with his plans for the block, and felt it would be a shame to make a cut in the marble before he was sure. He'd thought, originally, that he was going to carve something abstract, that he would let the form emerge out of the stone, after the ideal of Michelangelo. He'd read that some of the great sculptors claimed that the marble itself told the sculptor, in some mystical way, what it wanted to be. While he appreciated the analogy to his own work with patients, he found he didn't feel the relationship to the marble that such sculptors claimed to feel, nor could he imagine taking a whack at the cube without a plan of some kind.

He didn't have that kind of courage in the face of such uncertainty. He'd been to the Wisconsin State Fair with his daughter when she'd lived in Milwaukee during an internship, and he'd been fascinated then by the sure-handedness of the man who carved totems, badgers, bears and elves with his chain saw. Six or seven a day. The chain saw artist never paused to ask the wood what it wanted to be—he worked swiftly, knowing exactly where each cut should be, how deep, and in what order. The master of the chain saw had a plan. Haverill Richardson did not.

A few weeks after the call about his daughter's patient, a few weeks after Cecilia had entertained the boy and his family, Haverill's daughter called again in the little break he gave himself between Cecilia's 10 a.m. session and his next, at eleven-fifteen. "How's the marble coming?" she asked.

"It's coming along," he said.

"Wonderful," she said. "What are you doing with it?"

He paused.

"Oh," she said. "You're still planning?"

"That's most of the work," he said stubbornly. "The hardest part of the work." He felt his heart skip an angry beat. "So, what about my grandchild?" It wasn't fair of him, he knew, but he was hurt, and he'd just had a particularly difficult session with Cecilia, who had regressed to her sulking, silent stage, her interest in the boy, which had energized her for a few weeks, apparently now gone.

"Well, that's a mature response," his daughter said in a parental rather than therapeutic voice. "Lash out at me because you have artist's block?"

She was right, and he felt doubly defensive. "I'm entitled to work at my own pace."

"So am I," she said, which he understood as forgiveness. "It's Mom's marble. In some ways, it's the last thing you and she will create together," she said gently. "I understand. And I know you understand, too. Grandchildren take time."

"I'm sorry," he said.

"I'm not avoiding it, you know," she said.

"It takes time," he said, and was relieved to hear his daughter's amused laugh.

"We're all just a little crazy," she said.

"Diagnosable," he said, their shared joke.

"You can name it, but you can't cure it," she said, and they smooched into the phone.

That was, perhaps, the hardest part of his profession—he couldn't cure anything, and couldn't take credit for anything, either. Haverill Richardson had been trained in a Rogerian school of psychology, which held its clients in the highest esteem and which believed that clients, given the right conditions, would, in time, "cure" themselves. "Do and say as much nothing as possible" was, for Dr. Richardson and his colleagues, the equivalent of *Primum non nocere* in the medical community. A human being was a marvelously resilient organism. Left to its own devices, it would seek food and shelter, grow, reproduce, and die. Even in death, it would shut itself down in the order that would give itself the least pain: kidney, lung, brain, heart. Eyes shut, consciousness quelled, less and less breath to sustain less and less life. A self-protective winding down. So, too, the human psyche seeks healing and life. When the pain is too far beyond bearable it will deny or split off or alter its reality, preserving its "self" as best it can. So, as a therapist, Haverill Richardson had been taught a hands-off approach, an approach that believed that people must discover themselves within themselves. People know why they do the things they do. They just need to be encouraged to see the reasons clearly, so they can choose alternative behaviors, if they really want to.

Cecilia had shown a little progress, in his view, when she'd tried getting out of herself. Odd that she would choose the boy rather than some more traditional volunteer work, but perhaps not. Her mother's idea of volunteering was, no doubt, the Women's Board of the Lyric, and while there was nothing wrong with that—high culture needing all the help it could get—he could see why Cecilia would eschew her mother's way for her own. It was her sudden drop of interest in the boy that had surprised him. She'd reported singing with him and having him and his girlfriend and baby in her apartment, and then, for two weeks, she didn't mention him. It had been a true professional challenge not to ask what had happened.

He knew a catalog of reasons—practical, emotional, psychological—why a person would not get involved with a boy from the street. Mostly they boiled down to that great motivator of all human behavior, fear. If his daughter had done what Cecilia had done, he'd be seized with panic—Ros would've been on a plane immediately to check things out for herself—but Cecilia hadn't registered any fear regarding the boy, and no particular angst that he hadn't remained in her life. She hadn't said she missed him, or the excitement he injected into her life. She'd remained, at least in her therapist's office, excruciatingly passive. What would it take to motivate Cecilia? What did she really want? What was she most afraid of? He knew she wasn't yet ready to tell him, or name it, although eventually, to get better, she would have to.

For himself, he knew his fear—and it was only natural. What

if he made an irretrievable mistake? Who in their right mind would carve into a hunk of marble without knowing what it might become?

seven

Two weeks after the night Kix, Charmaigne, and the baby first stayed in Cecilia's guest room, Cecilia's doorman called her apartment just as the ten o'clock news was ending.

"A Mr. Kix Gordon here to see you," he said, with more than his usual prickliness.

"Alone?" she asked. "No one with him?"

"Yes, ma'am," the doorman said.

"Tell him I'll come down," she said. After her encounter with Dr. Richardson, she'd realized that she had taken an unusual risk, perhaps bigger than she'd fully appreciated, in inviting the couple to her home. Since then, she'd avoided the subway and Millennium Park. Kix hadn't called. She'd never been one for one-night stands, and she regretted Kix the way she regretted the few she'd experienced when she toured at out-of-town theaters, lonely and slightly intoxicated. There was slightly more dignity in her memory of Kix—more like a show that opened, played a few weeks, and then closed, good enough for its time and place, but not enduring.

She put on jeans and a light sweater, shoved a twenty and a few ones in her pocket along with her keys, and, having turned on almost all the lights in her apartment, waited in the hall for the elevator. She wasn't used to going out this late. She hoped that the coffee shop at the corner would be open. If Kix needed to talk, they could go there. More likely, he needed cash, and he could ask for that in the lobby. She could spare him another twenty and send him on his way. But that was it.

Downstairs, the doorman nodded to the reception area opposite his mahogany station, where Kix sat perched on his backpack, in dirty jeans and a faded White Sox T-shirt, as if he didn't want to spoil the leather couches, even though they were there specifically for the use of guests. He jumped to his feet.

"Miss M," he said.

"Hi, Kix," she said. "What a surprise," she added, loud enough for the doorman to hear, if he was eavesdropping, as he usually did. She hoped the doorman understood that Kix was not an invited guest. "What brings you out this time of night?"

"Don't have a watch," he grinned. "Can we talk?" He eyed the inner lobby door leading to the elevators. "Someplace else?"

"There's a coffee shop on the corner," she volunteered. "Looks like you could use a burger as well?"

"My mother used to say I was a bottomless pit," he laughed, his hand on his stomach, as if to suggest that he wasn't hungry, wasn't begging, necessarily, was just always, typically, hungry.

The doorman made a show of looking at his watch, as if he expected he would be called upon to testify as to his tenant's disappearance in the night with a scruffy adolescent about five seven in stature with dirty blond hair and very blue eyes.

As soon as they settled into a booth looking out on the street, Kix started to cry. Cecilia was speechless. It was rude to stare, but she did, silently, as the boy, leaning on his elbows, covered his eyes with his hands. She felt she should say something, but she could hardly say something soothing, even, "It'll be okay," without knowing whether "it" was the kind of thing that could be okay. Some things, she'd come to believe, were neither okay—whatever that meant—nor fixable.

Briefly she considered what Dr. Richardson would do if she were ever to start a session in tears. He would wait, that's what he would do, and so, not knowing what else to do, she decided she would wait, too. When the waitress came by, oblivious to the boy's distress, Cecilia ordered two colas, one diet, one regular, and a giant cheeseburger with fries and slaw. She ordered a toasted bagel with light cream cheese for herself.

After the waitress left, he croaked, "She's gone."

"Charmaigne left?"

Without looking up, he nodded.

"And took the baby with her?"

He barely moved.

"And you have no idea where?"

He raised his head three-quarters and faced the window. "I've been looking for two days. No place. She's nowhere. Not at any of our usual places."

"Have you told the police?"

"They wouldn't do anything."

She hesitated, afraid he might be right.

"Tell them a runaway has run away? No way, man." He leaned across the table, determined. "I've got to find her myself."

"Could she have gone home? To Wisconsin or wherever?"

"Naw. She'd never go home to that son of a bitch."

"Her father?"

"Who else?"

"That's why she left in the first place?"

"Yeah, and that's why she got started with the drugs, you know, to escape the pain and shit and then when she got pregnant she got clean and has been ever since and I thought we were doing real good, and now she's left."

The mention of drugs sent a needle through Cecilia's heart. She looked around, afraid he may have been heard, but the restaurant was nearly empty, and the waitress at the counter was flipping through the day's paper. "Were you married?" It was a silly question to ask, not particularly relevant to the fact that the girl was missing, not even relevant, really, to the question of paternity, but it slipped out.

"What difference does that make?" he said, slapping the table and rattling the silverware. The waitress, intent on her paper, didn't flinch.

She was beginning to appreciate Dr. Richardson's skill at getting people to say things they might not want to say. "Yes, I hear you." Cecilia folded her hands in front of her, but fiddled with her thumbs. "You've been very good to her, her source of support, acting like a father to the baby."

"Acting?" he said, insulted. The waitress put the burger in front of him. He took a huge bite. "I am her father."

"How did that happen?" she blurted.

"Like you don't know? Trust me," he said, with an overblown swagger. "I'm her father."

Cecilia paused. She remembered noticing the girl's blue eyes, as blue as Kix's. And she remembered bending down to the baby, and looking at her big brown ones. Would it ease the boy's suffering to know the baby was not his child? That he'd been conned by the girl, and didn't need to take responsibility for her mistake with another boy?

"What are you saying?" he demanded. "That she was banging somebody else? Doing another dude?"

The street language pushed her over the edge. She decided the boy should know.

"The baby has brown eyes," she said. "So, the father had to have brown eyes."

He stared at her. "You a biologist?"

"Basic, high school biology. Two blue-eyed parents rarely have a brown-eyed child."

His breathing was heavy, and he shoved a handful of fries in his mouth. He stared at her as he chewed, but she didn't see surprise in his eyes. She guessed that he was calculating his next move. If not a father desperate for the return of his child, then what?

He swallowed. "I'm the only father Abby knows," he said. "Doesn't that count for something?"

She nodded. Indeed, a father counted for everything. Her father, a businessman, had been her rock when she was young and struggling with her mother's ambitious perfectionism. Where her mother was never satisfied by the brilliance of her daughter's performance, her father, trained as an engineer and a tinker by disposition, was confident that whatever she did was the "best." He was tone-deaf, and his unconditional support rang false in her ears, but the sentiment of it, the unconditional love behind his praise and admiration, gave her the courage to meet her mother's gauntlet. She would have to tell Dr. Richardson her new insight, that the truth lay someplace between her mother's false humility—her drive for an unattainable perfection—and her father's ever-optimistic false excitement at each performance.

"Who will protect them?" she asked, almost to herself.

"That's my job," he said, throwing his shoulders back and scooting over, as if to leave.

"Stay here a minute," she said, struggling to catch her breath. "Let's think."

Kix leaned back, and he looked again to her like the skinny boy who'd borrowed a match on the street weeks ago, too young to protect anyone. "Look it," she said. "It's too big a city. You and I aren't going to find her. We need to go to the police."

"No police." He flung a leg out of the booth but stopped when she spoke.

"We'll say you were staying with me. Friends of the family. We'll say your parents are missionaries someplace. Whatever. The police don't need to know you are runaways. You never told me you are a runaway," she said, cocking her head as if to seal a secret.

The boy sat back in the booth, stirring his last fry in a pool of ketchup, considering. "She doesn't want to be found," he said, and his voice cracked again. He took an envelope from his pocket. "She's blowing me off, heading to New Orleans."

"Oh," Cecilia said, surprised. "Then the police aren't going to help. But why did she tell you where she was going if she doesn't want to be found? And why did you say you didn't know where she was?"

"You ought to listen better. I never said that. I said I've been looking for her, and she wasn't in the usual places."

"Now you are splitting hairs," Cecilia said, angry. "Why were you looking in the usual places if you knew she wasn't there?"

"Crazy bitch," he said, ignoring her logic. "I took good care of them. I really did."

"You did," she assured him, giving up on getting logical answers to her questions.

The waitress came over, tired and bored, and left a green check with Cecilia. She took it to the cash register and got change for her twenty, leaving the boy in the booth until she could come back with the tip.

What next? Should they each go their separate ways? It was midnight. Where would he go? What danger would he be in? No more than any other night, she decided. He'd taken care of Charmaigne and Abby, he could take care of himself.

Slumped in the booth, he looked younger than his seventeen years, and his face was again wet with tears. He slid out, shouldered his pack, and followed her to the door. The night was hot and sticky, and few people were about, making her feel suddenly lonely.

"Do you want to use the guest room tonight?" she asked him.

He gave a little skip. "You're the best, Miss M. That would be great!"

"I guess that would be okay," she said, although the invitation had already been issued and accepted.

The doorman opened the inner lobby door for them with his usual aplomb, and he had the further good grace and professionalism not to show the slightest surprise or interest in the young man Cecilia was bringing home at midnight. For his part, Kix followed Cecilia into the apartment and turned down the hall to "his" room without her having to point him in the right direction. Cecilia turned off all the lights in the living room and kitchen, and followed down the hall.

"There are towels in the bathroom," she said as she passed the guest room, and locked herself in her room. In bed, she tossed and turned, agitated. She got up and slid a chair in front of her door, but then felt foolish. Still, sleep eluded her. Having received the boy's confidence, she felt an anxious responsibility toward him. When you know someone's weakness, you have a fair amount of control over them, or so she'd learned from her mother, who could critique a performance by praising what Cecilia knew to be the weakest part. There was a little break in her voice between E and F above high C, and her mother thought it a compliment to offer, "It was hardly noticeable tonight." But Cecilia always noticed her mother's noticing, and felt sabotaged by the compliment, condemned to a life of parsing her mother's judgments.

When you had control or influence over someone, you had to act responsibly toward them. She knew the boy's vulnerability, and vowed not to exploit it. He might take control of his life by taking control of others' lives, the way he assumed responsibility for protecting and feeding the girl and her baby. He would not take control of hers. She would not permit him to know her weakness, to know her need. She might instead take care of him, if he would accept her caring. She wasn't sure she understood why she cared, but she did, and as she stared at the ceiling, she knew that they had formed a relationship. It wouldn't necessarily be an easy or explicable one, but for now, they were in each other's lives. He needed her. What she had yet to realize was how much she needed him.

She overslept the next morning, and when she awoke, she felt uneasy, then remembered she was not alone in her apartment. She pulled on jeans and a T-shirt and quietly moved the chair from in front of the bedroom door. With her palm covering the button, slowly she turned the doorknob, hoping to muffle the pop when it unlocked. When she appeared in the kitchen doorway, Kix was reading the newspaper at the kitchen table. He was wearing jeans, but no shirt, and he had a bit of a farmer's tan, his shoulders bony and soft above his weathered forearms. He sprang to his feet and punched the microwave start panel. "I'm heating the mug," he said. "With the AC on, they get cold."

"Yes," she said, and stared at the microwave with him, waiting for the seconds to tick off and willing herself not to blush. She didn't consider herself a prude, but something about having a partially clothed young man in her kitchen seemed wrong, vaguely unsafe. She'd thought adolescent boys covered themselves in front of their mothers, unclothed for their girlfriends. It was her apartment, and she was old enough to be his mother. To be in control, she had to be his mother.

With ten seconds to go, he seemed to remember himself, and sprinted back to the kitchen table, where he threw on the White Sox T-shirt from last night. "Forty," he said, running back to the oven as the buzzer buzzed. He splashed the boiling water into the sink, and poured the coffee into the warmed mug. "Good morning," he said, with a little bow.

"To your health," she said, raising her cup in toast, letting out the breath she'd been holding.

She took a sip. "Shall we do laundry today?" she asked, nodding at his T-shirt.

He gave himself an exaggerated sniff under each arm. "Maybe later, thanks," he said, and she immediately regretted having implied a future. She wasn't inviting him to move in, for god's sake.

Still, it was nice to have someone else around in the morning. She hadn't had a roommate since college. She'd had few overnight guests, and had found even those stressful. Her mother'd always used the best china and crystal for guests, even for breakfast, and brought trays to their room with a petite breakfast before serving brightly garnished eggs Benedict with homemade hollandaise. Guests were quite the production in the Morrison household. Small flaws evoked a barrage of apologies and incessant worries for weeks following. At such times, Cecilia's own self-confidence tee-tered on a precarious brink, as if, having managed to stand upright on a balance beam, she could not bring herself to slide her front foot even an inch forward. Kix's ease as a guest both unnerved her and put her at ease as a hostess. She'd have to remember to tell Dr. Richardson that when she next saw him.

"Feeling better this morning?" she asked.

"Dunno," he said. "I don't know what to do. Abby's not my kid, but so what? She needs me. I should head to New Orleans, go find her. But I dunno. It's a big place. Who knows if she even got there?"

"There's a lot to think about," Cecilia said, reminding herself of Dr. Richardson's studied neutrality. Part of her wanted him to leave, go find his friend, move on; part of her would miss him when he was gone.

"Yeah. I'm glad you understand," Kix said. Again, Cecilia real-ized it wasn't so hard to sound sympathetic even without saying anything. Perhaps that was the secret of Dr. Richardson's success—the patient, the person on the couch, heard in his neutral stance whatever they wanted to hear. She quickly tried to remember what ambiguous statement Dr. Richardson might have made to her that she had taken the way she wanted, but drew a blank. She would have to listen more closely next time. Kix wiped his eyes, and she understood, as he had suggested, that there could be a big differ-ence between what one person said and the other heard.

"Well, you don't need to decide today," she said. If he wanted to know what she really thought, she thought he should forget Charmaigne, stay in Chicago, get his GED, and go to college some-place. Get his act together. He was a bright, charming, responsible kid, and Charmaigne and her baby would only bring him down. It was Charmaigne's problem, not his. It was a shame about the baby, but there wasn't much Kix could do about it without sacrificing his own potential.

"Irregardless, I need to earn some do-re-mi," he said.

"Regardless," she said.

"Huh?" he looked at her, his body tense, his eyes wide, as if frightened.

"The word is 'regardless,' not 'irregardless.' A lot of people say 'irregardless' but it's wrong. A double negative? Regardless means without regard for, like unmindful or without concern for; so what would irregardless mean? Not without regard for, which means with regard for?" She was babbling, and he rolled back on his heels, again relaxed.

"I hear ya," he said. "Regardless, I need to make some cash. Wanna sing with me today?"

In the subway? Her mother would turn over in her grave! Her classically trained daughter, the winner of *Le Prix de la Société de le Public*, singing in the subway with a street urchin? She'd done it before, but not on purpose.

"Sure, why not?" she heard herself say. There were a million reasons why not but the boy's enthusiasm—or his need, whichever—made her momentarily forget them.

"Just a minute," he said and dashed from the kitchen. Before she could realize what she'd agreed to, he was back, a sheaf of wrinkled papers in hand. "The words," he said, handing her the stack. "You study. I'll shower," he added, and was off. She laughed to herself. For reasons she couldn't explain, the boy made her do crazy things.

She flipped through the papers, downloads of the lyrics and chord progressions for classics from the sixties and seventies, folk, early rock, a little gospel. They were familiar, but she hadn't sung any of them in ages. It was one of her talents that she had a nearly photographic memory, at least in the short term, for what she read, particularly scripts and song lyrics. She flipped through them and went to her own bedroom, thinking that if she were going to do this thing, she wanted to look professional, not as if she needed to sing in a subway for her supper. Her jeans and scoop-necked maroon T-shirt were fine. She thought about a belt of sterling silver links but decided that was too showy, might even look stolen. She chose instead an Hermes scarf in tan, gold and navy blue, which she draped around her neck like a collar and knotted loosely in front. She stood before her bathroom mirror, considering. Not everyone would recognize how expensive the scarf was—a gift from her mother, and, frankly, too formal and recognizable to be Cecilia's preferred style—but those who knew would know, and they might assume, more benignly, that she'd bought it at a resale shop that didn't know any better. Or they might assume it was a knock-off, but that she had good taste. Knowing then her expectations, they might drop a dollar rather than fifty cents.

She could see that there was a lot of psychology to singing on the street. Cecilia hadn't worked an audience in a long time, and while her last professional outing had been, in her mind, a disaster, this was decidedly not professional. It wasn't as if anyone would know her. Right? She quickly ran through her friends and their likely routes to and from work. No, she was unlikely to see any of them on the State Street subway.

"Lose the scarf," Kix said when they met in the hall.

"I like the scarf." The sound of her own whine reminded her of how she'd had to plead with certain directors to try a song her way. Of the half who caved and let her give it a try, more often than not, they insisted on their own direction. It used to aggravate her.

"But it's my act," Kix said, cutting to the chase, as if he were the money man, the producer with the big bucks who got to call the shots. "They gotta see we need the moola."

Her rationale for wearing the designer scarf suddenly seemed lame. She untied it and made quite a show of folding it just so, corner to corner, in half, then quarters, then eighths, folded but not creased. She returned to her bedroom and placed it in her drawer, then double-checked the top drawer to make sure she had indeed stored all her good jewelry in the hidden place in her closet. She'd left a few sterling bangles she'd purchased at art fairs, two gold chains and a rhinestone wristband, enough perhaps to satisfy a robber with a need for quick and easy loot.

It was midmorning when they headed out of her apartment, and, to her surprise, Kix headed north, not south.

"Gotta pick up the guitar," he said, although she hadn't realized it was missing. In her life, all the costumes, props, and instruments were at the theater. You didn't have to bring your own. "Besides, it's too nice a day to go underground," he said. "There's nothing going on there at this time of day," he said.

"Where are we going?"

"Water Tower," he said. "Nice acoustics."

"No way," she said. "I'm not singing with you there. What if I see someone I know?"

"You know Joshua Bell? Once he played in the subway in DC during rush hour and in forty-five minutes like only one person recognized him! He only made thirty-two dollars, and twenty dollars was from that one." She was surprised he knew the internationally acclaimed violinist. "So what if someone recognized you?" he concluded, and from his tone, she thought he wasn't being reproachful, he just didn't understand.

"I'm a professional," she said. "Not a street performer."

He shook his head. "A professional plays for money, right?"

Stopped at the corner of Michigan and Ontario, just a few blocks from the famous urban shopping mall, she didn't budge when the pedestrian light turned to walk. He was halfway across when he realized she wasn't with him, and turned back. "We are playing for money," he said finally. "What's the difference?"

The difference was that a real professional was chosen by a producer or director and was directed, coached, molded into the director's vision of an artistic piece or performance. Someone told you you were good, told you what they wanted you to be, told you you were fantastic, told you how to be better. A professional didn't play themselves; they played a part. Even when they met the press or were on nighttime TV talk shows, they played the character of the celebrity they wanted to be.

The boy touched her arm, like a toddler tugging on his mother's sleeve, urging her forward to the swings, the merry-go-round, the playground. "What's the difference," she muttered. Dr. Richardson had suggested—by look if not in actual words—that she wasn't going to find meaning within the four walls of her apartment. She needed to get out of her comfort zone, have new experiences, meet new people, try new things. Blah, blah, blah. The boy needed her.

They stopped briefly at an old brown brick hotel near Water Tower, where the doorman, costumed in green livery gear, held up a finger for Kix to wait a minute and then ducked inside and retrieved the guitar case, which previously Cecilia had only seen open. The top was covered in an eclectic collection of stickers, most likely from previous owners: "Honk if You Love Jesus," "On the Eighth Day God Went Fishing," "Question Reality," a yellow smiley face, a skull and bones, a Chicago Cubs baseball, "Hemp Is a Plant, Bush Is a Dope." Kix thanked the doorman, passing him a few dollars—Cecilia couldn't see how many—as they shook hands.

Remarkably, no other musicians had already claimed the sidewalk outside of Water Tower. What was nice about the location, Kix explained, was that both they and their audience could have the shade of the overhang and not obstruct the main entrance to the mall or to the Macy's store.

The foot traffic was light. While Kix tuned his guitar, Cecilia studied the Macy's windows, which were, despite the fact that it was only June, in the last throes of the summer fashion season. She could feel her heart pounding too fast a tempo in her chest, the way it did in the final minutes before a professional curtain. Her teachers used to say that a little stage fright was absolutely normal. Common, even. What would they think of this stage, or her current fright?

Kix called to her. "Ready?"

She forced herself to walk casually, slowly, in his direction. Not looking at her, he busied himself propping open the guitar case. He reached into his pocket and dropped a handful of coins and a few crumbled dollar bills onto the crushed red velvet.

"Priming the pump," he said to her. "One minute to curtain."

Kix opened with a solo, "Dock of the Bay," and Cecilia stood nearby, the beginning of an audience. A few folks stopped, and then more gathered for "Day-O," which he also sang alone, almost a capella, clearly and sweetly. She was a little miffed that he didn't need her, but was also feeling saved from her own foolishness, when he motioned to her. Ignoring the dozen or so who had gathered, she joined him, her back slightly to the audience. From his backpack, he handed her a beribboned tambourine for their first duet, "I've Got You Babe." She drilled her eyes into him as she sang, afraid to make eye contact with the small crowd of strangers around them. Kix looked at her, but then, experienced showman that he was, at the audience. He looked at her, and then out to the crowd, and then at her, and she could tell by the little furrow between his light eyebrows that he meant for her to follow suit. How dare he tell her, a true professional, how to perform! She knew how to work an audience, and she knew how to ignore one. The thought that she might see someone she knew, or worse yet, a producer or director or fellow theater person, sent a little chill up her spine. She remembered her old tricks, and fixed her gaze just inches above the heads of the first persons in their surrounding circle. In soft focus, she saw short-haired, stocky women in Bermuda shorts with youngsters by the hand, their purses tucked under their armpits, their crew-cut husbands in golf shirts and Cubs T-shirts, wallets bulging in their front pockets. Tourists, most likely, enjoying the sunshine, in no particular hurry. Cecilia herself was enjoying the music.

A gray-haired woman in a navy linen suit and pumps stood with her adult daughter, nicely dressed in khakis, a light knit yellow top, and a single strand of pearls. The older woman's lips were drawn tight, and when Cecilia dared to make eye contact with her, expecting a smile, she was shocked when the woman raised her hand and wagged her finger at her, as if she was doing something terribly wrong. Did she think the two of them were a couple? Ridiculous. Did she think Cecilia was the child's homeless mother, unable to provide for her child? How self-righteous was that? Did she just not like their singing? Then she should move on.

They finished to a smattering of applause and a drop of five or six dollars, plus change. Two of the mothers sent their youngsters forward with some quarters, and the children approached in ways that reflected their personalities, one shyly sliding forward, one eye on mother, one on the task at hand; another dashing to the front, dropping the money as if in a slam-dunk contest, and dashing back; a third marching up there, counting the contents of the guitar case, getting lost, starting over, and finally announcing to Cecilia, "Eleven dollars and twenty-five cents. Plus this." He squatted down and placed the quarters in the case. "Eleven seventy-five."

"Thank you so much," Cecilia said, bending down to shake the youngster's hand. He pumped it, turned on his heel, and marched back to his parents, where Cecilia heard him say, "Can we go to the Nike Store now?"

As the crowd dispersed, the older woman in the navy suit approached, without money in hand, and Cecilia prepared herself for some kind of tongue-lashing. How dare someone comment on what another person has to do to make a living! How dare she jump to unwarranted conclusions! How dare she criticize a performance that she voluntarily stopped to see, and that was given for free.

Cecilia noticed the woman's daughter, standing back, her head turned down the street, as if to disown the old woman. In seconds, the mother, though shorter than Cecilia, was standing too close to her, and Cecilia felt the adrenaline of fear freeze her muscles. The woman shook her finger under Cecilia's nose. Instantly, Kix was by her side, his shoulder slightly in front of hers, a protective barrier.

The woman was not deterred. "You're too good for this," the woman said, her voice low and raspy, betraying her age. "I know my music, young lady, and you belong onstage, not on the street."

"Yes!" Kix pumped. He slapped Cecilia on the back, as if she would feel congratulated by this woman's approbation, and retreated to guard his open guitar case.

"What's your name?" the woman demanded.

"Cecilia," she answered, glad to have been neither recognized nor criticized, but not particularly cheered, either. She'd enjoyed the singing well enough, but something seemed to be missing.

"The patron saint of musicians," the woman said, toddling away. Cecilia knew her mother had baptized her with such expectations. She'd always hated her name, as too formal, too stand-offish, and it amused her to think she was taking some of the shine out of it. Patron saint to a street musician. Her mother would be appalled.

Kix struck a chord or two and waited until several folks had stopped. The old woman joined her daughter in the stream on the sidewalk, and they headed north, perhaps to the Drake Hotel for lunch. Her own mother should've been so supportive! Cecilia remembered bitterly how her mother had crowed her way through the opening night party for *Rumplestilt's Kin*, overwrought with the expectations of her daughter's predicted future fame and glory, accepting the congratulations that were rightfully Cecilia's. And then she hadn't had the decency to contradict the critic who'd called the production "a waste of breath" and her own performance "amateur." Cecilia had never forgiven her that breach of loyalty. For a moment, Cecilia understood one thing that was missing from her performance with Kix, her mother's critique.

They played until midafternoon, taking short breaks for one or the other to run into the mall to the restrooms or to buy bottles of water from the drugstore down the block. Then Kix closed his guitar case and said they'd take a real break until the going-home crowd picked up again. They walked toward the lake, to a small, shady park that felt hidden, even though it was across from the imposing grid of the Museum of Contemporary Art. Laying his guitar next to him, Kix stretched out on the lawn, folded his arms behind his neck, and closed his eyes. Cecilia sat next to him, legs sprawled in front of her. There were some things she could not imagine herself doing. Sleeping in a public park was one of them.

She didn't have a book with her, and while there may have been people coming and going to the Museum, they were tucked in a corner of the park without a clear view. She wondered if Kix had slept here before. With the trees and bushes providing cover, he could have spent the night there, undetected. The thought frightened her. How did he get the courage? And how sad was it that at his tender age, he needed courage in order to do such a simple thing as sleep?

Kix's breathing eased, barely perceptible, his blond eyelashes lush and still and innocent. Courage or naiveté? He was too smart, too acutely aware of his surroundings—who would drop a dollar, who would walk by, who had kind eyes—to be naive to the dangers of his vagrant life. His concern for Charmaigne last night had reached near panic. But he was calmer today, at home on the street, doing what he knew how to do, and what he had to do. He hadn't given up on Charmaigne, but he was a survivor, and he made Cecilia feel that Charmaigne—striking out on her own—was a survivor, too.

She stared at a coffee stain on his T-shirt near his heart as if it were a Rorschach, and felt both a fuzzy tenderness and envy. He wasn't naive about the street, but perhaps he was about his own potential. He knew today. He couldn't think too far ahead, couldn't, perhaps, dream and have dreams crushed. He enjoyed a freedom that Cecilia had been denied. No one told him what to do or whether they approved. No one criticized. No one set impossible standards, disowned him if he failed them. He answered to his stomach, to his own sense of things.

Skinny, peaceful, sleeping, he seemed to her a good kid. He attracted Michigan Avenue crowds that she knew—she was one of them—didn't stop for every street musician unless they had something special. Kix had charm. He used his charm to con, but he didn't rob—at least, he hadn't robbed her yet. He worked, too. Singing on the street, standing and entertaining for hours—it was far harder than she'd ever imagined, requiring salesmanship as well as showmanship. But the show wasn't for the accolades: it was for food, and for his family. He cared about something outside of himself. He cared about Charmaigne, and the baby.

His backpack was between them, and an outer pocket was unzipped, the papers sticking out. She leafed through them, testing her memory. She wouldn't close her eyes, but she read one title after another, pausing after each to stare at a point just beyond her nose, as in meditation, silently singing the songs to herself. In precisely one hour, Kix stretched, yawned, and opened his eyes. He sat up, shaking his head like a puppy. "Ready?" he asked.

The meditation had relaxed her. She wasn't sure she had the energy for another performance, but Kix needed the do-re-mi. He could go alone, or she could finish what she'd started. "Only one more set," she said. "I'm union."

After the set, which ran more than twice as long as any union would've allowed, they started to walk south toward Cecilia's apartment, Cecilia aware that the boy expected to spend the night as much as she expected that he would, given that it was already early evening. They'd gone a few blocks when they came upon a casual restaurant with a few tables on the sidewalk.

"Hungry?" she asked, and he nodded. A couple was just leaving a table against the iron railing that separated the sidewalk from the eating area, and Cecilia and Kix hovered while the busboy removed the dirty plates. Cecilia ordered her usual, a Caesar salad with chicken, lemon wedge, no dressing, and the boy ordered the half-chicken dinner with mashed potatoes and gravy. The teenage waitress brought them an iced tea and a cola, and gave Kix a flirtatious smile. "Good color," she said, meaning his streaky-blond hair. "All mine," he smiled back.

"Was it what you expected?" he turned his attention to Cecilia, a surprisingly insightful question, she thought, coming from a teenager who she might have assumed had no concern other than the money she might help him earn.

"Good question. You first. Did you expect me to say yes?"

"Just a hunch," he said. "Although most adults wouldn't have, I don't think."

"Most adults have more sense," she said. She was vaguely aware of how surprised she was to be described as an adult. Dr. Richardson would say—when he would say—things like, "these are adult questions," or "adults have to make these decisions." Dr. Richardson assumed adults were autonomous. For someone trained to ask a lot of questions about parents, he seemed to think that his clients could grow up to be autonomous, free-standing "adults," free of parental influence. Cecilia wasn't sure she agreed. Wouldn't she forever be a disappointment to her mother? How could she ever correct that?

"Most adults need to grow up," Kix said. "Look at my dad," he volunteered. "He's like a spoiled brat, throwing tantrums when he doesn't get what he wants for Christmas or his birthday. He expects perfection. Named me after Werner Karl Heisenberg, as if that would make a difference."

"Werner?"

"Verner, to be proper about it," Kix said. "Something about the uncertainty principle. Anyway, he—my dad—can't stand that I'm not some mathematical genius that he can use to prove to the world how smart he is—why he should be a chaired professor."

"Being a professor is a big deal!" Cecilia said. "Surely . . . ."

"Not chaired. Not big enough," Kix interrupted. "Not nearly big enough. I think he expected to win the Nobel Prize before he was thirty-five, and since he didn't, he takes it out on us."

"Us?" She knew very little about Kix.

"Me, my mom, my brothers, and sisters. Did I tell you there were five of us?"

"Five! Are you the oldest?" She was surprised that a university type would have so many kids. That was her own bias, she understood, but she wondered if having so many siblings made Kix feel as if he hadn't been good enough for his dad from the get-go.

"Yes. I have a sister who's a year younger."

"Are they all at home?" She wondered if the other four were tense little overachievers, pleasing Professor Gordon in a way his first born son couldn't or wouldn't.

"Some are, some aren't," he said, and waved to the waitress, pointing to his glass for a refill of cola. "They're free here," he said to Cecilia, who rested her head in her palm, aware that she had treaded too close to one of Kix's sore subjects. "I asked you a question," he said, sitting back in the booth and pointing his fork at her between bites of soupy mashed potatoes.

She dropped her palm from her chin and leaned back herself. "It wasn't bad," she said. "It was like performing for a really small audience, like in a nightclub or something, except that the audience keeps coming and going." She laughed, picturing how odd it would be if between each song in a real musical theater the audience filed out and a new one filed in. "It's a little different, too, that the audience decides *after* the performance whether or not they want to pay for it. I'm used to it the other way around."

"Meaning you decide how good a performance to give depending on the size of the audience? Or do you give the same performance, irregardless?" He smiled broadly, a little gravy clinging to his chin. She wiped her mouth with her napkin, and when he didn't mimic her, she did it again, a bigger wipe, and he grabbed an extra paper napkin from the rectangular dispenser on the table.

"Okay?" he asked.

"Okay," she said, and a thought came to her. "It's very freeing to perform for an audience that doesn't expect anything from you," she said. "Did you see the look on that woman's face when we did 'Amazing Grace'?"

"Blew her mind," Kix said. "You know, you're very good. Why don't you get a job singing?"

"Why don't you?" she wanted to say back to him, but she didn't. She felt slightly insulted by his judgment that she was only "very good." She was superb! Amazing! Excellent! Head and shoulders above anything onstage this very day in all of downtown Chicago.

She was more than very good. She was the best. That was what her mother expected of her, and that was what she expected of herself.

"I used to," she said, as if she were a diva who'd retired, weary, at the top of her game. "That old lady at the beginning of the day told me I was too good for the street. That I ought to be onstage. But I've been away from it for a long time," she said.

"So if you went back you'd disappoint your fans?"

She was flattered now that he assumed she had fans. Maybe "very good" wasn't as damning as she'd thought.

"Oh, I don't know," she hedged. "The critics can be cruel," she said. She imagined that there would be at least a little mention in the press about her comeback, most of which would pitch the drama of it by referring to the devastating review that forced her out of the business in the first place. The critics could then set expectations: low, so they could pan her with tepid praise, "better than expected," "not bad after such a long layoff," "with more steady work, could again approach her as yet unrealized potential" or high, so they could blast her for not living up to their hyped, unrealistic expectations. She'd never asked for their opinions. She wondered why anyone paid them to judge that which they couldn't do themselves. Who made them the arbiters of art?

"Doesn't matter what the critics say, if people like you," Kix said. He put his fork down, his brow furrowed, trying to remember something. "I once had a shrink who tried to tell me it didn't matter whether people liked me or not," he said. "I told him he was full of sh—, full of it," he said. "If my father didn't like me, what was I supposed to do? How was I supposed to eat?"

"I'm sure the shrink—" she felt awkward using the word, in her mind it pertained to doctors for the mentally ill, and she certainly wasn't ill—"didn't mean it like that. He meant only that you need to have self-esteem—" again, she winced at her own use of such a touchy-feely word—"self-esteem that isn't based on what other people think of you."

"You believe that?" he asked.

"I do," she said gamely.

"That's why I left," he said, triumphant. "For my self-esteem."

eight

The next day Kix was still asleep when it was time for her appointment with Dr. Richardson, and she felt trapped. Sure, she could wake him up, but then she'd just have to kick him out, probably without breakfast, if she was going to make her session. But should she leave him alone in her apartment? Singing together out on the street, in public view, had been safe enough. Kix was always in her view. If she left, he'd be free to take whatever he could lift and leave—had he said why he'd been sent to a shrink? Did he have such low self-esteem that he would have to steal, or so much that he thought he could get away with it? She stood in her living room and looked at her watch. Her most precious possession, her Steinway, wasn't going anywhere. If she cabbed it to Richardson's, she'd be gone less than two hours. If he were a normal teenager, Kix could sleep 'til noon. Maybe she'd just check in with the therapist, not yak the whole time, and hurry home. Maybe she'd quit Richardson altogether. He was a waste of time.

Before she left, she went into her closet, moved the dial of her safe to the number fifteen, and rearranged the hanging clothes in front of it so that it was not immediately obvious upon opening the closet door. The other valuables in her apartment—her stereo, flat screen TV, and computer—were too bulky to be easily hijacked. She picked up her notebook computer and took it with her in a canvas bag with a book, as if she were headed for the library or a coffee shop. In the lobby, she spoke to the daytime doorman, Ali, and explained that, if her nephew, Kix Gordon, wanted to leave, he should ask him to wait for her, that she'd be back momentarily. "He's glued to the TV, but don't let him take it with him!" she said, hoping the joke would get her point across. She wouldn't be the first rich aunt in her building to have a few things walk off with visiting young family members.

"Kix is back," she told Dr. Richardson, who registered neither surprise nor dismay.

"Where was he?" he asked.

It occurred to her that she didn't know. "His girlfriend left him. I let him stay with me. In fact, he's there right now."

Dr. Richardson nodded.

"I think I trust him—we sang together yesterday, in front of Water Tower. My mother would've been so proud!! I think it was okay to leave him home alone. He needs me to make the do-re-mi, as he calls it."

"He wasn't making do-re-mi before you?"

She felt herself redden. Of course he was. She'd assumed Kix's success yesterday as her own, yet all she'd done, really, was to back him up a little. He didn't need her, for singing or for anything else. He'd got along just fine before he'd met her. How rude of Dr. Richardson to rub her nose in it. She ignored his question, in a rush to get the hour over with.

"It was kind of fun. We just sang, as ourselves. No pretense about it at all. So, that's what's going on. I'm okay, and I think, if it's all the same to you, that I don't need to come back."

"You've been here long enough?" She was glad that Dr. Richardson didn't protest.

"I think so. It's been six weeks. I certainly have done things in the past few weeks that I wouldn't have done before I came here, that's for sure!"

"How so?"

"You know. All this stuff with Kix. I would've been afraid about what people would say. Probably wouldn't have given him the sixty dollars, which got everything started."

"And now what?"

"What do you mean?"

"What happens next? Are you going to adopt the boy? Sing with him? Find the girl?" He sounded genuinely interested.

She thought for a minute. It wasn't like she'd found any great meaning in any of this, but she wasn't so depressed, and that was enough for her. "We think the girl went to New Orleans. The boy, no, I can't sing every day on the street like that. It was a kick, but no, that's not me. I'd like to get him into a program or something, I don't know."

"He'd live with you?"

"Oh, no, not that. Not that at all."

"He'd live at the program?"

She shrugged, frustrated with Dr. Richardson's persistence. "I don't know. He's not my problem." She immediately worried that she would find a problem at home, something missing, or worse, a boy transformed into a terrorist.

Dr. Richardson furrowed his brow. "You're not his mother."

She was indignant. Unfair of him to play the biology card. "No, I'm not." She stared at him coldly. "By choice."

Richardson nodded. "He must mean something to you. He's asleep in your home as we speak."

She pictured Kix, asleep on the grass in the park, young and innocent and trying so hard to survive. She let out a long sigh and muttered, "I shouldn't have. . . ."

"Shouldn't have what?" he probed.

"Shouldn't have told you he was there."

Dr. Richardson smiled out the side of his mouth. "Of course. Telling me was the problem."

"There's no point to it!" She was frustrated and angry at his nettling. Dr. Richardson had stopped smiling, but his eyes were still kind. She wanted out but had been brought up to exit gracefully. She sat forward on the couch. "And I should thank you." It was rote, and not particularly heartfelt, but she would indeed be grateful if he'd just let her go without a fuss.

"Ordinarily we would spend some time talking about your decision to leave," he said. "Kind of wrap things up, so we can be sure we're not avoiding something important."

"Well, I've never wanted to be 'ordinary,'" she said. "You know me well enough to know my mother wouldn't approve of the average, everyday ordinary!"

"Why wouldn't your mother approve?" he asked, jumping on the bone she'd inadvertently tossed him.

Perhaps, she thought, he'd be sorry to see her go. She was what Tyler called a therapist's dream, a private-pay neurotic, just crazy enough to be more interesting than dangerous. She nearly softened, feeling kind of sorry for the old man. She was sure that her encounter with the boy had spiced up his life, too.

"Superior. I was supposed to be superior, not ordinary. At any rate, I don't see a need to talk about not talking any more. I'm okay." She stood up. "Thank you," she said again and found the right words. "Thank you for your support."

"It has been my pleasure," he said with a slight bow of his head. "And do not hesitate to call me if you ever need to."

"Thank you," she said again, leaving fifteen minutes unused, like a tip for the good doctor, quite sure she'd not be needing him again.

She sped home in a cab and found the door to the guest bedroom still closed. She switched on the light in the guest bathroom. Kix's bath towel wasn't there. There was no evidence that Kix had been up. In the kitchen, the coffee level was roughly where she remembered it being after her two morning cups.

She knocked lightly on his door. When he didn't answer, she knocked harder. "Kix?"

Her hand on the doorknob, she hesitated. What if he was there, passed out, or even dead? What then? What if he wasn't there? Was anything missing?

The room was pristine; the guest quilt smoothed and straightened. The used towels were folded and stacked on the floor near the bed. Kix's things were gone. There was no note in sight.

She went back to the kitchen, confirming there was no note there, and checked the hall table, where unread mail and building notices accumulated. She found it hard to believe he would leave without a note. She could guess that he was going to New Orleans, but why wouldn't he just tell her? Of course he would. She squared her shoulders and headed to the last place she wanted to find a note from him.

In her closet, everything was exactly as she'd left it, except that the dial on the safe was at twenty, not fifteen. Tears came to her eyes. She'd trusted him, and he'd insulted her trust by robbing her! Or at least he'd tried. She spun through her numbers and opened the safe. One by one, she fingered the most important pieces, the brush set, her grandmother's diamond dinner ring, the gold chain, her birthday pearls. To her relief, everything was there. Under the last box, at the bottom of it all, there was a piece of notebook paper, folded formally and precisely in thirds. She sat cross-legged on the floor opposite the closet.

Dear Miss M:

Just fooling with you. I didn't take anything—wouldn't ever, not from you. You've been real good to me, and we appreciate it. I'm going to find Charmaigne and Abby. We might come back here. I'd like to. It sure was great to hang with you for a while. But it's up to Charmaigne, and whatever she thinks is best for the baby.

I hope I can find them. Charmaigne can be stubborn. She wants to be independent, but she doesn't have the street smarts that I do, and there's no way she can take care of

Abby without financial help. Charmaigne thinks I've got talent and could win some talent contest or something if I didn't have her and Abby to worry about, but I don't care about that. I care about them.

Yeah, I know it's not my kid. I told you my father's a bastard. He has brown eyes. No big mystery there, although our mom never got it and was mad at Charmaigne's boyfriend Charlie, but it wasn't Charlie. Anyway, it's nobody's business, and the kid seems to be okay so you don't need to let on to Charmaigne that you know.

Thanks again for everything. I'll try to write once in a while to let you know where we are. Remember, I know where you live!!

Yours,

KIX GORDON

PS: Go to auditions. You belong onstage—audiences love you!

PPS: Be more creative. When a person lives at 30 East and on the 17th floor and in unit 04, it's not that hard to figure out a likely combination.

She crumpled the letter. How dare he give her advice on how to live! Be more creative, indeed! Dr. Richardson would get a laugh out of that, wouldn't he? A homeless kid giving her advice. Telling her she had talent. Ha! That wasn't the issue, not at all.

She started to spin, her thoughts reeling around the pressure she felt to use her talent, please her mother, be creative, not fail, when she reopened the letter and smoothed it out. How self-centered could she be?

Anxious about Kix and worried about her things, she'd rushed past his horrific, heartbreaking indictment. The father!

A university professor committing incest? Could Kix be making that up? No, no. Perhaps only a university professor could get away with such a thing. Too horrible. No wonder the girl was sullen and withdrawn. How brave of Kix to take her away, to try to act the father, to provide, protect, parent.

What should she do with this information? What could she do? Did she have the courage to do anything? What would Dr. Richardson say? She realized with a start that she couldn't turn to Dr. Richardson for help. He no longer cared what she did or didn't do, whether she sang or not, befriended the boy or not, told him things or not. But perhaps he would care about this? Would he accept Kix's word for it? How could he remain neutral in the face of such a thing? Would he tell her to worry about herself, her own life, the things she could do something about? Her thoughts raced up and down an arpeggio of conflicts: Richardson, her mother, her career, her life. The boy.

Now, Charmaigne. She lay back on the carpet and stared at the dull white ceiling, horrified at the cruelty of life. She felt powerless over these young lives, powerless over her own. How did Charmaigne overcome such a heinous crime against her that she could make her way—any way—in this world? Charmaigne and the boy both did what they could with what they had. Even though Cecilia had everything to be grateful for, she'd been paralyzed. Something vital was missing from Cecilia's privileged life, and there were so many names for it, so many losses, she closed her eyes, overwhelmed, and cried.

For the rest of the day, Cecilia stayed home, sorting bills and papers and trimming dead leaves from plants in her southern window that were getting full, all-day sun. She moved a couple of geraniums to the east, where the morning light was filtered by a neighboring high-rise. By midafternoon she was anxious and expectant, and thought that she should shop in case Kix came back. Although he thought Charmaigne needed him, he himself needed to be taken care of. They were both just kids. They'd suffered unspeakably at the hands of their parents, who hadn't taken care of them. What about Kix's mother? Why hadn't she protected them, mothered them? Her problems with her own mother, her own mother's constant oversight and direction, seemed mild compared to the utter failure of Kix's folks. She hoped he would come back, and let her take care of him the way he needed to be taken care of. Charmaigne, too. She wasn't their mother, but she could take care of them. What would Dr. Richardson think of that?

As if her hoping could make it so, she hustled out to the upscale food emporium in her neighborhood, where she filled a basket with fresh fruits and vegetables, an overpriced olive oil in a stone crock, and a hunk of aged Parmesan. The fragrance of fresh basil so filled her elevator that her neighbor from the twenty-sixth floor asked— almost seriously—if he could come for dinner. She laughed, but, as she chopped the basil and spun it in her food processor with the pine nuts, garlic, expensive oil, and fresh cheese, she felt herself sinking into a dour loneliness. Kix obviously wasn't calling. She'd found her pasta machine, barely used, in the utility closet, and now, cooking for one, the idea of fresh pasta seemed silly. Stupid. A handful of linguini from the box would be good enough. If she felt like eating. Which she didn't, not just now. Perhaps a glass of red wine would stimulate her appetite. Wasn't that the purpose of an aperitif? She thought again of her mother, for whom wine was as necessary as water. She'd just have a glass. She'd tossed the last of that bottle from the laundry closet, but in her wine rack in her dining room there was a bottle of cabernet sauvignon with a lovely label, part gold foil, part black swan. She wasn't very sophisticated about wines, considering too much knowledge in that area more suspect than erudite. Cecilia's mother had used her knowledge of wines to conceal a growing addiction, perhaps on the theory that if you sent a bottle back every now and then that proved you were in it for the taste, not the high. In her twenties, Cecilia herself had suffered dates with men who thought that closing their eyes and naming a region and year made them cultured, although they couldn't sit through a piece of theater without checking their Blackberries at intermission. She opened the pretty bottle, poured herself a glass, and stretched out on her living-room couch to reread the morning's newspaper.

She awoke with her foot on a pedal, spinning yarn that dusted her hands with gold. She sat up on the couch and tried to remember when she'd slipped into sleep. She couldn't see the lake in the blackness, although the streetlights lit up Lake Shore Drive on her left and Columbus Drive on her right. In between, high-rises twinkled. Wine on an empty stomach! She'd slept for several hours. It must be nearing midnight. Kix hadn't shown up. It had been a wild hope.

But she knew that taking care of Kix was not the answer to her problems. She'd been overwhelmed by her own career angst and personal issues, which in comparison now seemed trivial. She'd never before felt like a spoiled brat, but now, the truth about Kix and Charmaigne and Abby made her ashamed of her own whininess. They were—at least Kix was—stronger and more resourceful than she in every regard. If she had any mothering skills, they were rudimentary at best, perhaps no more than the financial wherewithal to provide food and clothing and shelter for a family. She hadn't done much with her own life, and it was self-centered of her—Richardson had almost said as much—to think that she could help the kids. She cared, oddly, about them, about Kix, especially, but she didn't know how to help them. Her ignorance depressed her, made her feel like a poor excuse for a woman, her maternal instincts totally wrong. She got up and went to her bedroom, where she fell asleep in her clothes on top of the bedspread, exhausted.

The next morning, her dreams of *Rumplestilt's Kin* and spinning gold only vaguely remembered, she awoke with a new energy to do the things she could do something about. While her coffee was brewing, she went online and checked for upcoming auditions. Three or four were for sopranos in their thirties. Close enough. She had talent. She had experience. She'd told Richardson that she didn't need him anymore, and that she was sick of talking about not doing what she knew how to do. She should just go ahead and do it, right?

She limbered up at the piano, then drank two cups of strong black tea in her office while she sorted through stacks of sheet music, selecting her favorite audition pieces—showy tunes that showed her range and style but didn't invite the casting directors to compare her rendition to Streisand or Liza or Midler. The first suitable call was for Thursday. It was only Saturday. She could be ready by then. For three days, she disappeared into deep practice. Singing scales for warm-up, rememorizing words, singing for a half hour or more, full voice, then taking a break for a run along the lakeshore, a light lunch, and a repetition of the morning's practice. The first evening, she ate her pesto with fresh pasta she made for herself; the second night, she went to an open mike at a local club and listened to the competition—wretched; and the third, she suddenly remembered that all her songs were of the same style, and often at auditions, the director would ask, "What else you got?" or "Sweet, but give me something smoky." She needed to expand her repertoire. Panicked, she called Tyler, her former coach, and, for old times' sake plus the premium fee she offered, he agreed to come to her apartment both all day Tuesday and Wednesday afternoon to work on what he chirped would be her "glorious return" to the Chicago stage.

Tyler arrived at 9 a.m. on Tuesday, his throat wrapped in a beige silk scarf. He had a tickle in his throat but assured her he wasn't contagious. He was otherwise simply dressed, in pressed khakis and a stiffly starched white shirt with French cuffs and gold links, the top three buttons of the shirt open to reveal patches of smooth golden tan beneath the scarf. He declined the hot tea she offered, preferring plain boiling water instead—something he'd learned from Deepak Chopra, he said—and then warmed his hands in winter lamb's wool mittens for five minutes before sitting down to the piano.

"Such a beautiful instrument," he cooed, stroking the East Indian rosewood of her Steinway. "I am so glad, my dear, that you have decided to return to the stage. Never easy, mind you, but certainly within your grasp." He ran the opening bars of "What I Did for Love" from *A Chorus Line* and added, humbly and sincerely, "Thank you for remembering me. I've always been there for you, darling. Always." She smiled at him; a graduate student when she'd been a freshman, he'd helped her with her junior year recital and then moved to New York. When he returned to Chicago, they'd revived their friendship, and she'd hired him as her private coach all the way through *Rumplestilt's Kin*. He was patient, and kind, and understood the casting business. He was the one who'd first told her the old adage, "A professional actress is one who enjoys the bus ride to auditions."

On her behalf, he'd been outraged—unlike her mother—with the critic who'd slashed Cecelia along with the show. "Wrong! Wrong! Wrong!" he'd shouted into Cecilia's message machine the morning the review was published. "Do not read it, my dear! Do not!" He'd been too late, of course. Although, like many actresses, she professed not to care what the critics wrote, she read them as soon as she could get her hands on them. "I'm burning my copy as we speak. Hear that? It's my smoke alarm going off!" Tyler joked later that he'd barely avoided flooding his apartment by smothering the alarm in a wet towel before the sprinkler system kicked in. One step removed, he'd not taken the reviews to heart as deeply as Cecilia or her mother, and, while he wanted for her to move on, he'd quickly realized that he couldn't do it for her. He took her out for drinks, for dinner, to recitals by his other students, and when she declined the invitations to auditions that he had arranged for her, he pulled back, the ball in her court.

Now, he returned to coaching as if there had been no hiatus at all. They worked hard for a couple of hours, running scales, practicing her sight reading, then experimenting with a couple of different songs that Tyler knew the director of the show especially liked. By Wednesday afternoon, Tyler declared her ready.

"Will you come play for me tomorrow?" she asked as he was leaving her apartment.

"Oh, honey, I'd love to," he said, "but I don't think that would go down well."

"Why not?" she asked. She'd never taken her own accompanist to an audition before, but now the idea seemed so obvious. To do your best, why not perform exactly as rehearsed?

"Way too high-maintenance," he said. "Besides, since I'm not doing the show, you're gonna have to work with an inferior pianist, no matter what, so you better get started right off the bat!"

She laughed along with him but wasn't convinced.

"You don't want to look fragile," he said, taking her hands in his. "They all know you've been away from it for a while. You got to show 'em you've still got the stuff." He let go and her hands dropped to her side.

"Fragile? Is that the word on the street?"

Tyler hesitated, and Cecilia realized that there probably wasn't any word on the street about her. Until she showed up, no one would be thinking of her or anticipating her arrival. This was a cattle call, not an audition to which she'd been specifically invited. "Whenever an old face shows up after a hiatus, there's going to be a question: 'What've you been doing?' What are you going to say?"

She folded her hands in front of her and shook her head slowly. "I'm just going to say 'screw you, it's none of your business.'"

Tyler howled. "You go, girl!! Call me as soon as it's over!" He turned to go and, with one hand on the doorknob, turned back to her. "But remember, darling, that this is just one audition, and it has nothing to do with you. You're there to play the game, but win or lose, it's way out of your control. You're either what they're looking for or not. You been watching those talent shows on TV? Dreadful stuff, really, but you know what they all have? Guts and heart. It carries them through. Just sing your little heart out and knock 'em dead." He stretched to kiss her on both cheeks, European style, Tyler style. "Ciao."

Despite a ritual lavender-scented bubble bath and a warm massaging shower, Cecilia slept fitfully that night and dreamt another version of *Rumplestilt's Kin*. She was locked in a rehearsal room back at college, and her mother was onstage at the Lyric Opera House, in an ornate black and gold Elizabethan gown, arms outstretched to the audience, her mouth in an open O, holding a single note for well into an hour, without a breath. The audience was standing, amazed, but a couple of people in the front row, their faces obscure, were talking among themselves and shouting, "Poseur! Impostor! Sham!" In her room, Cecilia held her single note, beads of blood forming on her forehead, until her vocal chords popped out of her mouth like straws, her mother was silenced, and Tyler magically appeared to wipe her brow. Cecilia woke from her dream, her heart racing and her mouth crusted dry. She went to the kitchen and drank a glass of tepid water from the tap, then filled a mug, boiled it in the microwave, and sipped it like warm milk, hoping it would ease her to sleep.

She awoke again at nine only because her cell phone rang and she had to get out of bed to find her purse to stop it. She missed the call, from Tyler. His message was short and sweet.

"Before you leave the house, fifteen minutes of scales and run through both numbers twice. Enjoy the bus ride!"

She wouldn't be taking the bus, but she knew what he meant. She dressed in the outfit Tyler had chosen—a black silk skirt cut on the bias with lots of swirl to it and a simple black, light knit, long-sleeved top, V-necked with just a hint of décolletage. Even with the necklace of large silver balls that Tyler had selected, she felt the outfit too severe and redressed in a green print skirt with a short-sleeved lime T-shirt. Inspecting herself, she felt like an ad for a rain forest and went back to the black. "Let them dress you as they want," he'd advised. "Better not to have too much style of your own." After her night's dream, she heard his advice as a kick in the stomach. Perhaps that was her trouble with the whole profession—always having to fit someone else's notions of who you were or should be. At least the bus ride gave you a chance to be yourself.

The audition was at a small, storefront theater on Halsted Street, on the near north side of the city. Cecilia had been to the theater before, both for auditions and as an audience member, but she remembered it as being larger. Waiting in the lobby for her name to be called, she counted the seats on the seating chart near the box office—152—and rolled her neck in slow circles. A much younger woman, two younger men, and a man her age sat in folding chairs that had been scattered around the lobby, gazing at posters of past productions.

Cecilia took a seat not far from the younger woman, whose daisy-flowered flip-flops revealed neatly polished, pastel green toenails, who looked up from the sheet music on her lap and mouthed words. She smiled at Cecilia. "Have you auditioned here before?" she asked.

"Not in a long time," Cecilia answered. "Have you?"

"Never," the young woman answered. "I just graduated in June from Indiana. So I'm just learning how to audition. It's fun, though, don't you think?"

Cecilia smiled. One of the young men had stood up and was bellowing arpeggios at a wall; the one sitting rolled his head around like a demonized child. She'd never considered auditioning "fun," even at the height of her young career. If she'd been completely honest with Dr. Richardson, she would've said she dreaded auditioning, dreaded the critique, the imperfection, the rejection, the failure.

"I learn so much every time," the young woman bubbled on. "I haven't been cast yet, except as an understudy, but everyone I've met has taken so much time to show me the ropes, or get me to sing a little differently than I was trained, or even to tell me what to wear, you know. Stuff like that."

"This is a great theater town," was all that Cecilia could think of to say. "It's a very tight community." As she finished her words, a man with a clipboard called "Morrison."

"Nice to meet you," she said. "Good luck to you."

"Thanks," the woman said. "By the way, my name is Leigh Hunter."

Cecilia was halfway to the theater door when she realized she hadn't told Leigh her first name. Thank goodness she wasn't seeing Dr. Richardson. He'd probably want to analyze that.

The man with the clipboard took her headshot and résumé—both ten years old—and pointed to the stage. "Nice picture," he said. "But a little out of date?" He handed it to a middle-aged woman, a gray-haired man, and several younger people clustered together in the fifth row of the ten in the theater.

She shrugged.

The woman asked her, "So, Cecilia, tell me what you've been doing lately."

"Took a little break," she said with the nonchalance she'd practiced with Tyler. "Did some studying and some writing."

The woman didn't press her, and Cecilia handed the pianist her music. He ran a few chords—Cecilia thought it fairly well in tune, but not perfect—and then he looked to her to see that she was ready. Despite the moisture beading on her forehead, she nodded, assuring herself that she was too far from the directors for them to see it, and began to sing. She couldn't bring herself to look at their faces, so she focused above their heads, on the back wall, and tried to picture Tyler and her own living room. She was no more than a minute into her number when she heard her own voice—clear, on pitch, resonant, nearly perfect (considering)—and panicked. She stopped singing. "I'm sorry," she said. Without stopping to retrieve her music from the pianist, she hurried down the stage stairs and fled out the door, through the lobby, and to the street.

Her legs beating like a metronome, she sped down Halsted, cursing Tyler and his insistence on three-inch heels. At busy North

Avenue she headed east and pumped along, feet burning, until she got to the underpass at Lake Shore Drive. As she entered the tunnel, she felt a cold fear. What if the boy were there? How ashamed she was, that he could sing—off-key, thinly, mumbling the words—on street corners and underpasses, and after days, years, of training, she couldn't get through two minutes? She'd run out on an audition! How long would it take for that to get around? How could she expect ever to work again?

And if she didn't sing, what was she going to do with her life? She'd been doing nothing for years. What was wrong with her? And why hadn't that psychologist figured it out?

The tunnel was empty, and she stopped, letting her eyes adjust to its dusk, listening to the grind of traffic overhead, and trying not to breathe the underground air.

nine

It was summer, and no new patients called that week to fill Cecilia's hour, so during the slot she'd abandoned, Haverill took a sketch pad and went down to the plaza of his building. He was feeling sorry for himself. Cecilia's abrupt departure felt like a failure on his part, even though he'd been trained to consider that as his own ego issue. His role was to be there and be of service. To respect the patient enough to believe that she knew what was best for her. Many neurotics quit therapy prematurely, and many returned—if not to him, to someone, in which case his success was that they still sought therapy, still had the capacity to ask for help. The fact that they didn't return to him specifically was not his failure. It was hard, though, for him not to take personally a patient's leaving. Who wouldn't? He told himself it was only natural. How would a lawyer feel after years of working on a case, only to be fired on the eve of trial in favor of a famous name? Or what about the parish priest, counselor to a family through disputes and illnesses and funerals, replaced at a wedding by a visiting monsignor?

He bought a coffee in the lobby and sat outside at an iron table under an umbrella. He opened his sketch pad in the middle, although most of the first sheets were also blank. He poised his pencil in the center and stared at the passing crowd. Nothing came. He put his pencil in the center of the page and forced himself to move it, a pinpoint becoming a slanted oval, dark on the growing outer edge, lighter in the middle, but still miserly, uninspired. A doodle. Nothing.

Disgusted with himself, he closed his eyes to the blank page and tried to conjure up Roslyn's marble block. The nuances of the grain escaped him, but he felt his hands subtly flexing as if he were molding clay. Clay was an easier medium—you could instantly fix your mistakes. He'd not made a mistake with Cecilia, had he? He'd listened intently as she'd steadfastly tried to convince him that she was okay, that she was as good as she said she was, and that she had only appreciation for her mother's support. Cecilia bent over backward to make excuses for her mother, who anyone could see had been domineering, perfectionist, and conditional in her meting out of love. If Cecilia could name this resentment, she could probably get past it.

Haverill had seen *Rumplestilt's Kin*. A dreadful play, but at the time he and Rosalyn had agreed that the actress who played the daughter was extraordinary. He was afraid he may've looked surprised when Cecilia walked into his office a few months ago, but he'd never told her that he'd seen the fateful performance—that would've been unprofessional. She didn't need his validation. She needed to develop the ability to validate herself. Cecilia lacked the essential self-confidence of an artist—the ability to stand apart from her art and judge it, good and bad, without extending those adjectives to herself. An artist had to weather wrong criticism and false praise, to set her own standards. A coach could tell you whether you were on pitch, but the artistry, the artistic statement, was solely yours. And it was the artistry that gave rise to the joy, the joy Cecilia seemed to be lacking.

Why was he even thinking of Cecilia? He'd never himself produced a satisfactory work. He'd taken secret pleasure in the few clay models he'd managed, but he'd never declared himself in a more permanent medium—not wood or bronze or tin or stone. What was he afraid of? He wasn't trying to create something for public display, so what could possibly be holding him back? He could name Cecilia's fear—fear of displeasing her mother—but he couldn't name his own.

Perhaps it had something to do with permanence. Everything in Haverill's life was so ephemeral, so intangible. His relationships with the patients he knew the best were still one-way, once or twice a week affairs; his professional relationships were not social; his social relationships were mostly his wife's. Without Ros, many of those were a bit wary of friendship with him. People didn't like the idea that he might be analyzing them. He wasn't. They weren't that interesting. But still, sometimes he felt lonely, as if huge hunks of life were passing him by.

His daughter had lived with him for barely eighteen years and then gone off to her own life. The woman to whom he pledged "'til death" had died way too young, way short of "forever." Everything seemed so transient. Cecilia's art, also. She could perform onstage, make a big or small mistake, continue, forget, move on. It would disappear. That notion appealed to him. Why wasn't that comforting to Cecilia? Why didn't that free her to perform with complete abandon, come what will? The performance ephemeral—over, only a memory, no permanent record—even the newspaper reviews buried in archives, irrelevant. That was the essence of live theater, that it was, like life itself, like life's problems and life's triumphs, transitory. But sculpture? It defied death. It was deathless. It intimidated him.

He looked up from his blank page and saw a man ten feet away, facing him. Despite the predicted summer heat, he wore a heavy sweater and dark, dirty pants, torn at the knees. He wore no socks, and one leather boot had only half a shoelace. Before he could avoid it, the man made eye contact and darted forward, paper cup outstretched. Haverill shook his head and held up one hand in a stop position. Disappointed, the man halted, searched Haverill's face for any softening, and then shuffled off, leaving a trail of "God bless you's." Haverill didn't feel blessed. He was irritated to have been put in the position of saying no to a direct request. He could spare a dollar, but if you gave to one, wouldn't you have to give to all? He gave to collective efforts, the Salvation Army and such—shouldn't that absolve him from responding to each and every beggar on the street? He hated being so judgmental, but the chances were high that the man would've spent the dollar on liquor or cigarettes. He'd not been a druggie; those were easier to spot. He wouldn't think twice about saying no to an addict.

It was near the end of Cecilia's hour, and Haverill closed his sketch pad. How could she have given that homeless boy sixty dollars, befriended him, even, and brought him home? She'd put herself in danger. She'd survived that night, but how could she be sure that was the end of it? She was clearly still in danger. In his entire career, he'd never called a terminated patient to follow up, but this was different. Cecilia's personal safety was at stake. He would call her right away.

Getting up from his table, he saw the man with the paper cup, standing as stiff as a Buckingham Palace guard, nearly catatonic, fifty feet behind him. Whether he'd forgotten Haverill or was stalking him, Haverill didn't know, but he reached in his pocket, where he'd put the change from his overpriced coffee, and went back to his table, where he anchored two singles with a quarter and hurried away, hoping no one, other than the man, noticed him. Before entering the revolving doors of his building, he peeked back and, to his relief, saw the man standing over the table. He turned around and lifted his hand in the same stop sign that Haverill had used earlier, but Haverill understood the man's sign to mean peace. He nodded slightly, although the man would probably not notice such a tiny gesture, and rotated inside.

His phone was ringing as he unlocked his office door. His daughter's usual time. If he answered it, he might blab what had just happened on the plaza, or worse, she would talk him out of calling Cecilia, and despite himself, he was curious. He let the call go into voice mail.

"Hi, Dad. Surprised you're not there! Wanted to say goodbye.

You know I'm taking vacation. Barging through France. Two weeks! How about that! I'll email you all the contact info in case you need it. Be good! Love ya!"

She must've said before that she was going to France, and the barge trip sounded vaguely familiar—she may've tried last year to interest him, but he judged it way too slow—he spent so much time in his profession sitting, he wanted something more active in a vacation: more sightseeing, or more activity, like sailing or golf or hiking, something like that, something at which he would set his own pace. Who did she say she was going with? A girlfriend? A boyfriend? He couldn't remember. Maybe her email would say.

He saw two more patients—a gambling addict and a depressed commodities trader—and had another break. He called his daughter, who was in a rush. Her flight to Paris was that evening out of Detroit, and her plane left New Orleans at five.

"Aren't you going to ask?" Maddie said.

"Ask what?" he said. "You said you'd email me the details."

"I will. Just in case."

"You'll be fine," he said. When she didn't answer right away, he realized that there had been a non sequitur in the conversation, but he couldn't for the life of him imagine what it was. In therapy there were often long pauses, but their father-daughter conversations always flowed, two busy people who understood each other perfectly and knew how to say the sorts of supportive things that got the other one to talk. "You're not worried, are you?"

"No, no," she said. "I'm going to have male protection."

"A boyfriend?" he asked.

She giggled like a girl. "Yeah, I guess so," she said. "It's been a whirlwind three months. I didn't tell you earlier because, well, you know."

"I didn't know I was so pushy," he said.

"Sometimes," she said. "Anyway, you better stay in shape so you can walk me down the aisle."

Tweaking the feminist in his daughter, he laughed, "He better ask for my permission!"

"If he does, please say no!" she shot back.

"Okay," he said. "Will I approve of him?"

"Probably not," she teased. "He's a pediatrician, plays bass in a swing band, writes a little poetry, plays a decent game of tennis, has an eight handicap, father's a past commodore of the yacht club, loves me."

"That's the ticket."

"And he's only five years younger!"

He thought immediately of Cecilia and her infatuation with the teenage boy. "What's with you women and younger men?"

"Five years is hardly younger. Besides, it means we'll have a longer time together."

"I know." He wished her well and hung up, realizing with a start that her "just in case" concern was not for her own well-being but for his. He might need her, rather than the other way around!

His desk clock chimed, time for his next appointment. He hadn't called Cecilia. He shouldn't and he wouldn't. There was no valid reason for calling her. To call her might suggest that he had some stake in her therapy. He didn't. Well he did, to the extent he earned his living on the backs of other people's problems, but most people did, didn't they? Doctors, lawyers, plumbers, even. It wasn't personal. He needed patients, but he didn't need for Cecilia to be a patient. And he didn't know she was really in danger, or that she was in any way a danger to herself or others, so it would be unprofessional, unethical, even, to pursue her. If he thought she was sexually involved with the boy, he might make an exception to his long-standing rule, but he doubted she was, although there'd been a number of well-publicized cases about female school teachers and their young lovers. In fact, Cecilia didn't present herself to him as a particularly sexual person, and he couldn't remember that she'd ever talked about a boyfriend or ex-husband.

Over the years, he'd had plenty of female patients develop what

he told Rosalyn were adolescent crushes on him, some overtly flirtatious, some attempting to tease him with graphic descriptions
of their passionate encounters, often casual and alarmingly easy,
others just unctuously eager to please. Unlike some of his colleagues, he'd never succumbed to any of his patient's charms. He
had Rosalyn, his steadfast companion, the passion of his life, to
thank for the fact that he'd never once felt tempted by any of his
female patients, no matter how voluptuous, how slender their legs,
how long and silky their hair as they tossed it back or drew a strand
across their lips. Now, however, whenever Cecilia popped into his
mind, he wondered if he was more vulnerable, if he was losing his
professional distance, because Rosalyn was gone, had been gone,
unbelievably, more than a year. Unlike some of the others, Cecilia
didn't flirt with him—far from it—and she didn't seem particularly grateful to him or attached in any way. She'd quit him without
the slightest tremor of insecurity or sense of loss.

The end of a therapy was often like a small death—the two
people, once bound in the intimacy of the therapy room—never to
speak or socialize again, the patient embarking on her new life, the
therapist sitting behind, laboring on, the two dead to each other.
He was certain Cecilia wasn't mourning, but he had to admit to
himself—so that he wouldn't do anything about it—that he kind
of missed her. Why? He should probably look at that, but he didn't
have the energy. He was a widower. Wasn't that in itself a sufficient explanation? In the past year, every ending, every loss, every
empty hour echoed in the canyon of the loss of Rosalyn.

He saw his next patient, and two more, and left midafternoon,
his failure to sketch and the news of Maddie's boyfriend still
weighing on his spirits. He would've liked to have had a social
commitment for the evening, something to take his mind off his
loneliness, but he didn't, and so he prescribed for himself the "self-
care" he promoted to his patients. He decided to make himself a
good meal. He had become, out of necessity, a good cook and now
found the process both creative and soothing.

There had been no time to say goodbye to Rosalyn, or to prepare for life without her. He'd woken up one morning, surprised that she was still in bed, that there was no cup of fresh coffee waiting for him on the night table. They'd not been out late. There was no particular reason for her to have overslept her usual. He'd called the paramedics hopelessly. He was a medical doctor, and he knew death, but he had never slept next to it. He'd been terrified, angry, devastated, despondent.

In the horrible weeks after his wife's death, it came as a shock to him just how dependent he'd been on her. He'd thought of himself as a mature, authentic, autonomous adult who made few, if any, demands on others and was fully functioning, integrated and independent. He was professionally self-aware. He never acted impulsively but was willing to be flexible when the occasion demanded it. His temper was under control. He wasn't jealous. He was self-confident yet humble, given his exceptional background and talents. Within a few weeks, a stack of bills had piled up, he was out of starched shirts, and his pantry was close to empty. He'd finished the spaghetti casserole Maddie'd left for him when she'd gone home the week after Rosalyn's funeral, and, with two servings a day, he'd ploughed through the last of the six boxes of bran flakes Ros had brought home one day when they were on sale, as well as the last of four large cans of peaches. He dreaded the idea of going to a restaurant alone, and after a few weeks of suppers of cheese and crackers, fried eggs, and peanut butter and jelly sandwiches, he'd learned, with Maddie's help, to cook.

Tonight, he had a taste for vichyssoise and decided to walk home both to pass the time and to stop by a grocery store with an especially good selection of fresh vegetables. Not that he would know a gourmet potato from an ordinary spud, but he wanted potted chives and fresh watercress. At home he stripped off his tie and rolled up his sleeves. In the kitchen, he felt like he was spending time with Ros, remembering the way she sliced a celery stalk vertically in half and half again, then made the smallest and most precise horizontal cuts, or how she broke an egg with a quick tap of a knife rather than just whacking it on the edge of the pan. He flipped through his cookbook, *The Joy of Cooking*, pausing every few pages to read Ros's margin notes: by a paella, "Made this for the Steeles, 7/12/89"; by a tomato-soup cake, a notation, "really takes 48 minutes."

He found the recipe, one he'd never made, and read it through. He remembered Maddie telling him, during a weekend visit toward the end of his first month of widowhood, "Mother always said, 'if you can read, you can cook.'"

"I can read, but I can't sing," he'd said.

"That's totally different," Maddie said. "She didn't say that."

The recipe for the soup proved easy. He minced three leeks and an onion and sautéed them in butter, no longer the kind of cook who had to look up the verbs or guess at how large medium potatoes were or how thinly to slice them. He simmered the vegetables and chicken stock and whirred the mixture in his blender with a generous amount of cream. In a hurry to get the soup chilled enough to eat, he poured two cups into a larger measuring cup and put it in a larger bowl of ice cubes. He liked his soup ice cold, dusted lightly with mace, and sprinkled liberally with chives.

After downing two bowls—it was excellent, and he was proud of it—he bounded up the stairs to his rooftop garden, inspired by his culinary success. It was a benign summer evening, not at all humid, and the garden was in full bloom. The north brick wall was obscured by a variety of oversized red-orange clay pots, tubs of red and white impatiens and geraniums, and baskets of iridescent light green sweet potato plants and trailing vines in a luminous black-purple. He sat at a glass table with his sketch pad, a dozen subjects calling out to him, but again he couldn't start.

He was torn, as, he suspected, many fathers were torn. His little girl was getting married. No, she hadn't said that, but he assumed that he and Rosalyn had had a good enough marriage that his daughter would want to get married, not just live together until the going got tough. He wanted her to get married. He wanted to see his grandchildren. What an old man he was becoming! Rosalyn hadn't lived to be mother of the bride or a grandmother, and he assumed that she had wanted those things. He thought about that. He remembered Rosalyn saying once that she "dreaded" having grandchildren, she'd thought it no concern of hers. What she'd wanted for Maddie was for her to get through all her schooling without the interference of a man or marriage or children. "You get that degree," she'd say to Maddie, when she'd call home from college unhappy about another breakup with a boyfriend. "You worry about boys later."

Rosalyn had always called Maddie's dates "boys," as if to emphasize that Maddie wasn't grown-up enough yet to settle down, as if getting married was both "settling" and "down"— giving up some of her own dreams to settle down with a boy. Had Rosalyn felt that way? Why would she have? Haverill had never stopped her from having a career—having a child had been the deciding factor. Working nights in the big city while trying to raise a child in the suburbs? They'd wanted children, no question about that. They both had. They'd both agreed that the timing for Rosalyn's career was not, in the early years, and then in Maddie's adolescence, right. Later. That's why they'd moved to the city, later, so that Rosalyn could pursue that acting career.

Had it been the other way around, Rosalyn pursuing her career first and children later, there may not have been a Maddie. Instead of being Maddie's mother, Rosalyn may have ended up like Cecilia, talented but lonely, directionless, searching for meaning in dramatic and possibly dangerous ways.

Well, Maddie'd waited, she was clearly old enough now, and she wouldn't be sacrificing her career—one could always see a few patients—but Haverill still felt torn, in the most fatherly of ways, because her young man would become the man in Maddie's life, and he would be number two. As it was supposed to be. But still. A second major loss, so quickly on the heels of losing Rosalyn.

He thought about the marble. Perhaps—if Maddie did get married—he could sculpt something for the couple as a wedding present. Would that be too narcissistic? Too homemade? Why would she want a piece of sculpture from him? It would only be the thought, the gesture, the significance in the eyes of the beholder: a collaborative wedding gift for a precious daughter, from her mother, who'd bought the marble, and her father, who would shape it. If only he could begin.

ten

She'd had nowhere to go, and as soon as her eyes adjusted, she made her way through the dank tunnel, eyes fixed on the light at the other end, alert to the possible sound of footsteps behind her, gradually assuring herself that she was safe, that Kix would not be in the tunnel or at the beach. Up the stairs, on the other side, she sat on the beach wall and stared at the horizon, seeing nothing.

The midday sun hung like a spotlight over her right shoulder, so that her right side was burning while her left was cooled by a northeast breeze off the lake. Her phone buzzed but she couldn't bear to see who was calling. She shooed away the flicker of hope that the director was calling after her, begging her to come back. This was a tough business, and that would never happen. She didn't want to talk to Tyler, and there was no one else who would normally call her midday. Normal people had normal jobs and worked during the day. Perhaps what they did wasn't exceptional, and perhaps they weren't exceptionally talented, but at least they did what they could do. They didn't run from auditions and sit on beach walls during the day.

She hung her head and cried silently. In a few minutes, her mind went blank, and her tears stopped. She wiped her face with her hands and turned into the breeze with her eyes closed. When she opened them, she saw a shabby old man in a worn suit and knit cap pushing a shopping cart toward her, and she hopped from the wall down to the beach, where she stripped off her sandals and waded into the shallow water. It was freezing. She retreated, her feet stinging from the cold. Nearby, a couple of children splashed, oblivious. She waded back in and felt her feet go numb.

The phone buzzed again. She waded out of the water and fumbled in her purse.

No name came up on the screen. Wearily, she answered.

"Mrs. Morrison?"

"Yes," she said, slightly irritated but not bothering to correct the caller. She wasn't a "Mrs."

"Do you remember me? This is Charmaigne. Kix's friend?"

Cecilia ran her free hand through her hair, using her thumb to massage the base of her neck. "Yes, yes, Charmaigne, of course."

"Where is he?" she asked, part plea, part challenge.

"I don't know, Charmaigne, he's looking for you." She put her right finger in her ear, the better to hear Charmaigne and get a hint of where she was calling from. If Charmaigne were in New Orleans, maybe Cecilia would hear street music in the background or a riverboat calliope, and at least she could report that much to Kix—if she ever saw him again. She felt herself beginning to think clearly for the first time since running out of the audition. "Where are you, Charmaigne?"

"Yeah," she said. "Tell him to call me."

"I would if I knew where he was," she repeated, "but tell me, how's the baby?"

Charmaigne hung up in the middle of Cecilia's question, and Cecilia snapped her phone closed, angry to be so dismissed by the girl. Where was Charmaigne? Why hadn't she told Kix where she was going? If, as Kix thought, Charmaigne wanted not to be a burden to him, then she ought to not cause him worry, either. Selfish girl, she owed him that much, after all he'd risked and done to try to take care of her.

What a terrible day this had been! How had it gone so wrong? She'd looked out to the back of the theater, avoiding the director's eyes, and had seen—vaguely, clearly, then undoubt-edly—her mother, grimacing in the back row. Then she'd fled, and Charmaigne had called, looking for the boy who, a week ago, also had fled. Cecilia drummed her fingers on her phone. She wanted to call the girl back, find out where she was in case Kix called, but the number was blocked. Probably a phone booth someplace. Perhaps in a shelter. The noise in the background had sounded like inside noises—a little hollow, no horns or engines or sirens to suggest she was near traffic, but voices, cadenced voices, as from a TV or radio.

The cell phone vibrated in her hand. Now or never. "Tyler," she answered.

"Honey," he said.

"I don't know," she said, knowing the question but not the answer.

"Meet me at the Sofitel." She could rely on Tyler to pick some-place elegant and show-offy, not in his price range, but easily in hers. She'd caused this mess, and he'd talk her through it, but he'd make her pay.

"Give me half an hour," she said.

"Where are you?"

"North Avenue Beach," she said.

"In that case, walk south until you come to the palm trees, and I'll meet you there."

"Where?"

"There's a beach bar in the elbow there, around Oak Street," he said. "They've put a bunch of palm trees in the sand. It's a hoot. Let's go there."

Palm trees growing in Chicago. This she had to see.

As she walked, her irritation with the afternoon sank into cyclical despair. There was something terribly wrong with her, and a drink with an old friend at a beach bar wasn't going to fix it. Her entire body felt scorched with embarrassment. If she couldn't audition, how could she think that performing again would be in any way fulfilling? And if not singing, then what? Despite her sour mood, as soon as the palm trees came into view, Cecilia smiled. The open-air restaurant was elevated, built on wooden planks on several levels, with canvas sails providing some shelter from the sun and umbrellas shading many of the tables. The bar was filled with white plastic chaise lounges. Flowers were everywhere, posts covered with vines of pink hibiscus, window boxes with orange marigolds, hanging baskets with trailing purple flowers. The owners had indeed imported an island atmosphere, and, in celebration, Cecilia ordered a frozen strawberry daiquiri. Tyler arrived, gave her a little peck on the cheek, and quickly ordered.

"Charmaigne just called," she said, hoping to deflect Tyler's inevitable anger.

"What did she want?" he asked, with no particular interest.

"To find Kix." Tyler watched the waitress deliver his beer. Cold sweat streamed down the sides of the glass, and Tyler used his napkin to dry it off. Cecilia sighed. "But I don't know where he is, and she didn't say where she is, so it's kind of a mess."

"I'd say so," Tyler said, taking a long sip through the dense reddish head of the beer. He put down the glass and leaned across the table on his elbows. "So how bad was it?"

"Pretty bad."

"How bad?"

"Don't torment me," she said. "You know very well how bad."

"Yes, but you need to say it out loud."

"It was bad," she said, fairly shouting at him as she fell back in her chair.

"What specifically was so bad?"

She picked up her drink as if to throw it at him.

"You have to say. Out loud. So you can let it go."

Tyler was full of self-help aphorisms and they drove her crazy. "I've never understood that."

"It's just that it never sounds so bad out loud as it does bouncing off the walls of your brain, getting bigger and louder and bigger and louder until you explode."

She let the daiquiri melt in her mouth, then sighed. "I started singing, and it sounded good. I wasn't looking at anyone, just singing my song, when my mother came in and sat in the back row, shaking her head."

Tyler, bless him, threw his head back in a howl. "From the grave! Will she ever stop haunting you? When she died, you should've given her room to someone else—to a fan! To me! For god's sake, girl, let the old woman go!"

"Won't need to. When this gets around, I'll never work again."

"Not true, and you know it."

"Who would hire someone who can't get through an audition?"

"No one," Tyler said, reaching across the table for her hand. "No one." He dipped his chin and smiled up at her. "But they do hire those who do."

Not convinced, she ordered another round.

"I can see I'm going to have to take charge of your rehabilitation," Tyler said.

"You do that," she said, with a little more edge than she intended, but she knew that Tyler knew that she would be grateful. Stars had managers to advise them on their careers—which coaches to hire, which auditions to give, which roles to take. Artists, Cecilia thought, managed themselves. Unasked, Cecilia's mother, Francine Morrison, had assumed the role of manager; now that she was gone, Cecilia would have to reestablish her career before she could manage herself. "Long road?" she asked, this time more humbly.

"Not long, but it might be bumpy," he said. "You have to want it. Do you?"

She put down her glass. "What else could I want? Remember, you're the one who sent me to therapy."

"I keep forgetting you're a first timer."

"You've been more than once?"

He held up four fingers and pulled them down one by one. "In college. The year after graduate school. When I was in New York. And now."

"Oh."

"It's common in my community," Tyler said. "The only alternative when you're alternative."

It amused her how frequently Tyler felt compelled to remind her he was gay. His teeth were perfect, his tan was perfect, his white shirt was perfectly pressed and its long sleeves folded back just so. For whatever reason, straight men just never looked quite so perfect. But Tyler was loyal and fun and talented and supportive, and if he weren't gay, she would definitely consider him date material.

"Well, I've stopped. It wasn't helping me very much, if at all. I still can't think of anything specific that would make me happy—anything that I really want like that—so I don't know. By default, I guess it has to be singing. That's what I was groomed for."

"Not even marriage or kids?"

"That's different," she said.

"Usually one of the things people want in life. A relationship," Tyler ventured. "Did you ever?"

"Who knows what I wanted back then? I was all about my career. No one asked."

"No one asked what?" Tyler was reminding her, annoyingly, of Dr. Richardson.

"No one asked me to marry them," she said, exasperated. "Kids never entered my consciousness."

"They have now, apparently."

"No." She signaled to the waitress, who didn't see her wave. "Why would you say that?"

"These kids, Kix and Charmaigne, they seem to have a bit of a toehold."

"What?" She hadn't seen Kix in a week, Charmaigne even longer. She was surprised Tyler bothered to remember their names.

"I don't know, you seem a little hurt that they've been out of touch."

"No. Look it, they're gone. Both of them. That's okay." Tyler stuck his lower lip out and frowned at her. "I mean I hope they're safe and everything, but I wasn't looking to them to save me from myself. How did we get started on this?"

"Relationships." A few tables away, the waitress twirled her finger in the air, and Tyler nodded, held up two fingers, and pointed to Cecilia and then himself.

"Yes, well, I was just saying that I don't have a lot of control over who I meet and who wants to dance, and whether to have kids, so I better pick something I can do for myself."

Having recently broken up after a six-year committed relationship, Tyler sighed. "I hear you on that one, honey," he said. "I'm just saying that to have a singing career, you have to want it more than anything. More than a boyfriend, maybe. And, here's the kicker." He leaned across the table and looked both ways, a parody of a spy passing national secrets. "Getting it won't make you happy."

She opened her mouth to protest, but he held up his hand, blocking her unspoken words with his palm and a cock of his head.

He put his hands at ten o'clock and two o'clock on an imaginary steering wheel.

She nodded.

"I get it."

He smiled.

"The bus ride," she said.

Tyler's version of the bus ride was a vigorous couple of weeks of singing, running, singing, dieting (for the removal of toxins as well as what he perceived to be her five extra pounds), singing, dancing, scene study, and practice auditions. They spent more time at his loft/studio, and every couple of days he'd bring in friends and other students to critique each other. Most of his students were younger, and eager, and hung on every word Tyler uttered, without push-back. Cecilia hated the public nature of the critique and went along with whatever was said for the sake of moving the focus off her and on to the next student. But she had ideas of her own, and, finally, the third time they met for mutual critiques, Tyler gave an instruction with which she strongly disagreed. She may need coaching, and she hadn't been the world's greatest success lately at auditioning, but she did know a thing or two about singing and decided to say something.

"I think it would sound more natural with a pause," she ventured, after he'd said to sing the first eight bars without one. Facing the group, she saw a couple of the students nodding tentatively.

"We're not going natural, darling, we're going for dramatic effect." The nodding students looked from him to her as if the matter were settled.

"What if the dramatic effect we want is natural?" she shot back. "Listen." She sang the two phrasings, his way and hers.

He smiled. "I see," he said and turned to his students. "An artist is usually right," he said. "But you need to know why you're right, so that you will be right more often." Cecilia had tried not to beam, but later Tyler gave her a ride home.

"Pretty proud of yourself for that one?" he asked.

"I just . . .," she started.

"You should be," he said. "By the way, next week there's a season audition I want you to go to at Lincolnshire."

"I don't know, Ty. I can sing it, sure. But mentally, I don't know."

"It's like a horse," he said.

"Sooner or later you get a concussion?"

He reached over and took her hand. "Sooner or later we're all dead," he said. "The question is, what are you going to do in the meantime?"

That was, indeed, the question, Cecilia thought. She figured that all kinds of work had downtimes between high points: between lifesaving diagnoses and a string of common colds; between death penalty acquittals and drunk-and-disorderlies; between multiple homicides and routine traffic stops. But this theater profession had a lot of nonproductive waiting involved. Even if you got a part, you could wait through an entire first act to make your entrance in the second—a vital, but tiny role. What were you supposed to do in the meantime? Crosswords? Sudoku? How many classics could a person read?

Tyler performed two or three times a year, and taught and coached between shows. She thought she could do that, if she was looking for something to do. They had similar university trainings, but that wasn't what she'd been groomed for. Francine Morrison had wanted her daughter to be in the spotlights, not backstage.

As she entered her apartment, turning on lights and putting on a kettle for tea, she realized that Tyler's criticism was far different from her mother's. Tyler's was gilded in the optimism that the artist's work could be improved. Whether she'd intended it or not, Cecilia's mother's criticism had implied that the artist wasn't up to the work. If she ever were to teach, she'd want to be like Tyler. She'd never want to treat a young artist the way her mother had treated her.

Exhausted, Cecilia sipped her tea while reading the unread morning paper, then watched a talent show on TV. The contestants, for the most part, were, as Tyler had said, horrible. "A lot of guts and heart," she heard Tyler's voice in her head. Something positive to say, something encouraging. That was, she understood, the essence of Tyler's success, and she felt hopeful to be under his tutelage. When the show was over and a singer who lost smiled through her tears to say it was the greatest experience of her life, Cecilia turned off the TV and the lights and went to sleep.

It was midnight when she was buzzed awake by her phone, vibrating on her nightstand. She turned on the light, noted the time, and flipped it open. It was from an unidentified number, and she couldn't imagine who it was, unless something had happened— God forbid—to one of her brothers. Before she could say hello, the caller said, "It's me. Sorry to call so late, but I'm in trouble."

"What kind of trouble?" she asked. Knowing Kix as she thought she did, it must be big trouble if he couldn't handle it himself and had to call her, after a month of silence, let alone after midnight. "Where are you?"

"Jail," he said with a slight irritation, as if that were just as obvious as why he'd asked for a light a few months ago.

"Is Charmaigne with you?" She prayed she wasn't.

"No, haven't seen her. They probably wouldn't have brought me here if she'd been with me."

Cecilia thought to say that she'd heard from Charmaigne, but she had so little information, and if Kix really were in jail, his time on the phone might be limited. "Where are you?" she asked.

"Town Hall," he said.

"Where?" she repeated, trying not to sound alarmed.

"3600 North Halsted," he said, sounding as if he were reading.

"Why?" she asked, as much annoyed as concerned. She'd thought him too smart to get caught, his crimes minor. Something serious must have happened for the police to have arrested him.

"'Cause that's where the cops brought me," Kix said, but she heard a slightly higher register than his usual tenor and knew that his bravado was false. It was juvenile and irritating.

"Charges?" she asked, urging him to focus on the serious business at hand.

"They think I took money from a bum," he said.

"Did you?"

"No," he said emphatically. "I asked him for some help and he gave it to me." Implicit was the challenge to her that she help him.

"How much?" she asked.

"Hundred. Two fifties. He must've thought they were twenties."

It didn't sound like much of a defense to her. "What do you want me to do?" she asked.

"Get me out of here," he said. "It's full of creeps and perverts." There was some commotion on his end and the line went dead. She closed her phone and shook her head, not knowing what to do. Did he expect her to go bail him out? Had bail even been set, or would he have to go before a judge first? She had no idea how the criminal justice system worked at this petty level. All she knew were the big crimes of newspaper headlines and the sensationalized sketches of TV dramas. Even as adolescents, her brothers had never gotten in trouble with the police. Now, they had lawyers—business and estate lawyers, she guessed—but not criminal, and besides, she couldn't begin to explain to them why she needed a criminal attorney for a boy she barely knew. She could hardly explain that to herself, but the less she had to explain to anyone the better. They didn't understand an artist's life at all.

She dialed Tyler.

"Did I wake you up?"

"Heavens, no!" he said. "Actually, was just on my way out for a bit to meet friends."

"At midnight?"

"I know, it's a little early, but it's a school night," he laughed.

She told him her story, and he said he'd swing by and pick her up. He knew a couple of guys who knew the police station and could maybe do something. He'd make some calls.

In the car, Tyler didn't ask about Kix, so Cecilia felt compelled to tell him the whole story.

"Talk about guts," Tyler said. "It's totally dangerous out there for a kid his age. Drugs, prostitution, you name it. He's lucky he conned you and not some gangbanger."

"What am I going to do? Am I stuck with him just because he conned me once? Isn't the second time 'shame on me?'"

"Maybe the third," Tyler said, "and from what you've told me, you're way past that!"

"Seriously, Ty, what am I going to do?"

"You're going to do what you can do and nothing more," Tyler said. "Let's just take this real slow, and see what unfolds."

She was a little startled when Tyler stopped in front of the police station and told her to go in by herself. "I'll park the car," he said.

"You go play damsel-with-son-in-distress. I'll be in the background so we don't irritate the cops right off the bat. I have a feeling I'm not their type."

He was right, but she hesitated, afraid.

The car behind them blew its horn angrily. "Go," he commanded, and reflexively she got out. She ignored the young men who loitered outside, smoking cigarettes, and entered the station. Inside, she was met with the salty odor of tension and anxiety.

A dark-haired man in a navy blazer, red tie, and gray slacks, approached her. "Miss Morrison?"

"Yes," she mumbled, not sure she wanted anyone around her to hear.

"I'm Jack O'Malley. Tyler called me. I'll be representing your friend. Kix, is it?" He handed her his card.

"I don't know what name he gave the police," she said, and Jack held on to his card a second longer than normal, as if reconsidering his representation of the alias.

Jack told her to sit on a chair in the hallway, and he disappeared through a set of doors. There was a security officer standing there, but he didn't look at her or otherwise acknowledge her presence. She had thought—from TV, she supposed—that there would be others in the hall, that the place would be teeming with activity, but it must be a slow night, because the place seemed quiet, almost lazy. She looked at her watch. It was nearly one. Perhaps there was more activity when the bars closed, at two or four. Fifteen minutes passed, and then Tyler came in and sat next to her.

"Impossible to find a place to park," he said.

"But you did," she said.

"Eventually." He pointed toward the doors. "Jack here?"

"Yes," she said. "Seemed to know what he was doing."

"He found the place," Tyler laughed. "The trouble with professionals like lawyers and accountants and doctors is you don't know enough to know if they're any good or not. But Jack has an excellent reputation, and he's a good guy. Hot, too," he said and winked.

"You!" she laughed.

"Make lemonade," Tyler said, just as Jack came through the doors with a smiling Kix.

"Thanks, man," Kix said. "I'm free!" he shouted to Cecilia and Tyler, spreading his arms like wings. They stood up, and Kix took a giant step toward her, as if to hug her, but stopped, dropping his arms, when Cecilia pulled back.

Lawyer and client stood facing singer and coach, and after an awkward moment, Tyler said, "Coffee, anyone?" and together they left the station, following Jack to the closest twenty-four-hour diner, Cecilia anxious to hear Kix's side of the story.

eleven

The four of them squeezed into a booth at a diner not far from the police station.

On the way out of the station, Kix had started jabbering about the cops and how they'd tried to scare him, but how they had nothing on him, and the other perverts were downright sick. The three adults had walked ahead, Jack leading the way, Tyler and Cecilia behind him, Kix bringing up the rear. He'd dodged to the side to get even with Cecilia and Tyler but fell back, quiet, when his efforts met only with stony silence. The adults still hadn't spoken when the waitress came by for their orders.

"Coffee," Jack said.

The waitress, middle-aged, older than Cecilia by probably ten years, hair unevenly dyed a reddish brown, pursed her lips.

"And a piece of the lemon meringue," Jack said, eager to please.

"Out of lemon meringue," she said wearily. "French silk or apple."

"Apple," Jack said quickly.

"Same," Tyler said.

"Just coffee," Cecilia said, because Tyler was there and he'd fuss if she ordered pie. The waitress sighed and looked at Kix.

Kix raised his eyebrows at Cecilia and smiled weakly. "They didn't feed us in there," he said.

Jack laughed. "That's a good thing," he said.

"Go ahead," Cecilia murmured.

"Cheeseburger, fries, large Coke," he said. "Please."

"No Coke," Cecilia said. "Give him a glass of milk." She had no idea why she'd intervened, except perhaps to show him who was boss. She felt like her own mother, who routinely amended Cecilia's orders to less fattening foods and foods she perceived as better for her voice. Her own mother, and Tyler himself, had vetoed milk before any important performance—something about coating the vocal chords. On her own, she found milk soothing. Kix probably found it punitive. So be it—he should know he'd hurt her feelings.

"Cool," Kix said.

"That's it?" the waitress asked, looking around the table.

"Okay, the pie," Kix said, and Cecilia couldn't keep herself from laughing.

"You're a bottomless pit!" she said.

"Aren't we all?" Tyler said. "Food," he said, pointing to Kix. "S-E-X," he pointed to himself. "Praise," he pointed to Cecilia. "And what? Must be money!" he pointed to Jack.

"Not the satisfaction of helping the disadvantaged to get a fair shake from the system?" Jack asked. He wasn't smiling, and to Cecilia he looked hurt.

Tyler laughed "I call 'em as I see 'em."

"You calling me disadvantaged?" Kix asked.

"You paying for my services?" Jack asked, his voice calm and matter-of-fact.

Kix sat up straight. "I will," he said. "I will. I pay my debts. Ask Cecilia."

Cecilia bristled. There was no need for Jack to know about the sixty dollars; she'd only told Tyler that night by way of explanation of her relationship to Kix. "The point is," Cecilia said, "you shouldn't have needed Jack in the first place."

"That's what I say!" Kix jumped in. "No way they should've arrested me, man."

Tyler propped his chin on his elbow. "In my experience, Kix, and this is just me talking, the police usually have some kind of basis for arresting somebody. They've got too much to do with real crimes to go around making them up."

Jack, still in his lawyer's role, said, "Tell them what you told the police."

"Okay, so I was coming off of doing my gig at Belmont and Broadway, and this old dude comes out of this bar, and he looked friendly. . . ."

"And a little looped?" Tyler asked.

"Yeah, maybe. So anyway I just told him I'd been robbed on the El, and that I was trying to get the train back to school in Ann Arbor, and that I needed fifty bucks, and that I would send him the money as soon as I got home. And he looked at me real hard, and I showed him the train schedule, and he started talking about the Wolverines, and I played along like I was a great fan and knew all about bowls and shi . . ." he caught himself, "bowl games and stuff like that—and then he opened his wallet and gave me two fifties, kind of stuck together." Cecilia busied herself with cooling her coffee. "I asked for his card, and he started to pull one out of his wallet, but then his driver's license and his Visa card fell on the sidewalk, and I went to pick them up—just to be polite and all—and then he started hollering and got real mean, and there was a cop on the next block and next thing I know, man, I'm in cuffs and they're smashing my head down in the backseat of a car, and they're hollering at me and calling me a little shit and throwing me in a lockup with a drunk guy who stinks to high heaven and a couple black kids who are all jittery, man, flying high and talking trash, and you know the rest."

Cecilia's face burned. She herself had fallen for him because of the pink slip he'd used to verify his story. She knew the answer, but she asked, to let him know she was on to him, "Why did you have the train schedule?"

Tyler dropped his arm from under his chin and peered at her as if she'd focused on exactly the wrong question.

"Ya gotta have something," he said. "Goes to credibility." He smiled sheepishly at Jack. "It's hard to get somebody to part with twenty bucks." Cecilia drank her coffee, hoping to keep secret her own gullibility from the lawyer, who, she'd noticed, was handsome and ringless, and not as perfect as Tyler.

"That is, of course, the point," Jack said, and Kix cocked his head, not exactly following. Jack rubbed his forehead. "Look, kid, when a guy with no apparent means of support shows up with two fifties in his pocket and a guy in a suit starts hollering, it's logical for the cops to think they belong to the guy in the suit."

"Things aren't always what they appear," Tyler cautioned, wagging a finger at his friend.

"You are such a bleeding heart, Ty," Jack said. "Do you think the kid never picked a pocket or lifted a pack of gum from a 7-Eleven?"

Tyler looked at Kix hopefully—he was such a dear, Cecilia thought—as if he expected a denial, but Kix shoved the last bit of hamburger in his mouth, ignoring them.

"You can't be certain," Tyler said.

"That's my Dad's thing," Kix said, washing down the hamburger with a gulp of milk. "The 'uncertainty principle.' Werner Karl Heisenberg."

"I remember," Tyler said. "Something about not being able to know both the position and the velocity of an electron at the same time."

Jack questioned him with his raised eyebrows.

"Physics teacher was a dream," Tyler said, and Jack laughed as if he should've guessed the answer.

Kix nodded vigorously. "Heisenberg figured that out when he was twenty-three. That's why my dad named me Karl. He wanted me to win a Nobel Prize or some shi . . . . I think he forgot that Heisenberg's whole theory was about errors."

"What are we talking about?" Cecilia asked, irritated that Tyler appeared now to be siding with Kix's version of his brush with the law. Jack was clearly right on this one. Even if the kid were innocent on this particular charge, there must have been plenty of times he'd gotten away with petty, if not grand, theft.

Tyler ignored her, and he leaned across the table, his hand outstretched. "You're not an error, kid."

"I've just made bad decisions?" Kix said, leaning back in the booth with a sarcastic smirk and staring at the ceiling.

"I don't know," Tyler said quietly, withdrawing his hand.

"Damn right you don't know!" Kix said. "My dad. He's the error!" Kix's voice cracked, and Cecilia, next to him, thought she saw his lower lip quiver. Red blotches were creeping up his neck, and his left ear was blood red.

"Hey, parents do the best they can, man," Jack said, as if he were the mediator. "You gotta—"

"No. I don't gotta nothing when it comes to him. I did what I had to do. I got Charmaigne out of there. I'm taking care of his baby. And I don't need nobody telling me what I gotta do now. I should've killed him when I had the chance." He wiped at his left eye, but his jaw was set and he locked his gaze on Jack. Cecilia saw Tyler's eyes widen. She signaled him with a small wave that she would fill him in later. At the moment, she turned to look at Jack's face to see if he thought Kix's threat to kill his father was real. The four of them sat in a stunned silence, the relentless velocity of the atoms of their bodies imperceptible. Cecilia felt as if in a staged tableau, about to explode.

Kix bumped against her. "Let me out."

Across from her, Jack shook his head. "Let's take a minute here," he said.

"Let's not," Kix said, mimicking.

Cecilia put both hands on the table. "Please, Kix. Just let's all take a deep breath and then we can figure out, together, what to do."

"Do? About what? What could any of you do about anything?"

"We could help," Cecilia started.

"Help? I didn't ask anybody for help."

She was furious, still hurt by his running off and not calling until now. She forgot about what Jack and Tyler knew or didn't know, eager to say her piece. "Of course you did! You took sixty bucks off me, you spent a night at my apartment, you asked the drunk in the suit for fifty, and you called me tonight—for what? To chat? No, for help. Show a little gratitude, for god's sake. You could be stewing in your own juices behind bars, if it weren't for Tyler here, and Jack. That's help. You needed it. And they gave it. Say thank you."

He held her gaze, blinked back a tear, and mumbled, "Thank you." Jack was looking at her in a curious admiration.

"Louder," she said, like mothers she'd heard in grocery stores making kids apologize for a minor transgression, like picking a grape from the produce stand.

"Thank you," he said, louder, recovering himself to look each of them in the eye, no longer a scared adolescent but a young man who could, indeed, have murdered his father when he'd had the chance.

"You're not on the lam, are you?" Jack asked. "I mean, from the law. You didn't have the chance. . . ."

"No, man. Just got the hell out of there."

"Any other sisters, besides Charmaigne?" Jack asked, sounding just like the lawyer he was, assessing the facts.

"Baby girl, three years old." Surely, Cecilia thought, there was time to get the three-year-old out of her father's home. As soon as possible, but not necessarily immediately. Someone else— someone professional—could be asked to deal with that, and she could disentangle herself from Kix and Charmaigne. She was already involved with this boy more deeply than she'd ever intended.

Why not let him go? Kix had said thank you, so now he could split. She shouldn't stop him. He had things to do, his sister to find. Jack had plenty of nonpaying clients, Tyler a hundred causes of his own. She had an audition to get ready for.

"Well then," Tyler said, "the way I see it, you can go find your sister, or you can stay here and start your life."

"Where would he live?" Cecilia asked, a slight panic running through her, as if finding a place for him were her responsibility and she had to start looking right away.

Jack waved her concern away. "There are places. Some special schools. That is, kid, if you want to go to school. I could make a few calls."

Kix rolled his head around, like a swimmer limbering up for a race. Tyler jumped in, "You don't have to decide today," he said. "Listen, why don't we call it a night. You can come back to my place—there's a pullout bed in the living room—and tomorrow you can do whatever you want. You know the three of us will help you any way we can. But you gotta decide what you want to do. We can't decide for you."

"That's right, man," Kix said. "Hey, and I do thank you all for everything," he said. "I really mean that. I really do."

The kid was good, Cecilia thought. Damn good. He knew when and how to act sincere. The question was, did she believe him? His left earlobe was colored blood red, as if in terror, and she knew she wanted to.

She slept late the next morning, and at about ten the phone rang. "He split," the voice said.

"Of course," Cecilia said, so tired still that his words weren't fully registering. "Just like before."

"Hey, we do what we can do," Tyler said. "Have you run your five miles yet?"

"Yeah, yeah," she yawned.

"You will?"

"I'm not awake yet!"

"Take a run, call me later," he said.

"Ty?"

"Yes?"

"What are we going to do?"

"About Kix?" He hesitated. "Let him go. You don't really have a choice. You've done your bit. Maybe you should go back to Dr. who-ever and figure out your obsession."

She listened tight-lipped.

"Are you there? Honey, I'm sorry. Obsession. Too big a word. You know me. I just mean you've been good to the kid and he's moved on. People come and go in our lives. That's all. Are you there?"

"I'm here, Ty," she exhaled into the phone. "I hate it when you're right."

"You'll go back to therapy?"

"Heavens, no. I just mean you're right, I've been a little obsessed, and I can easily un-obsess. I'll call you later."

She lay back in bed, staring at the shadows on the ceiling, noticing small cracks and wondering how long high-rise buildings lasted, anyway. She'd bought a quarter of a floor in a building that someday could crumble to the ground, or, worse yet, be bulldozed floor by floor like the old hospital buildings nearby, the salvage value of the land underneath worth more than the sum of the floors. Her building was only twenty years old. She satisfied her-self that she wouldn't live long enough to have to worry about it. Still, she should call maintenance, and let them know her home was falling down.

She should also get up, eat, run, shower, sing. It was easier to do what Tyler told her to do than what her mother had told her. Her mother had hounded her with a litany of shoulds—all versions of what she would do, if she'd been given Cecilia's talent, which she hadn't. It hadn't been fair of Francine Morrison to appropriate it as her own. Cecilia'd gotten that much of a hint from Dr. Richardson. But she had yet to feel she owned her own talent or knew for her-self what she wanted to do with it.

Was Kix looking for a chance to kill his father? She could under-stand the impulse—what a beast the father must be, all that Karl Werner Heisenberg grandiosity, and then such perversion. But where was the mother? How could she have let him do that to Charmaigne? Why hadn't Charmaigne asked her mother for help?

Her own father had been such a kind man. Always calm in the midst of his wife's storms. Farsighted and visionary where her mother was nearsighted and blinded by ambition. Although born to privilege and inflationary prosperity, he remained humble, hardworking but satisfied. He had no desire to sell his business to a conglomerate for a hefty multiple. He accepted his good fortune as just that. He neither apologized for it nor felt compelled to prove his entitlement. He was the sole owner of his company, but half the annual profits were bonused to his one hundred and twenty employees. His half, wisely invested and modestly spent, grew to a substantial sum, and he'd been grateful. It had pleased him that his business would support his daughter's exceptional talents.

Francine Morrison, on the other hand, had grown up needy— not in poverty, but on that insecure rung of single-income middle class that always appeared more prosperous than a middle-school principal's salary could provide for a free-spending wife and her three children. Francine had inherited both her own mother's taste for the finer things and her anxiety. Although she no longer had to worry financially, her relief became instead a campaign to demonstrate her worthiness, and her exceptional daughter, Cecilia, was her best proof. A good child by nature, Cecilia had understood that she would be loved in direct proportion to her ability to bring glory to her mother. Whether her brothers felt that way, Cecilia didn't know, but she did know how frequently she'd fallen short, and how she'd dreaded the cold shoulder of her mother's disappointment.

How could Kix's mother not notice what was going on in her own home? What kind of woman allowed her husband to rape their daughter? What kind of woman, having so failed her children, still earned the love of a son who wrote home once a month, who would sooner kill the father than worry the mother? Why hadn't her own father come to her defense against her mother? He must have, Cecilia consoled herself. She didn't remember that he'd ever intervened, that he'd ever told his wife she was wrong or that she should say or do any specific thing, but his defense was his unconditional love, the antidote to her mother's, and that had saved her. Kix's mother may have been weak, stupid, fearful, naive, but she loved her children, Cecilia was sure of that. She'd raised a son who had saved her daughter.

Why did she even believe Kix? Perhaps because he had no proof, no piece of pink carbon paper, no train schedule, no proof other than the baby and a somewhat sullen sister, who, if Kix were telling the truth—why would he make up that particular horror?— could be forgiven every weary sigh and every ungrateful glance. Wherever they each were, it was vital that they not be near their father.

twelve

I'm guessing Charmaigne is on her way to New Orleans, but she could've gone to Ann Arbor, too. One or the other. She'd always wanted to go to the University of Michigan, at least until she dropped out. She was more of a student than I was. Come to think of it, I bet she went there. It's too damn hot in New Orleans this time of year. There are a lot of bleeding hearts over there in Michigan. I hope someone is taking care of her, and of Abby.

Had it been up to me, I would've gotten the abortion. I could've gotten the money together, but she didn't tell me until it was too late. I don't know why she wanted to keep the baby, given the circumstances. Maybe she just needed someone to love. Me? I am her brother. Used to be I could be a pain in the ass sometimes. Not anymore, though. Not now.

How did I not notice? You know, she was so afraid of my Dad, she always tried to hide herself. She was real quiet—in my family, you'd hardly know she was there. She didn't make friends, really, except for this boy Charlie who she'd been friends with since grade school, and he was a shy guy himself. Cecilia didn't ask my mom for anything, not even new clothes. No makeup or earrings or concert tickets or any of the stuff the other girls in school got into. She went to school, tried not to be noticed, snuck into the house after. My mother stopped coaxing her to talk and get out more. She thought it was just a phase Charmaigne was going through and that it wasn't personal. My mom is kind of quiet herself.

I didn't know myself why Charmaigne was the way she was, until she told me she was pregnant and asked me to take her away, and I felt so dumb, man, that I hadn't known. How was I supposed to know, I said to her. You never told me. She told me I should have seen what was going on. But no one saw what was going on, even Mom. She said Mom was in denial. That we all were. I told her I had my own problems with the old man—although he never touched me—that it was just me being such a disappointment to him. She said I was just self-absorbed. I said I'd never be self-absorbed again. I told her I would take care of her.

She said she didn't want me to take care of her, just to help her for a little while, 'til she figured out what to do. Maybe she has. But if she has, she should've told Cecilia that when she called that time, because if she doesn't want to be found, that leaves me, trying to figure out what to do—about me. If she's gone for good, then I have no choice but to be self-absorbed again, do I? Who else am I supposed to worry about?

thirteen

Obsessed. Now it was Tyler who was obsessed. The audition for the show he had recommended to Cecilia was less than a week from the long night when Kix was in jail. That night was like a dream for her, a bad dream she couldn't shake. Again, she felt abandoned by the boy, by his refusal to accept her help, and by the way he bounced in and out of her life.

"We're putting way too much time into this," Cecilia told Tyler one evening over salads at a sidewalk café. "You know as well as I do that it has more to do with looks than talent, with the director's preconceived idea of what the character looks like. He's probably precast the damn thing, and the audition is just for show. Or worse, just looking for an understudy."

"I'm assured it's not precast," Tyler said. "Even if it were, the point of the audition is to get in front of some of these people who might precast you next time."

"Yeah, right," she said, so that he would know she didn't believe that was possible.

"You want instant success in a business that's terribly risk adverse yet takes immense risks every day. It's a notoriously fickle business, loyalties are thin, and you're only as good as your latest work. The business ain't gonna change just because you're ready for a triumphant return. You need to get some good work behind you, even if it is only the good work of an understudy."

"I don't want to understudy, for god's sake."

"You'll take the understudy if offered," he said.

Cecilia's stomach growled. She was hungry, and the seventh day of the strict salad diet Tyler had prescribed was killing her. Why was she taking orders from Tyler?

"Because I've been in the trenches for the past ten years, while you've been holing yourself up," Tyler said, answering the challenge she'd thought but not said.

She stabbed at a carrot that slipped off her plate. She put down her fork and picked it up, swirling it in the small container of poppyseed dressing that Tyler had insisted be served on the side.

"It's not just your reputation, you know," he said. "I have something at stake here, too."

"Oh? What's that?"

"I want to be known as a coach that does the right things, whose people can be counted on to do the right things. To warm up. To drop five pounds when they have to. To not drink during a show. To take direction. To be on time and cheerful. To support the lead role. To be ready, to be steady, but not wish the star deady." He grinned from ear to ear and reached out to take her hand. "I think you are going to be terrific, honey. I really, really do. I've got twenty on your getting cast."

"With whom?"

Tyler opened a package of Ry Crisp and motioned to the waiter for more iced tea.

"With whom?" she glared.

"Kix," he said meekly.

She felt her heart race. "Do you know where he is?"

"No, no. So, it's a safe enough bet. He's not around to collect!"

"Kix bet against me?" She was suddenly furious. "What does he know?"

"He said he didn't think you were hungry enough. He wasn't sure you wanted it enough."

"Where would he get that?"

"Who cares? He's a kid who sings on the street, literally, for his supper. He sings because he absolutely has to, if he wants to stay out of jail. You? He sees you as someone for whom singing is a luxury. You can sing or not, depending on your mood."

"My mood," she mumbled. "I am a professional. It has nothing to do with mood." She was hurt that Kix thought her so—what? Spoiled? Shallow?

"Exactly!" Tyler cried. "A professional. The real point is, I am also a professional, and I put my money on you."

She twirled her fork and pushed aside a weary piece of lettuce. She swallowed hard and looked Tyler straight in the eyes. "The point is, I'm so afraid. Of what happened last time. What if?"

"Don't let it."

"I can't help it if she haunts me."

"Well, actually you can."

"How? How do I stop a ghost?"

"One of my therapists used to say, 'If you can name it, you can cure it.' Shrinks can help. But you gotta stick with it." He stopped to notice a young man walking his mahogany-colored boxer, with a showy white flash. "Beautiful," Tyler sighed and winked at Cecilia, who said only, "You're incorrigible."

"I love summer," he said and raised his iced tea in toast. "I love beautiful men and beautiful women and talented men and, especially, talented women." He clinked her glass before she could even raise it.

"What would I do without you?" she said, genuinely touched to have a friend as loyal and upbeat as Tyler.

"You'd think of something," he said. "Maybe spend a little more time with that shrink of yours."

"I'm done with him," she said more firmly than she intended. She didn't feel negatively toward Dr. Richardson, but she couldn't identify any particularly positive or life-changing things he may have said to her. Secretly, though, she missed the visits that for a short while had been the focal point of her week.

"That's fine," Tyler said. "Just so you know it is always an option. Meanwhile, let's keep our eyes on the prize."

"You got it," she said. "It's only a minute or two, right? I can fend her off for that long, can't I?"

"Of course you can," he said.

But she couldn't. For the next few days, she heard slides and breaks and wavers and missed pitches that even her mother, rest her soul, might have missed, even at her most hyperattentive. Tyler tried to reassure her that she was wrong, but she lashed out at his inability to hear.

"I have perfect pitch," she said.

"So do I," he said.

"I don't think so," she said.

"Your perfect is better than my perfect?" Tyler said, peering over reading glasses he sometimes used to follow a score.

"Yes," she said, unequivocally, and he pounded on a high C on the piano and she hit it perfectly, though not perfectly enough to suit her. She sang, he pounded on the key. He pounded, she sang.

"The piano's off," she said.

"No," he countered, then abandoned the piano and sang the note himself. She sang, he sang. After battling their perfection for a few minutes, Tyler caved. He struck the high C on the piano with a normal force and peered at her. She sang, and her voice blended with the piano. "You'll hurt your voice," he said. "It's not quite perfect,but perfect enough."

"It's very close," she conceded.

"Honey, I think you need to relax. Perhaps we've overdone it, eh? It's just an audition. You're imposing standards that are way beyond the average director in this town. You're going to drive yourself crazy."

"You're right," she said, and Tyler pushed his reading glasses back on his head.

"All-righty then," he said. "Let's call it a day, you rest tomorrow, warm up Thursday morning, and then we'll meet at the audition at eleven. My treat for lunch after."

"Good," she said. She didn't want to sing for Tyler anymore. He was obviously willing to let her settle for less than what she knew herself to be capable of. She was grateful to him for getting her started again, but she didn't think his standards high enough to take her to the next level. He didn't enforce the standards of Francine Morrison. Come to think of it, he didn't even enforce the standards of Kix Gordon, who'd had the nerve to bet against her!

She didn't follow Tyler's advice. On Wednesday, she didn't rest. She ran five miles, sang for hours, skipped all meals, drank only juice. She shaved her legs, took an hour to pluck her eyebrows, redid her makeup three times as a trial run. She fell asleep at midnight, on top of her bed, and woke at four. She went to the gym on the third floor of her building, swam laps for half an hour, and sat in the hot tub for twenty minutes. Back upstairs in her apartment, she showered, made some coffee, surprised the paper boy by opening the door as he dropped her *Tribune* in front of it, and by seven was so charged with nervous energy she put on her running shorts and headed up the lakeshore at faster than her usual modest pace. By the time she got to the palms at North Avenue Beach, she was winded, and she stepped off the path to the sand, bending over and holding her knees.

At her feet were a million grains of sand, mocking her with her own insignificance. What did she think she was doing? What difference did it make if she got the part or not? What difference did anything at all make, if, in the end, we left a trace no greater than a grain of sand? She was overcome by a sophomoric, but paralyzing, angst. So this was her midlife crisis? But which? Wanting to return to the stage, or being afraid of it?

Tyler would be angry, but she wasn't going to go to an audition that he picked out for her just because it would please him to have his student make good. If he picked easy enough parts, then what would be the vindication in that? Her mother would say the material was beneath her, the equivalent of singing on the street with Kix. Obviously, she could play the part, probably better than most, but playing an easy part well wasn't much of an achievement, was it? Certainly not the kind of achievement her mother had envisioned for her. And what if Kix won the bet—what if she didn't get even so easy a part? How great would be that failure? To have lost not only the boy but also the part? No, she wouldn't let Tyler choose her parts. She would choose her own, when she was ready.

She walked the lakeshore for a few hours, avoiding the 11 a.m. audition and what surely would be Tyler's repeated, frantic phone calls. She was surprised, when she returned home about three and there were no messages. Tyler must be absolutely furious not to have called. She felt she should call him, but she couldn't. She looked at the phone as if it were a twenty-pound weight. She was starved—Tyler's fault—and in her freezer found a carton of fuzzy chocolate chocolate-chip ice cream with caramel pieces, something she'd bought long ago for the kids. Standing in the glare of the light from the open freezer door, she dug in with a tablespoon.

Would Dr. Richardson find her behavior self-destructive? He'd never said those words to her, but even she could see that what she was doing was undoing whatever good Tyler's "cleansing" diet had done. The ice cream felt good on her throat, dry from days of singing and running, as if she'd inhaled the sand from the beach, even as she'd held on to all the tension building over the audition, now missed. Would word get around that she'd skipped out on a second audition? Not necessarily, she comforted herself. Maybe they'd assume she was merely rude, that she'd been cast in another show and failed to cancel. She scraped the last of the ice cream from the carton, closed the freezer door, and burst into tears.

She sat at her kitchen table, staring out at the patch of Lake Michigan that she could see between the nearby high-rises. Tour boats cruised just off the shoreline, no doubt pointing out buildings like her own, naming their architects, discussing the genius of Burnham and the city's planning, a fine balance of preservation and creation. Cities could be planned, but not individual lives. In hers, how had things gone so terribly wrong? With everything a girl could want, how had it come to this?

Her father had assumed she would get married and have kids. "It's too hard a life," he'd said of performing. "Enjoy yourself. Enjoy your family. Sing on the side." Her mother, of course, had thought that "boys" could wait until later. Later had come and gone, and if it came again, she feared it was going to come in the form of a guy ten years older than herself with weekend visitation rights, child support payments, and divided loyalties. It wasn't about men, she thought. Or about children. She'd tried to make friends with Kix and Charmaigne, hadn't she? Had almost taken them in! Might have, if Kix hadn't left, or if Charmaigne had said where she was. But even that wouldn't have been forever. Getting married, having children, adopting children—those would work for some people in her position, but she knew deep down those weren't her answers.

She'd always been kind of a loner, and at one time, she'd wanted, she'd really wanted—hadn't she?—to sing. When had she lost that desire? The *Prix* was a thrill; so was winning the lead in *Rumplestilt's Kin*. After that, perhaps, it had become a chore, the weight of the show on her shoulders, the strain to be not just good enough, but great, perfect. Would Dr. Richardson agree with that analysis? If so, what would he tell her to do about it? Lower her standards? That seemed to be Tyler's answer. She was surprised at herself for feeling so much anger toward him, but he'd gotten her into this auditioning frenzy, and where was he now? Didn't even care enough to call and see if she'd been run over by a bus on the way to the audition. Cecilia shut the blinds in the kitchen and in her bedroom and, still in her running shorts, pulled a sheet over her head and forced herself to sleep. For the next two days, she rose only as necessary for the bathroom, a glass of water, the last of a carton of raspberry sorbet. She didn't collect her mail. No one called. She was finished.

On the third day, the doorman called up, and her first thought was of Kix. But in fact Tyler Baron was in the lobby, and she said to send him up. She considered splashing water on her face and brushing her hair but then thought better of it. He should see the havoc he'd wreaked on her life. Tyler knocked, and when she opened the door the powerful scent of a bouquet of fragrant pink stargazer lilies startled her, they were so aggressively alive. He smiled silently and went to the kitchen, where he opened the blinds and then found a clear glass vase on the top shelf of a hard-to-reach cabinet over the sink. He held his wrist under the tap until he judged the water to be of appropriate temperature. He made a show of arranging the lilies, adding a packet of long-life flower food, and then marching them to the front room, Cecilia following, where he tried several different positions before settling for the obvious, the center of her dining table. He then sat himself, uninvited, on the couch and tapped his hand on the seat next to him, as if calling a pet to join him.

She stood her ground next to the dining table. It was obvious that, like Dr. Richardson, he thought she should speak first. She thought he should open, say, "I'm sorry," or "How are you?" or even "You look terrible, honey." He stopped tapping and leaned back against the armrest, comfortable, patient. Easy for him! He wasn't the one who'd failed to show. If you have a date, and someone stands the other up, shouldn't the stander-upper be the one to apologize first? Yes, Cecilia thought. Unless it was the other person's fault. And how could that be? What had he done except to arrange the audition, coach her, bring her flowers?

"I guess you deserve an explanation," she said and sat opposite him a comfortable leather chair. He leaned forward, attentive, but silent.

"I didn't sleep well the night before," she started, hoping that would force him to say something simple like, "Oh, I'm sorry," or "Why not?" Faced with his silence, she braved on. "I went for a run. There are a surprising number of people out running at seven o'clock in the morning." He registered no surprise, didn't ask how many people, didn't ask why she was surprised. "I got to thinking about all the people in the world, and how many have ever lived, and I just got paralyzed." She'd been thinking about grains of sand, actually, but she didn't want to admit to such an obvious metaphor. "I didn't feel good enough." She was getting angry at his silence. "I'll never be good enough, and it's plain old egotistical to think otherwise."

"She reappeared?" he asked quietly, and she thought she heard some sympathy in his voice.

"No," she said. "No ghosts. Gosh, I wish I hadn't told you about that. Now that's all I'll hear from you. That was a one-time thing. No. I was just tired."

"She might as well have been there, frowning and whispering criticisms in your ear. You should've called me. At least I could've joined the debate."

"What's good enough for you," she started, but he jumped up, startling her.

"Is good enough! Stop insulting me and the entire city theater scene just because you've concocted the perfect excuse for yourself. Grow up, Cecilia! You can't please your mother anymore—if you ever did—so you've got to please yourself. From the looks of things, you have no standards of your own, just a soul full of fear. You're a selfish brat, you know that? It never once occurred to you, did it, that your failure to show up might make me look bad? That maybe I'd called in some favors to get you this audition? That you owe some others—including maybe even your mother—a little effort? That even if it's not perfect, it's better than many—" she winced, and he corrected himself "—and maybe even better than most, and you owe the rest of us poor slobs an occasional listen to your gifts? And here's another news flash, honey—you're good. You're great. But you ain't the only one, so get over yourself and get out of bed, and—" he was about to run out of steam, "—smell the lilies." She sat stunned at his tirade and couldn't meet his eyes.

When she heard the door close, she looked up and stared at the place on the couch where he'd been sitting. The spicy smell of the lilies permeated the room, reminding her of the wreaths of dying roses at her mother's funeral.

fourteen

It's not a great gift to have the talent but not the desire. It would be worse, she realized, to have the desire but not the gift, or not enough of a gift. But many of those of only average talent don't know they don't have enough of a gift, and they succeed beyond their wildest dreams on gumption and luck rather than God-given talent. Cecilia spent two weeks in limbo, isolated, undecided, unmotivated. She was the lonely runner on the lakefront, stuck behind groups, passed by couples, outpaced by individuals with far more determination. Still, filling her mornings and evenings with listless runs down to Burnham Harbor, up to Montrose, and back to where the river flows out of Lake Michigan, she lost the extra weight that Tyler had suggested she drop, expanded her lung capacity, and relieved the panic of what she was calling her midlife crisis. She tried to assure herself that this was a phase; that soon, like the summer, it would pass, she would turn forty in February, Tyler would forgive her, Kix would be a distant memory, her life would return to normal, and the crisis—such as it was—would be over. It was already the end of August, some schools were back in session, and whatever shows were opening in September were cast and in rehearsal.

It had been a hot and muggy afternoon, even by the lake, and she flipped on the TV as she cooled down in her bedroom. The early evening news was on a special report about a shooting of a college professor in Normal, Illinois. She paid it little attention—apparently the shooter had missed and had disappeared into the campus crowd, but the authorities were asking the students for descriptions and leads. There was no apparent motive for the shooting, and the professor, a tenured professor of physics who'd been teaching at the university for fourteen years, had been lecturing on the uncertainty principle when two shots were fired. Not one student could say for sure from where. The TV reporter showed a still picture of the lecture hall, a steeply tiered semicircular room with seats for probably three hundred. It was half full, and the professor used assigned seating for the first eight or so rows. It was agreed that the shot had come from the top row, and one or two students, who had looked in the direction of the sound rather than hitting the floor, claimed to have seen a male with a brown baseball cap, long-sleeved brown T-shirt, and blue jeans rushing out. They couldn't say if the person fleeing was white or black, Asian or Hispanic; they didn't remember seeing any hair, let alone the color, and had not seen any facial features; if pressed, couldn't say for certain that it was a male except that that was the impression they had.

Tired, Cecilia sat on the edge of her bed and watched the story, wondering what kind of craziness was going on on college campuses that students would bring a gun to a classroom and start shooting. What kind of anger did such a person have? What did they think would happen if they shot a professor? Did they even think about the consequences? Had they no moral compass whatsoever? Were they on drugs? Or just desperately depressed? She could, in her own way, identify with the depression, but she couldn't imagine lashing out randomly like that. She'd done some self-destructive things this past summer, but she assured herself she hadn't hurt anyone else. Tyler would get over it. He hadn't been hurt. Not like the professor, who was in shock and being treated at the hospital, and who would forever be just a little nervous when he faced his class. The TV reporter said that classes would continue, they would not be intimidated, and the professor would return to teaching as soon as possible. That was the kind of person Karl Gordon was, the university president said into the camera, and Cecilia grabbed the remote, hoping they would say the name again and that she'd heard wrong. Back in the studio, the anchor moved on to a different story, and Cecilia flipped channels.

Another channel was just beginning its coverage and this one named the professor right off the top. "Shots rang out in Professor Karl Gordon's Introduction to Nuclear Physics class today at Illinois State University, narrowly missing him but terrorizing the campus. . . ." Cecilia felt her heart sprinting. What had Kix said that night he'd been in jail?

The phone rang and she rushed to answer. The voice launched in as soon as she picked up. "Have you heard from Kix?"

"No," she said. "Have you?"

"No, no. I'm here with Jack, and he said to tell you that if Kix calls, you should meet him somewhere and call the police."

"Don't harbor a criminal," she heard Jack say in the background.

"What happened to innocent until proven guilty?" She heard the phone being passed.

"Cecilia, this is Jack. We've had our one brush with the law. Right now I'm advising you to stay out of it. If he's a suspect, you don't want to obstruct justice. They will appoint an attorney for him. If he's innocent, fine, but Tyler and I don't want to visit you in jail. Got it?"

Cecilia felt her stomach muscles tighten in fear. It hadn't occurred to her that Kix would be a suspect—he wasn't in Normal, at least as far as she knew—and she'd never thought him the type to fire a gun, even at his disgusting, deserving father. Surely, Tyler and Jack had rushed to judgment. "Well, I wouldn't harbor him, but I don't know that I would call the police, either," she said. "If he calls, and if we have coffee in a public place, let the police find him, if they're looking for him. It's not my job to tell the cops where he is."

"Fair enough," Jack said. "Just don't get in deeper than you already are." He handed the phone back to Tyler, who was on the line when she asked, with a little tremor in her voice, "Do you really think he did it?"

"Oh, honey, I don't know," Tyler said. "He said that night, 'I should've killed him when I had the chance.' Jack says that's a bad fact. He's the most logical suspect."

Cecilia realized she'd been holding her breath and took a deep gulp of air, filling her diaphragm as if to hold a note for an eternity. "None of this is logical," was all she could think of to say.

"Do you want to join Jack and me for supper? We're going to see a friend's workshop at the Theatre Building. There might be some people there for you to meet."

The thought of seeing anyone who might have heard about her disastrous summer gave her goose bumps, but she didn't want to be around if Kix were to call, even though she knew that was a long shot at best. "Sure," she said. "You and Jack an item?"

"Heavens, no! Just friends. Frankly," he whispered, "I thought he'd be a good catch for you."

"Oh," she said. She hadn't thought of it quite that way before, but of course her gay friends had friends who weren't themselves gay, just like she had friends who were and who weren't straight. Tyler knew better than to try to actually fix her up. She should have guessed his motives when he didn't talk about Jack as his own love interest.

They met at a rib joint on the north side that gave its patrons plastic bibs and a stack of warm terry-cloth fingertip towels rather than antiseptic alcohol wipes. Tyler and Jack seemed relaxed, but she couldn't get the news story out of her mind.

"It just doesn't seem like something he'd do," she said, as soon as they'd ordered a bucket of ribs and a family-style bowl of slaw.

"As we say in the biz, he has motive and opportunity," Jack said.

"But why? Why in a classroom? Why not when he was alone in his office or taking out the garbage or whatever?"

"The public scene is more dramatic," Tyler said.

"More likely to get caught!" Cecilia countered. "Besides, Kix is a pickpocket. Wouldn't he have better hand-eye coordination? I can't imagine he'd miss."

"Shooting a gun isn't that easy, Cecilia," Jack said. The waitress put the bucket and slaw on the table and returned with a platter of fries.

Tyler grabbed a handful and winked at Cecilia. "Dig in," he said.

Cecilia reached for the fries, and Jack continued, "Maybe his intent wasn't murder."

"Then what would be the point?" Tyler asked.

"To publicly humiliate the guy," Jack suggested. He placed a cleaned bone on his plate.

"And lots of people could have a motive for that," Cecilia said. "Bad grades, bad recommendations . . ." She wasn't sure what else would anger a college student.

"Sexual harassment," Tyler said. Jack dipped his chin and looked at Cecilia with a little lift of his shoulders, the pointer of suspicion swinging back around to Kix, revenging his sister.

"Why now? Why not when he first discovered it?"

"He got Charmaigne out of harm's way, was taking care of her, and then she up and left him. Maybe he just got fed up with everything and everybody," Tyler said. He gnawed on a rib and wiped a splotch of sauce from his chin.

"I guess it's possible," Cecilia said. "But I choose not to believe it." Even though the ribs were the best in the city, and she hadn't had a French fry in months, she put down the one she'd been holding, not hungry.

There were about thirty people at the workshop, friends of the author, the director, the composer, and the young actors who were walking through the piece for the experience and the exposure to the theater community. She would've slipped into the back row of the small, hundred-seat space, but Tyler knew many of the people and sat in the middle of the middle row, flanked by Jack on one side and Cecilia on the other. He introduced her around, and fortunately she saw no one she knew.

At forty, Tyler had paid his dues and had outlasted many of his fellows—once young hopefuls like the ones involved in the evening's production. He'd earned some right, if not to judge, to offer sage advice. He brought with him a clipboard and a thumb-sized LED light, the kind used discreetly in restaurants to read menus, and as soon as he was seated, a lanky young man, who looked to Cecilia to be not much older than Kix, handed him a script.

"Congratulations," Tyler said.

"You haven't seen it yet," the young man murmured, the muscles of his face stretched tensely over his protruding cheekbones. The kid looked as if he hadn't eaten in days. Cecilia felt the urge to take him to the closest diner and order a cheeseburger, fries, and the pie of the day. She thought again of Kix, of the secret pleasure of watching him feast, of being the recipient of his appreciation and gratitude.

"Congratulations are still in order," Tyler said enthusiastically. "Not everyone writes a full length musical. And not everyone has the guts to put it out there." Cecilia winced. "You've come this far—it means to me you can go all the way. Listen real well tonight, as openly as you can. If you have to kill your babies, so be it."

The young man bowed his head, grinning broadly, then hurried off.

"You are really a good coach," she said to Tyler. "I think you saved that kid from a nervous breakdown."

"Well, at least he might get something out of the workshop. A lot of people are so nervous and so anxious to get to the end and hear the praise, they can't make good use of it. If you're the author, you have to sit in the back like the most vicious critic in the city and tear your own work apart. Sometimes you gotta kill your best lines. You gotta hear every whack-o comment from every moron who falls asleep in the front row or who wouldn't get the point if it were addressed to them in a memo from God, and you have to sort through it all, take what you want, and leave the rest, and make the whole thing better, if only by a single word. And some still aren't going to get it or like it. Mostly, you gotta remember it's not about you. It's about the work."

Jack laughed. "Not my ox," he said. Cecilia and Tyler looked at him blankly.

"What? All I'm saying is criticism is a lot easier to take if it's not directed at you."

Tyler shrugged. "Of course!" he said, laughing and patting Cecilia's knee. "Advice is easier to give than to receive."

"No doubt more blessed, too," Cecilia said.

Tyler started scribbling on the cover of his script, a large X, an O, and a question mark.

"What are those?" Cecilia asked.

"X for doesn't work at all, a circle for a word or phrase that could be better, a question for something too obtuse. U is for unnecessary," he said, continuing to write his chart, "and P is for more punch."

"In your opinion," Cecilia said flatly. She was still bothered by Tyler's and Jack's rush to judgment about Kix.

"Yes, obviously," Tyler said, a little prickly. "The author is only one-half the equation. No matter how perfect that side, the other half is the audience. It might be smart, interested, boozed up, bored to tears, politically opposed. You take 'em as you find 'em. It's art, it will never please all the people all the time. If that's your idea of perfect, better get over it. Pick an opinion that matters to you."

"Pick your own," Jack said, just as the director came onstage to introduce the night's effort.

After the show, the audience applauded vigorously, some on their feet, and then the author, director, and composer sat on folding chairs onstage and answered questions and asked for comments. Cecilia squeezed her hands together, as if to keep them from trembling. She hated public criticism. When it was her performance, she felt as if in front of a firing squad and now hoped no one would say anything the least bit critical of the show. It wasn't perfect, but it was good. Good enough, she thought. If anyone there could do better, they ought to do it. Tyler was right. It took courage just to finish the work and put it out there. For a moment she relaxed. If Kix did pull the trigger while his father, at the front of the room, pleaded with his students to understand uncertainty, it had taken a lot of courage.

The three onstage, dressed in jeans and T-shirts, the director and composer also with summer blazers, looked relaxed and poised, but the young author tapped his foot. Cecilia assumed he was, like her, nervous; then she realized it could be impatience, that he really didn't care what people said but just wanted to get through the obligatory critique session and then go make the changes he'd picked up for himself. Like with Kix, you could never tell what was really going on with another person. It occurred to her that Kix had deliberately missed, not just to avoid murder charges, but to force his father to know the real meaning of uncertainty.

The first couple of comments were highbrow and beyond the reach of a normal audience member. Someone asked, "Why not close that sixth song in the first act on a C Major seventh?" A young woman begging for attention in a low-cut fuchsia leotard and short-short black skirt with a sequined belt stood up to praise the show effusively, saying how fun the role of the ingénue should be to play (implying of course, that the ingénue had failed to convey that she was having fun), and closed with, "Every time I heard that E in the third song, I saw yellow. You could do that scene in yellow!"

Cecilia rolled her eyes at Tyler. She'd been in her twenties the last time she'd gone to a workshop and she'd forgotten how self-serving the critiques could be. The young woman obviously wanted to establish her own credentials, to let the director know that she had perfect pitch and so could play the part. Cecilia had learned in music school that one of the hallmarks of being able to recognize musical notes is a strong association of the note with a color, and frequently E was associated with yellow, which, of course, had nothing whatsoever to do with the work in progress.

In the short silence that followed the yellow comment, Tyler rose to his feet, and all eyes turned to him as if they expected him to give the definitive critique. Tyler was positive and generous and concluded that one scene in the middle could be crisper, move more quickly toward the climax, and that they could slow down the denouement for the audience's enjoyment. From Tyler's point of view, the main issues had nothing to do with the music, which he loved, or the book, which was very solid, he said, but pacing, and with more time to rehearse a fully staged show, he was confident the director could get the pacing right. The author onstage sat back in his chair and finally stopped tapping his foot. After one or two more comments, derived mainly from Tyler's, the group broke up, and Jack, Tyler, and Cecilia walked to the corner to a quiet bar for a nightcap.

Although exhausted and slightly inebriated on the two chocolate martinis she'd had with Jack and Tyler, Cecilia found it hard to sleep that night. They hadn't talked again about Kix and the shooting in Normal, but as she got in a cab to come home, Jack had leaned in and said, "Don't forget. It's called 'obstruction of justice.'" She'd nodded, but she was troubled. She wanted to hear Kix's side of the story. She wanted to hear him say he didn't do it. Although Jack and Tyler and she knew Kix's possible motive, no one on campus did, and since Kix was known locally to have run away, perhaps the police there had not yet identified him as a suspect, and so, despite Jack's advice, she would not be obstructing justice, if only he would call.

The phone rang the next day, midafternoon. Cecilia had lunched with her brothers, listened patiently to their projections for the business, expressed her gratitude, sincerely, if not extravagantly, for their dedication and effort, and gladly escaped with the knowledge that she would again be compensated well for their hard work. Her brothers were decent sorts, although she had little else in common with them. It was as if their mother had not influenced them in the slightest. Either she'd felt unable to mold male children—that that was her husband's role—or they were of little interest to her, having no talents as easily displayed as Cecilia's. They were unscathed and, perhaps as a result, slightly uninteresting to Cecilia, although she appreciated their stewardship of her father's business and their generosity in providing, as he had, for her.

She was tying her shoes for her evening run when she picked up the wall phone in the kitchen.

"Miss Morrison?" The voice was tiny and far away, but without a trace of an accent.

"This is Cecilia Morrison," she responded, still on guard against an unwanted solicitation.

"This is Charmaigne, Kix's friend."

"Kix's sister?" she corrected her.

The voice hesitated. "I didn't know he told you," she said.

"You have the same eyes," Cecilia said.

"My mother's eyes," the girl said. "We both do."

"Do you know where Kix is?" Cecilia asked. "Is he okay?" She wondered if the girl knew about Professor Gordon, but she didn't want to be the one to tell her. Even though she must hate her father, she would be alarmed that the police might be looking for Kix.

"I haven't seen him since I left town," she said. "That was more than a month ago."

"He was looking all over for you. Where are you now?" Cecilia asked.

"Here. I came back. I want to find Kix."

"You should've told him where you were going. Where were you?" Cecilia asked. She had a right to know.

"Ann Arbor," she said. "Miss Morrison?" Charmaigne started, her voice tired and frightened. "Could we stay with you tonight? Me and the baby? Without Kix, it's not as safe. . . ."

"Of course, Charmaigne," Cecilia said. This was not obstruction, she said to herself. Charmaigne was not a suspect, she was only a girl, and she had a baby. They couldn't be left to wander the streets.

"Come over whenever you want. Come now."

"Thank you, Miss Morrison," the girl said. Cecilia took a deep breath. Kix would find Charmaigne, would find the baby, would find her, and then . . . and then what? What would Jack say? What would Tyler say? What would Dr. Richardson advise?

She remembered Jack saying, "Pick an opinion that matters to you."

"Well, Jack," she said, as she replaced the phone in its cradle, "I guess I just picked."

fifteen

Cecilia still had a few jars of baby food from when Charmaigne and Kix had spent the night a few months ago, but otherwise her refrigerator was rather spare. She'd been living on cartons of cottage cheese and frozen bagels, and even those modest stores were depleted. She had time before Charmaigne could possibly get to her apartment, so she told the doorman that should her cousin arrive early, he should have her wait in the lobby. She rushed to the closest grocery store, a block and a half away, where she filled two shopping bags with a Broasted™ chicken, some bakery rolls, a bag of prepared salad, and a tub of chocolate-chocolate chip ice cream, plus eggs, cereal, milk, orange juice, whole wheat bread, and a hunk of sharp cheddar cheese.

After she put the groceries away, she sat at her kitchen table and leafed again through the morning paper, expecting that at any minute Ali would call from downstairs to announce Charmaigne's arrival. The story about Professor Gordon was on page one, bottom right, under the headline, "College Professor Shot During Class." She wondered if Charmaigne had seen it. If Charmaigne were truly looking for Kix, the subject would have to come up. Finding him could put him in jeopardy.

By six thirty, Charmaigne still hadn't arrived, and Cecilia was beginning to feel taken for granted. Did the girl think she could just come bounding in before the shelter doors closed for the night, as if she owed the hostess no courtesy whatsoever? She felt like the dutiful wife who'd put the kids to bed and kept her husband's supper warm, only to be told when he came stumbling home at midnight that she was a silly, sentimental cow.

Kix would've arrived on time, perhaps brought a flower, even if pilfered from one of the planters on Michigan Avenue, sat on her couch, and talked a while, like a real guest, not a vagrant. She was, she knew, romanticizing him. He, in fact, had not brought a flower either of the two times he'd been there and rather had broken into her safe, even though he hadn't stolen anything. She had to confess again that she didn't understand herself, or why she was so anxious to forgive this boy all of his transgressions. At times, she even thought him brave for having taken a shot at his brute of a father, possibly bringing Professor Gordon's unspeakably vile behavior to an end. She completed the crossword puzzle and uncorked a bottle of red wine.

It was eight o'clock and she'd finished her second glass when the doorman announced Charmaigne. Cecilia rinsed her glass and put it away. When she opened the door, Charmaigne pushed her stroller into the front hall before turning and saying hello.

"I need to change her," she said sheepishly. The girl looked terrible. Her jeans were dirty at the knees, as if she'd been kneeling in a garden; her blondish hair hung in oily threads; her light pink T-shirt was faded, grimy along the neck; and there were scratches on her arms. "Same place," Cecilia said as brightly as she could muster, pointing down the hall.

The girl lifted her baby from the stroller, and it started to cry.

"Let me get you some towels," Cecilia said, following Charmaigne. "Maybe you'd like to give the baby a bath?" To herself, she sounded maternal, but Charmaigne stiffened at the insinuation that Abby was dirty. Cecilia braved on. "Let me see if I have a tub." She'd never in her life given a baby a bath, but she recalled rubber bath sets given as gifts at showers for friends. In her utility closet, she had a square rubber container that the cleaning service sometimes used for washing the floors or windows. It would have to do. She rejoined Charmaigne in the bedroom, where the baby lay on Cecilia's treasured quilt. Cecilia bustled in. "Here's a towel," she said, spreading one next to the baby on the bed so that Charmaigne might get the hint. "I'll put the other in the bathroom with this tub. She should fit nicely," she said. "And here's a washcloth." She felt herself babbling nervously, but the girl was completely quiet.

"Okay," Charmaigne said finally. "You can give her a bath if you want. I'm just so tired."

"Perhaps a shower for you, too?" Cecilia suggested.

The girl hesitated, considering, then ran her hand through her hair and wiped it on her T-shirt. "Yeah. Sure," she said, as if she were doing Cecilia a favor.

"Well, then, use my shower," she said, pointing the girl to her bedroom. "There are clean towels on the rack in there." It seemed to Cecilia that Charmaigne didn't know about the shooting, that she was looking for Kix because she needed him to help her with Abby. Cecilia hoped she wouldn't have to be the one to tell her.

The girl took her backpack and shuffled to Cecilia's room. Alone with the baby, Cecilia bit her lip. "Abby, Abby, Abby," she murmured. The baby squirmed on the bed, her chubby arms darkened by a light silt, probably from being on the city streets these past however many days. "We'll give it a go," she said, lifting Abby like a paper bag with a leaky bottom and gently putting her down in the rubber tub. With one hand, she turned on the faucet and filled a glass with tepid water, using the other to keep the baby upright in the container. She poured water from the glass into the tub until it was half full, then took a washcloth and gently wiped the baby's arms and chest and back and neck. Remarkably, Abby seemed to like the water, laughing as if the bath were a great game. Cecilia was feeling proud of herself for having gotten this far, when she realized she needed to do something about the baby's hair. She thought about dumping a glass of water over the kid's head, but she herself would find that shocking, and she could hear Abby's wails even as she discarded that idea in favor of just lightly rubbing the baby's head with a washcloth. She did what she considered a good enough job and then wrapped the baby in a towel and, back in the guest room, waited for Charmaigne. She could hear the shower running. For someone who didn't want one, Charmaigne was certainly taking her time. The baby needed a diaper and fresh clothes, but she'd have to wait for her mother. Afraid that the baby would soon realize her mother was missing, Cecilia began to hum softly, her repertoire of lullabies coming back to her from a project her junior year in music school. Holding the baby, she swayed as she sang and was startled when Charmaigne appeared in the doorway. The girl dumped her backpack on the floor, and it thumped against the wall. Charmaigne bent over the pack, blocking it from Cecilia's view, and after some rummaging, came up with a diaper and a blue sleeper. The baby woke long enough to be dressed and placed in the stroller.

Cecilia pointed to the door, and Charmaigne pushed the stroller out into the hall and back to the kitchen. The girl sat at the table, and Cecilia lifted up the Broasted chicken. Charmaigne nodded. Cecilia worked silently, preparing a plate of salad, cottage cheese, and slices of the chicken for each of them, and put a basket of rolls on the table along with two glasses of water. She settled into the silence, which before the baby's bath had seemed awkward, but now was almost familiar.

When she was finished, the girl surprised her by taking her plate to the sink and then coming back for Cecilia's. Charmaigne rinsed them and set them in the drainer, then leaned against the sink and looked sideways at Cecilia. "Are you sure you haven't seen him?" Charmaigne asked.

Cecilia shook her head no, glimpsing for a moment the power of silence to elicit a person's deepest feelings. The secret, no doubt, to Dr. Richardson's success—the ability to withstand the silence.

Avoiding Cecilia's gaze, the girl said, "I'm worried about him."

Did she mean about her father? Should she ask? Cecilia said, "Do you think he's in trouble?"

Charmaigne turned and picked up the front section of the newspaper. Cecilia held her breath as Charmaigne flipped it over and her chin pointed at the headline Cecilia knew was there. "They missed," Charmaigne said, before she'd even had a chance to read through the story, but her tone was not a question.

"It's attempted murder," Cecilia said. "My friend Jack says Kix has motive and opportunity."

"Bastard," Charmaigne said. Cecilia didn't know if she meant Kix, Jack, or her father. "End of story. I want to go to sleep now."

"Of course," Cecilia said. But she wanted to know more. "Does Kix have a gun?" It chilled her to think that all this time, the times he'd stayed at her place, or at Tyler's, he'd had a gun in his backpack.

"No," Charmaigne said. "He doesn't believe in them."

"Do you?"

"Yeah. Sure. I believe in protecting yourself. And your kids."

"I mean, do you own a gun?" Cecilia asked.

"Nope," Charmaigne said, picked up her baby, and went down the hall to her room.

Alone again in her kitchen, Cecilia felt a mixture of anger and curiosity, compassion and resentment. She wanted something, but she wasn't sure what: the girl to act thankful, Kix to come back and prove his innocence, someone to tell her how this would all turn out. She opened her cabinets, looking for cookies, and then remembered the ice cream. Just because the girl had left before she'd offered dessert, that didn't mean Cecilia couldn't have some, and so defiantly she dished herself two scoops of chocolate chocolate-chip and sat back at her kitchen table, trying to imagine how Charmaigne found the courage to get over her own traumatic agonies enough to care for a baby so forced upon her.

When Cecilia woke up the next morning and shuffled into the kitchen, a little later than usual, Charmaigne mumbled good morning but continued to feed her baby in silence. Cecilia noticed she'd made the coffee.

"I have some of these," Cecilia said, opening a cabinet and putting her stash of baby food on the counter. "If you need them," she said. "They're for you. For Abby, actually." Cecilia forced a smile, then poured herself a cup of coffee. She noticed that the paper was on the counter, so she retrieved it and sat opposite Charmaigne, who continued feeding Abby. Living alone, she was used to quiet mornings, and being silent was, in Cecilia's opinion, by far the lesser of two evils. Her mother had been chatty and took morning silence as a personal affront. With her brothers off at an early morning swim practice, her father had hidden in the business and sports sections and grunted in response to either her mother or a score with a regularity sufficient to satisfy Francine, which got Cecilia off the conversational hook.

To Cecilia's relief, the story about Professor Gordon was not on the front page, which meant, she was sure, that there'd been no arrest. However, there was a follow-up on page three, and the story mentioned that the Professor had two teenagers who didn't live with him, leaving the reader to speculate as to whether they were in military school, on the streets, with a stepfather, or born out of wedlock. If they were thought to be suspects, the story didn't say.

"They're not looking for him," the girl said without looking up.

"It doesn't seem so," Cecilia said. "But you are. Do you have any idea where he could be?"

"Anywhere," she said.

"Kix didn't do the shooting," Cecilia said, her inflection sliding up, testing Jack and Tyler's theory.

"No," the girl said emphatically, which is what Cecilia had wanted to hear. She'd gone out on a limb for Kix, a couple of times, had tried to trust him when others were skeptical. For whatever reason, and perhaps just for pride, she wanted to be right about Kix.

"Charmaigne," Cecilia said. "I know you know this is serious. If Kix didn't do it, and I don't believe he did, then who? Who else would have a motive?"

"Anybody who knew him," Charmaigne said. "Anybody."

"Your mother?"

"My mother," Charmaigne scoffed and wiped her baby's face. She put the baby over her shoulder and rubbed her back.

"Kix said your mother didn't know."

"How convenient for her." Charmaigne didn't seem surprised that Cecilia knew her secret.

"Was she abused also?"

"Everybody wants to take her side," the girl said wearily.

"Who, everybody? Who else knew?" Cecilia thought that if others knew, there could be other suspects. The girl didn't answer, and Cecilia realized that the girl's shame was so extreme, probably no one in fact did know. There were no "sides" to be taken.

"Could it be one of his students?" Cecilia asked.

Charmaigne didn't answer.

"Did your father ever abuse a student?"

"Probably. The bastard."

"I was thinking they could be suspects, too."

"What difference does it make who did it? They missed."

She could understand the girl's logic, as far as it went, but there were broader implications. "Two things, Charmaigne," she said. "First, we can't have people taking pot shots at other people, particularly in public places. It's attempted murder, for god's sake. It is a big deal, even if the guy deserves it. Second, and I'm just now thinking of this one, if the point was that he is a bad guy and needs to be stopped from hurting his children or students, today, in the press, he's the victim. No one knows why anybody would want to shoot him. The paper says his classes are among the most popular in the whole university."

"No one would believe the truth," Charmaigne said bitterly.

"There must be ways to prove it, DNA and such."

"And then what? They'd lock my father up, my mother and my younger brothers and sisters would have no income, and who would support them? Kix?"

Cecilia swallowed hard.

"The faculty wives could come by with casseroles and coq au vin," the girl said. The baby began to fuss, and Charmaigne paced the kitchen, trying to soothe her. Even after a shower and a real meal last night, the girl looked to Cecilia like someone worried sick. She was so skinny—skinnier than last time she'd seen her—that her wrist bones stuck out like knobby tumors; her skin, though tanned, had a yellowish tint, and the cuticles of her thumbs had been picked raw.

"What if we don't find Kix?" Cecilia asked. "What are you going to do? It's hard to be a single mother, let alone . . ." She was going to say, let alone "a single mother living on the street," but she didn't want to rub the girl's nose in it. The girl knew she needed help. She was looking for Kix. She needed Kix to run his cons and sing his songs and be what her own father should have been, someone to protect and provide and care for her.

"We'll find him," Charmaigne said. Cecilia nodded her head in concerned agreement. Even if they found Kix, according to Jack, the boy would almost certainly be detained as a suspect.

Every adult in the girl's young life had failed Charmaigne, and now Cecilia, too, felt helpless. "I don't even know what the options might be," she said. "But I know some people who might know. There's this lawyer, Jack, who helped Kix a while back."

"No," the girl rushed. "We're figuring it out."

"Can I ask you what's the plan?"

"No," she said stubbornly. "I'll find Kix. That's the plan." She continued walking the baby, and when she got to the doorway, she kept going, into the dining and living area. Cecilia decided to give the girl her space, and finished reading the paper over a second cup of coffee.

Just as Cecilia was rinsing her cup in the sink, Charmaigne appeared in the kitchen door. "Would you mind if I ran to the store? I need to get a few things for Abby. I could take her with, but . . . She'll sleep," she said.

"I guess that would be okay," Cecilia said. Of course it would be a lot easier for the girl to get diapers and food and such, if she didn't have Abby with her. "But don't be gone long. You know I'm a rank amateur at this."

The girl rolled her eyes. "Like, it's not rocket science," she said. "I'll put her on a blanket on the floor in the living room, so she can't fall out of bed."

"Oh," Cecilia said, immediately insecure. The possibility of the baby squirming her way out of the middle of a double bed had not occurred to her. Together, they settled the baby, and then Cecilia offered Charmaigne two cloth shopping bags. The girl looked puzzled.

"Save a tree," Cecilia said brightly, and Charmaigne nodded.

"It's even easier to put stuff in my pack," Charmaigne said, as if sharing one of the secrets of street survival. She removed half a dozen jars and some diapers from the seemingly bottomless pack, along with an unopened package of baby wipes and a small pink bottle of baby lotion, and put them on the kitchen counter.

"Do you have enough money?" Cecilia thought to ask.

Charmaigne reached in her pocket and held up a crumpled ten-dollar bill.

"Silly question," Cecilia said. "What's enough? Wait a second and I'll get . . ."

"That's okay," the girl said and shoved her hair under a baseball cap. She smiled toward the living room and turned quickly to leave.

With the midmorning sun streaming in the southern windows, the baby slept peacefully. It occurred to Cecilia that the sun was bright enough to burn the child's delicate skin, so she lowered the blinds to filter it. In the half-sun, her apartment was warm, and she found it hard to keep her eyes open. She lay back on the floor next to the blanket and dozed.

She probably was asleep for less than twenty minutes when the baby cried. Panic shot through her, and she knelt over her, shushing and saying it would be okay, that mommy would be home soon. At the sound of her voice, the baby stopped, stared, then started in again. Cecilia shushed for another minute, before it occurred to her to pick the infant up. She did, and the baby quieted. Cecilia put her over her shoulder, the way Charmaigne had done, and then stood and paced the room until the baby seemed to be asleep. Charmaigne should be home soon. She'd been gone an hour, more than enough time to get to the grocery store a block and a half away and back. Her pack wouldn't hold more than an hour's worth.

The baby slept and Cecilia grew bored. Charmaigne had been gone now two whole hours, and Cecilia was again feeling that the girl was taking advantage of her generosity.

"Where's your mommy?" Cecilia whined. Abby squirmed and opened her eyes. "She's been gone more than two hours! Where do you think she is, huh? Does she think I'll look after you all day, like I have nothing better to do?"

As if picking up on the edge in Cecilia's baby talk, Abby started to cry, and when Cecilia leaned down to comfort her, she realized that the inevitable had happened. Abby needed to be changed. Tears came to Cecilia's eyes. "You really have the worst luck, kiddo," she said. "Of all the women in all the world . . ." She felt like the only woman in America who didn't know how to change a baby, and yet it had to be done. How hard could it be? "Not rocket science," Charmaigne had said.

It occurred to Cecilia that she could probably find a website that would offer step-by-step instructions, but the child was wailing, and the thought of getting Abby to the study, logging on to her computer, and ignoring the infant's howls long enough to read them was more than she could bear.

"Don't you dare move," she said and rushed to the kitchen, where she found the wipes and the couple of diapers that Charmaigne had left. Back in the living room, she took off the baby's damp sleeper, gingerly opened the tabs of the diaper, and slid a towel under the baby's bottom.

"Don't move," she said again and ran back to the kitchen to dump the diaper in the garbage can and throw the sleeper into the washing machine. Back in the living room, she opened the wipes, cleaned the baby's bottom, and fitted the new diaper, which turned out to be self-explanatory. Abby smiled at her, and Cecilia momentarily forgot her irritation at Charmaigne. Sitting cross-legged on the floor, she played with Abby for a while, letting her grab her fingers and reach for her face.

"Aren't you strong," she exclaimed, when Abby curled her tiny hand around Cecilia's little finger. The baby's brown eyes were alert and curious, and Cecilia found herself wondering what Abby saw, what Abby knew about her circumstances. Did Abby know the difference between Cecilia and Charmaigne? Of course, Cecilia told herself, a child would know her mother. Would Abby get used to . . . Cecilia dropped Abby's hand, horrified. What if Charmaigne were not coming back? What was she supposed to do then? Report Abby as abandoned? Charmaigne as missing? What would happen to the baby? Foster care? Horrors! And if they then found Charmaigne, would they put her in jail? Would they then find Kix? Would Cecilia be somehow at fault?

Hurriedly, she flipped open her phone and speed dialed Tyler. No answer. "Damn," she said out loud. It was just one, usually he'd still be lunching at this time, but maybe he was in a lesson. She waited until one thirty and tried again. Again, no answer. Her legs cramped. She crawled to her feet, stretching her arms over her head and then touching her toes. She needed to go for a run. She needed to play the piano. She needed to sing. Because of Charmaigne's total selfishness and irresponsibility, she couldn't do what she needed to do, and she had no idea what to do about the problem in front of her.

She squatted down to make sure Abby was asleep. So peaceful, so oblivious, so trusting, ultimately, of the world around her. Selfish? Cecilia felt a twang of guilt. It was possible she was the one who was selfish. What did it matter if she ran that afternoon or not? There were other things she could do. And didn't Abby need her more?

Careful not to disturb Abby, she did squats, leg lifts, crunches, windmills for her upper arms. Forty-five minutes passed, distracting her from her growing certainty that Charmaigne wasn't coming back. She picked up the baby, who was half-awake, and went to the guest bedroom, hoping to prove herself wrong. If Charmaigne had left anything of importance, then she would be coming back to claim it. Perhaps the time had just gotten away from her. Perhaps she'd walked down to the lake and was lost in the rhythm of the waves and her dreams of a different life.

In the bedroom, there was a small pile of Abby's clothes and a folded piece of paper torn from a notebook. She put the baby, still only in her diaper, in the center of the bed and sat on the edge, reading. "To whom it may concern: Professor Gordon was shot at because he is a rapist and has raped his own daughter. I have a five-month-old to prove it. If no one stops him, he will rape my little sister, and who knows how many others. He should be arrested. My brother Kix didn't shoot at him. I swear. Signed, Charmaigne Gordon."

The penmanship was neatly balanced on the paper's blue lines, as clean and without flourish as the writer's bare prose. Cecilia read the letter over and over. What was the girl thinking? Saying Kix didn't do it was as good as pointing the finger squarely at him! Worse yet, did she really intend to leave her baby with Cecilia? What did Charmaigne expect Cecilia to do? What should she do?

She dialed Tyler, but no answer. Angrily, she threw the phone on the bed, narrowly missing Abby.

"I'm sorry, I'm sorry," she murmured at the startled child and quickly picked her up, searching the baby's face for some sense of what to do, some sense of a future, for the baby, and for herself. Instantly, Cecilia saw Charmaigne's calculated plan. Cecilia had said, just that morning, that no one knew why Professor Gordon had been shot at. Charmaigne left the note so Cecilia could tell her story, and she'd left her baby, the most helpless victim in all of this, in the hands of a rich woman with no one else to worry about. Cecilia could take up Charmaigne's cause, and, as Kix would say, Abby could live at the Ritz. Cecilia wasn't sure about either one, but Abby cried, and, unlike the burden of what to do with the note, the task immediately in front of her could not be put off.

Abby's second diaper change was less intimidating than the first, and this time she cracked open the baby lotion as if it were a bottle of champagne. She rubbed the lotion between her hands to warm it, and Abby gurgled pleasantly as Cecilia rubbed it on. She glanced at her watch. It was already after four, and she had no idea where the day had gone. A nap, leg lifts, two diapers. Babysitting was far more time-consuming than she'd ever thought. But the evening loomed ahead, and she couldn't spend every day like this. She called Tyler.

"Where have you been?" she demanded.

"Out of juice," he said. "My bad." She wondered what was going on with him that he'd let his cell phone battery go dead. "What's up?"

She blurted out a short version of her news.

"Ohmygod," he said, all one word, his voice rising. "I'll be right over. Have you eaten? I'll bring Chinese."

"That's okay, Ty. I'll call for a pizza."

"Heavens, no! We don't use food to relieve stress."

"Please don't lecture me," she said, guilty about the chocolate chocolate-chip.

"Of course not, darling. How old is the baby?"

"How would I know?" Then she remembered the note. "Five months. Do you think I should call Jack?"

"Not just yet, honey. There are tons of issues here, to be sure, but let's sort out the emotional ones first."

Ty arrived loaded down with baby gear: a bassinette, what looked to Cecilia like a month's supply of diapers, a cloth shopping bag of jars, and a pink stuffed puppy. He handed Cecilia a quilted pink and white bag with a daisy on it. "For you," he said.

"For what?" she asked.

"Baby gear!" he said. "Can't leave home without it."

"Where did you get this stuff?"

"I'm an uncle," he said. "My sister has three of the little rug rats. Where's ours?"

"Ours?" Cecilia said.

"You should never leave her out of your sight."

"That's impossible."

Tyler shrugged and charged to the living room, where he found Abby squirming on the blanket from the morning. Immediately he picked her up and held her over his head, and she smiled and laughed for him. "What a pretty little girl," he said in a baby-talk voice. Cecilia went to the kitchen and brought back two glasses of wine.

Tyler put Abby back down and took the glass Cecilia offered. "Just this once. Usually, it's a rule. No drinking in front of the kids."

"Then you better turn her around," Cecilia laughed.

"And you better call your therapist."

"I can quit whenever I want," Cecilia said.

"Oh honey, vino's not your problem," he said, then lowered his voice to a whisper and pointed, "she is."

"Hopefully Charmaigne is coming back."

"Let me see the letter."

Cecilia found the note in her study and brought it to him.

"*Phew*," he breathed out. He read the letter again, although she'd read it to him on the phone. "Sounds like a confession," he said.

"What?"

"She has the most personal motive, and how would she know for certain Kix didn't do it, unless she did it herself?"

"With a baby? On a college campus? Where would she get a gun?"

Tyler pursed his lips, as if she were naive. "You're the one who likes strong women characters."

"So Kix would be off the hook," Cecilia mused. She could almost forgive Charmaigne for taking her revenge, but still, she found it hard to fully sympathize with the girl. Kix was charming, but Charmaigne was cool, even cold. You'd have to be cold to shoot someone in broad daylight, and to leave your baby with a stranger.

"She's not coming back," Tyler said.

Cecilia sipped her wine. He was probably right. "So then what do I do?" she said quietly.

"Call the Department of Family Services or the police," Tyler began, but there was reluctance in his voice.

"No!" she said in alarm, the liquid in her glass sloshing.

"Or—I don't know, we'll call Jack. I suppose we ought to give the mother a chance. We'll keep the baby until she smells like fish."

She hesitated to be sure she'd parsed the old adage. "Three days?"

"Just to be sure Charmaigne's not coming back. She could change her mind." He put down his glass and leaned back on the couch. "So could you."

"Me, what?" she asked. "Change my mind about what?"

"Better call that therapist."

"What for?"

"Because in three days, you will be so attached to this baby that you will have convinced yourself that she is the meaning you've been looking for, and you'll be hounding DFS to let you keep her, and—my luck—I will lose you to the Diaper Wars."

"And I couldn't do both? Be a mom and be on the stage?"

"Of course you could. But would you? You, who needs no excuse whatsoever to cancel an audition? 'The baby's asleep, cancel that call.' 'The baby burped, call the understudy.' It's too hard to do both, unless you are one-hundred-percent committed to both, and I don't see that in you." He picked up his wine and swirled it before taking a sip.

"So you've got it all figured out."

"No. Or yes. Whatever, darling. Even if I do, you're the one who needs to work it through. Call him. Now." He reached in his pocket and with one hand flipped open his cell phone. "I'll baby-sit while you perseverate."

"Perseverate?"

"Fancy medical term for beating your head against a wall, repeating yourself. You go tell the good doctor your story until you figure out what it is you want in life. And then you come to me," he winked, indicating he knew, "and I help you get it."

sixteen

"I'm here because Tyler says I should be," she said.

"Another 'should'?" Dr. Richardson mused, and she sighed in exaggerated disgust.

"I could use some advice."

"Not my line of work," he smiled, but she ignored him, rushing on to tell the story of all that had happened since she'd seen him last: the letter from Kix, telling her about Professor Gordon and that she had talent; Tyler's efforts to help her get ready to audition; the story about Professor Gordon getting shot; Jack's worry that Kix was the prime suspect; Charmaigne leaving the baby and the ambiguous note about Kix not doing it. Where was Kix? Could he possibly be guilty? What would happen to Charmaigne on the street? What about the baby? She couldn't possibly be expected to keep it. What would happen to it in foster care?

To her surprise, Dr. Richardson asked, "Did you go to an audition?"

"What difference does that make? Charmaigne took a shot at her father and left her baby with me. Where are your priorities?"

Dr. Richardson held her gaze, but softly, as if he were considering the very question she'd asked. "I suppose that's a question you might ask yourself," he said.

What were her priorities? The truth be told, the past few days had been engaging enough, but exhausting. Moving in to the guest room, Tyler had assumed the roles of nanny and doting dad. Playing mommy was an entirely new experience for her, and she found herself both consumed by concern for Abby's every possible need—how long she slept, how much she ate, how many times she needed to be changed, how alert she was, how happy—and resentful. She had no time for herself, and she was used to having nothing but time for herself. Was she just selfish? Or totally unsuited to being a mother? But what could possibly be more important? How could she call the police or Social Services and leave Abby to be bounced from foster home to foster home in an overburdened, underfunded system that would destroy what little chance the infant had in life? But wouldn't she be a fugitive herself, if she failed to report the abandoned child? How could she fill her time that would be more meaningful or fulfilling than caring for Abby? How was she to know what else that would be, what her priorities should be?

What did Tyler think she was going to get out of talking to someone who wouldn't talk about the things she wanted to talk about? She wanted the doctor's advice on what to do about the baby, and he wanted to talk about her priorities. She'd told him about an attempted murder, and he'd asked about auditions. She sighed heavily, to let him know that she felt pressured into telling him the whole truth.

"I practiced, and I was ready, but I didn't do the first audition." His neutral expression didn't change. The trouble with beards and mustaches was that they concealed so much. If the corner of his lips turned down in disgust, she couldn't tell.

He looked neither disappointed nor angry, but he must be curious. "Don't laugh, but I saw a ghost."

"At the audition?"

Of course the ghost would get his attention, she thought, just like a wildly complicated dream. "I was about to start, and I saw my mother in the back row. She was wearing her favorite black knit suit with very showy gold buttons—St. John's—and her gray hair, which was always so tightly coifed—every Thursday with the same hairdresser on Oak Street—was skizzed out, cartoonlike." She laughed. "Funny. At the time, I just saw her eyes, so dark and critical," her voice cracked a little, and she hoped Dr. Richardson didn't notice, "that I didn't see how funny she looked, as if she'd been electrocuted."

"How did she get electrocuted?" he asked, his voice betraying a mild curiosity.

"For god's sake, that's not the point," she said. "I have no idea. It was a ghost. Well, it wasn't a ghost, I don't believe in ghosts. It was just an image in my head."

Dr. Richardson seemed to nod slightly, as if she'd said something true.

"Shall we meet next week?" he asked.

"Depends what happens with the baby," she said. "We didn't make much progress on that," she said, "and that is what I wanted to talk about." She scooched forward on the couch to leave.

"We talked about other things that were important to you," he said, with just the hint of a question. He glanced at his watch and tapped the air with his right hand, indicating she should sit down. "We have a few more minutes," he said. "How do you feel about what's happened with Kix?"

"Nothing's happened with him," she said sharply. It seemed to her that everyone was piling up on the kid except for Charmaigne and her. "I mean, I don't believe he shot at his dad, but it's possible Charmaigne did, or they both did. I don't know."

"Charmaigne?"

"Maybe it's too much TV. Tyler thinks it's a possibility."

"I was wondering if you felt—I don't know—responsible, implicated, betrayed, maybe in danger yourself?"

"Just because Kix has motive and opportunity doesn't mean he has the character. Charmaigne might have the character— the passion even—and she has motive, too. It doesn't mean she did it. Either one of them could have and neither one of them could have. I think Kix still sees me as a friend, someone to turn to when he's in trouble. He wouldn't hurt me." He hadn't hurt her when he had the opportunity. It made no sense for her to be afraid now. And Charmaigne had just put her child in Cecilia's care.

"I hope not," Dr. Richardson said, perhaps skeptically. "Next week then?"

"I suppose Tyler would say I should," she said.

Before he stood to see her out, he said, "You're right, you know, you probably should get some advice—from a lawyer or social worker or someone like that—on the baby and what you know about Charmaigne and her father. You know, Cecilia, my only concern in this therapy is you. There are a lot of issues around Charmaigne and the baby that have nothing to do with you."

Cecilia smiled through gritted teeth. She was both touched that he would say the therapy was only about her—her!—and angry that he could be so obstinate. How were they supposed to get to issues only about her when there was a baby involved? How could he say that the baby had nothing to do with her, when it was, at this very minute, at her home, in the charge of her friend? She would have to resolve the baby thing first, she thought, if she were ever to get to issues about herself.

Closing the door behind Cecilia, Haverill felt more responsible for Cecilia's mess than he knew rationally he should. Actually, he'd been surprised to hear from her. Although it was not unusual for a patient to declare victory and run just before getting to their most important secret, fear, hurt, or problem, he hadn't counted Cecilia among those in enough pain to return. She'd called two days ago, and he'd had a cancellation. While his first inclination had been to give her an appointment for a week from now, to see if she really wanted to come back, she'd mentioned something about a baby. He hadn't gotten it totally; there'd been street noise down below and the volume on his telephone had inadvertently been turned down, probably by the night cleaning crew, and with a baby involved, he'd been inclined to believe Cecilia's matter was urgent.

In fact, her therapeutic reasons for returning to therapy were

betrothal. Still, he was surprised by his daughter's fear of commitment, this tiny flaw in her otherwise impeccable character.

He abandoned the notion that the marble would become Maddie's wedding present. He turned on his stereo, thinking the music might inspire him, and he was greeted with the stirring clarinet trill of "Rhapsody in Blue." It was a fanciful and then a soaring piece. No wonder it had been usurped by that airline for its commercials. He turned it up, full blast. He picked up a sharply pointed chisel and hammer from the professional, hand-forged set of tools Rosalyn had given him and stood over the block of marble. He poised the chisel over the top right-hand corner, then backed away. He needed his goggles. The music dove into its self and rose again, and he set his jaw and lifted the hammer one more time. George Gershwin's masterpiece came to a repetitive and rousing end, there was a beat of silence, and the soothing tones of the deejay announced the orchestration and recording by a Czech Radio orchestra.

How do you write something like that, he asked himself. How do you hear the melody? How do you add harmonies and other instruments and playful repetitions? At least, he thought, you have notes and sounds to work with, a large, but more-or-less fixed set of choices, like the words used by a playwright or novelist. But ultimately, how do you trust that someone else will re-create what you heard in your head?

With sculpture, the thing is what it is. People might see it differently, but they can't change it or botch it. The sculptor has the total responsibility. All the more reason to be absolutely certain you get it right. Perhaps with music, you can manage one recording that is as it should be; with writing, you have unlimited use of the delete key. If Cecilia gives a wrong interpretation, it's over, gone, forgotten. On film, there is the possibility of another take, or even a remake. But here, as a sculptor, he was expected to wield the chisel with intended but unknowable results, creating something permanent and immutable. As a sculptor, he would have to repeat himself, like one of his perseverating patients, nick after nick, hoping to figure something out.

He put down the chisel and hammer and removed his goggles. He wasn't ready yet.

In the corner of the studio Rosalyn had designed a small library nook, with two maroon leather easy chairs, a small oriental rug, and built-in bookcases of warm mahogany. On a small table between the chairs, there was a reading light and on one of the bookshelves, a Waterford decanter of single malt scotch and two snifters. He poured a small glass and lowered himself into the chair, contemplating the marble and the story of his life.

seventeen

Cecilia left therapy with no notion of what to do about Charmaigne, the baby, or her career, and as she walked out of the building onto the plaza, she found herself hoping, almost expecting, to run into Kix. Like a movie where you get to start the whole day over again, and take it in a different direction: Kix stopping and asking her for a light, her turning and seeing the fuzzy chin of his youth, her ignoring him. Well, that would've been uncommonly rude—she hadn't been much of a smoker, but when you need a light, you need a light, and a light is nothing, a bit of friction, a spark of heat and fire. She couldn't imagine denying the boy the match. But the money? That had changed everything. She'd been different after that, had done crazy things. She'd been floundering, as she saw it, when Tyler pushed her toward Dr. Richardson, awash in a universe of abstract possibilities. She was, today, still floundering, but there were specific things right in front of her that needed immediate attention. The abstract had become concrete. Abby, for one, was real.

She rushed home in a taxi, as if she were afraid the baby would forget her if she was gone too long. Tyler'd been a great help. He knew more about babies than she did, and fed and changed and bathed and played with Abby with a carefree confidence Cecilia envied. Jealous, she wanted the baby to bond with her, not Tyler. Still, the truth was, she was relieved not to be solely in charge. She was afraid of doing something wrong—giving the kid too much food, getting soapy water in its eyes, flipping its floppy body in the wrong direction, and suffocating it. She just wasn't very knowledgeable, and she wasn't feeling that reliable or dependable, either.

This was the third day of their caring for Abby, and as she opened the door to her apartment, she was greeted with the wonderfully fresh smell of baby powder, not dead fish. She might not be good at it, and it might make her nervous, but having this little one to take care of was giving her a sense of self and well-being that had escaped her these past few years.

"Honey, I'm home!" she sing-songed, pumping up her own spirits.

"In here," Tyler called from the living room, where he sat on the floor, playing with Abby, a bottle of baby powder behind him on the coffee table. He got to his feet. "I've got some lessons this afternoon. How about if Jack and I bring over some chow, and we can figure out what to do about," he nodded in Abby's direction, "you-know-who."

"Absolutely," she said. Tyler'd canceled classes the day before, but if he canceled he didn't get paid, so he needed to resume his schedule. "You deserve a break. How about if I make dinner?"

"You'll have your hands full," he said. "Call if you need me."

She was glad to be left alone, and to have some time to recover from her encounter with Dr. Richardson. At first, he hadn't seemed interested in the baby at all. They just talked about auditions and ghosts—abstractions, both—not the real flesh-and-blood problem lying on a blanket in her living room, and then he'd asked about Kix and her being in danger. She didn't even know where Kix was. New Orleans, possibly, but more likely still in town, making money for the journey. He was a smart kid. No doubt he'd heard the news about his dad, and, if innocent, he'd stay just as low as if he were guilty. There was, she thought, little chance of his coming back. She felt a twinge of sadness about that, but she could see how that would be for the best.

Abby was asleep, and Cecilia sat on the couch, watching her, wondering what to do. For three days it had been as if she and Tyler were on vacation, he running out to shop yesterday or today to give a class, as if playing a round of golf, and then coming back to home base to sit by the beach and watch the waves. They were on hiatus from real life. Going forward, there was no way they could keep this baby. They weren't a couple. Theirs was not a family. Neither of them had careers particularly suited to parenthood. The kid had enough problems starting out in life without becoming a group project, like the production of a world premiere. But if Cecilia called Social Services—and Jack was pretty cold in his advice that that was what she and Tyler should do and the sooner the better— then what real chance would Abby have? A round of foster homes? Lost in a system that clearly could not provide for her as well as she could, at least materially?

As if absorbing Cecilia's anxiety, Abby fussed all afternoon, feeding, not feeding, crying false alarms on diaper changes, sleeping, squirming, unhappy. In the late afternoon, Cecilia took Abby to her bedroom, where she flipped on the TV and lay Abby on the bed. The anchorwoman promised a follow-up on the Normal shooting after some commercial messages. Abby started to cry, and Cecilia shushed her. Abby cried the louder and Cecilia turned up the TV. Abby had to stop crying so she could hear the TV news. When she didn't, Cecilia grabbed her roughly and marched her to the guest room, where she hurriedly put a pillow wall around her and returned to her own room, just in time.

"Normal police have confirmed that they have reason to believe that the shooting in Professor Karl Gordon's physics class earlier this week was personally motivated," the anchorwoman said. Knowing her audience would want more prurient details, the anchor added, "They said they may look at family members and former students as persons of interest, but would not say more at this time." She was glad for the use of the phrase "persons of interest" rather than the more ominous "suspects," and they were looking beyond family to include students. If they asked the

Gordons, they'd say Kix and Charmaigne had been gone from town for more than a year. Cecilia imagined Normal was small enough that it would be hard to slip back into town unnoticed. Of course, she thought, it would be especially hard for Charmaigne, with a baby, but, on the other hand, Charmaigne, being a more quiet and less public person, might find it easier than Kix. She couldn't imagine, really, that Charmaigne would want to ever set foot in Normal again.

Cecilia moved the newscast over to sports and then, filled with guilt and a sudden panic, rushed to the guest room, where Abby was nestled, not suffocated, between the pillows. Cecilia picked her up and cradled her in her arms. Despite the horror of her conception, she seemed to be a perfect little girl in every way. Who could abandon such an innocent and helpless life? Cecilia could hardly imagine the conflict Charmaigne must have felt every time she looked at her baby. The baby would be fine. It was Charmaigne's life that had been forever changed, whatever dreams and plans and hopes she'd had for herself now totally undone. No wonder she'd been overwhelmed by this unwanted responsibility. She'd done what she could, had kept her baby safe these many months under exceptionally trying circumstances, and had just this week both reached a breaking point and a heart-wrenching decision. By giving Abby to Cecilia, Charmaigne had saved her baby and herself. Cecilia couldn't help but wonder whether that decision would also save her.

It was both too easy an answer to her ennui and not the answer she wanted. Her own mother had tried to live her life through her daughter, and what good had that done anyone? Perhaps for a while Francine Morrison had taken meaning from her psychic investment in her daughter's career, but at the end, it hadn't mattered much, had it? Even Dr. Richardson didn't seem to know. Was Cecilia better off or worse, for all of her mother's focus and attention?

Tyler let himself in around six, Jack trailing with cartons of fettuccini and chicken Vesuvio from an Italian delicatessen nearby. He was wearing chinos and a navy blazer with a club tie, a casual day for him at the office.

"Adult food," he said, plopping two white bags on the kitchen counter and rifling through a drawer for a corkscrew. He opened a dark bottle of cabernet sauvignon and poured three stubby glasses, not knowing where she kept her wine glasses.

Tyler lifted the baby from Cecilia, and she took a long drink of the wine. They went to the living room, where Jack settled himself on the far end of the couch and crossed ankle over knee. "When are you going to call Social Services?" he asked, ignoring Tyler and looking straight at Cecilia at the opposite end of the couch.

"Not yet," she said, switching her gaze to Tyler, who was nestled with Abby in a wingback chair facing them. She hoped that Jack would be satisfied but wasn't surprised when he wasn't.

"You two know this can't go on," he said matter-of-factly. "It's sweet and all, but it's not right."

Tyler let Abby grab his index finger. "Not now, Jack."

"When?"

"Later."

They sat in a tense silence, which was shattered by the ringing of Cecilia's cell phone.

She picked it up off the coffee table and said, "Hello."

"If it's Kix," Jack started, but Cecilia closed her eyes. She said "yes" and "okay" a couple of times and flipped her phone shut.

"Don't tell me," Jack said, shaking his head.

"He's not a fugitive," Cecilia said. "He can't be a fugitive unless he's guilty or there's a warrant for his arrest, and he's not and there isn't."

"A technicality," Jack said, putting down his glass. "How do you know he didn't do it? Are we to take Charmaigne's word for it?"

"You can ask him. He's coming over."

"Not good," Jack said. "Look, Charmaigne doesn't give him an alibi, she only says he didn't do it, which means, most likely, that she did. At the very least, Kix is probably an accomplice, possibly a coconspirator."

"So what if Charmaigne did it? The bastard deserved it." Between the two of them, Cecilia thought she'd rather Charmaigne be the guilty one, revenging her own violation. "You can leave if you want to."

Jack rubbed his forehead. "How can I leave?" he muttered, as if to himself. "You're in over your head." She gave him a nasty look, pointing silently toward the door. "We all are."

"You're staying?"

"As long as you need me." She couldn't deny she needed help. Separate from Kix's problems, was the problem of Abby. Cecilia couldn't imagine her life going forward with a baby in it, but she couldn't imagine giving her up, either. Whatever Kix or Charmaigne did or didn't do, she didn't see that the baby should suffer. She looked to Tyler, hoping he would have a solution.

"I don't know, Cecilia, but Jack is probably right. I can't see you doing this for life, and since Paul and I aren't together anymore, I can't see my doing this alone either. We ought to let Social Services find her a real home."

The phone rang again and Cecilia said, "Thank you." She took a deep breath. "Guys, do me a favor here. Let's not jump on Kix all at once. Let him ease in, see Abby. Let's hear him out."

"I trust he's not armed," Jack said, but it wasn't clear to Cecilia that he was joking. Tyler scolded him, rubbing his right index finger over his left, as if peeling potatoes. Jack took his cell phone out of his breast pocket, flipped it open to check the battery, and then put it in the outside pocket of his blazer.

There was a knock on the door, and Kix came in, his grin wide, but serious. "Thank you, Mrs. M. Where's Abby?" He dropped his backpack and rushed toward the living room as she pointed in that direction.

Not stopping to say hello to Jack, he knelt on one knee next to Tyler's chair, and Tyler lifted Abby over his head and down to Kix, saying "Look who's here! Da-da's here!"

"Uncle," Cecilia glared at Tyler.

Kix ignored all of them, *goochie-gooing* Abby and telling her he was back to take care of her. Tyler refilled his wine in the kitchen and brought the bottle back for Jack and Cecilia. No one spoke until Kix said, "Oopsie!" and took Abby off to the bathroom, presumably to be changed. Tyler and Cecilia looked at each other, Cecilia feeling chastised and Tyler crossing his arms across his chest, perplexed.

"Must've just happened," he said. "Trust me, if there had been the slightest . . ."

"I know," Cecilia said.

"Not something you should be arguing over," Jack said.

"We're not," they said in unison.

"I meant, there are more important things," Jack said, and Kix, coming back from changing Abby, put her on the blanket on the floor and stood over Jack. "I'm not a fugitive. I didn't do it. And I don't know where Charmaigne is."

"Then how did you know Abby was here? And how did you know Charmaigne was gone?" Jack asked.

Kix didn't miss a beat. "She called me and told me she was coming here. I figured out the rest."

"Where were you three days ago?" Jack asked, his courtroom voice low and steady, as if setting a snare.

"At City Hall, getting my busker's license."

He held up a plasticized card hanging on a lanyard around his neck.

"Morning or afternoon?"

"Afternoon. Got busted in the morning."

Jack raised his eyebrows in a shrug and nodded without actually assenting, the trial lawyer indicating his understanding of his client's planned testimony. It didn't really matter where Kix was on the afternoon of the shooting. What mattered was what could be proven (or not) about his whereabouts.

"And Charmaigne?" Jack continued.

"Haven't seen her, actually, since she first went missing, back in July," he answered. He eyed their wine. "Hey, can I . . . ?"

"No!" Cecilia said. She picked up the bottle and handed it to Jack to put on the end table near him, away from Kix.

"That's cool," Kix said. "Got any milk?" Tyler held up a hand and went to the kitchen.

Kix's nonchalance angered her. Did he not understand that his word was not good enough for them? That the truth—if he were innocent—was not sufficient, once the authorities pieced together enough circumstances, including runaway and other criminal behavior, no matter how petty, to make you look motivated enough to be guilty? And what if he were innocent and the only way to create a reasonable doubt were to point the finger at Charmaigne? Did fingering Charmaigne, or, for that matter, Charmaigne's guilt, bother him at all?

Jack sighed. "Okay, kid. Listen up. You're both in trouble, whether you know it or not. If you didn't do it—and the jury's out on that one, as far as I'm concerned—your sister's in big trouble. Maybe they can't prove attempted murder or assault or anything having to do with the shooting, but they could for reckless endangerment of a child."

"She never endangered Abby! Never!" Kix said, standing up. "She gave her to Cecilia."

"Sit down," Jack said. "She didn't ask Cecilia if she wanted her."

"You do, don't you?" Kix looked at Cecilia, and his eyes were moist.

Cecilia opened her mouth, thinking to say how complicated a decision it was, but Jack waved his hand to stop her. "Here's what you're going to do. You're going to find Charmaigne, bring her to me, and the three of us are going to take Abby, drive down to Normal, and straighten this out."

"That would be endangering us," Kix said.

"You're going to have to trust me."

"What will happen to us?"

"Once we find out how old everybody really is, we can explore options," Jack said.

"I'll be eighteen in October," Kix said. "Charmaigne just turned seventeen."

Jack nodded his acceptance. "We'll find a home, for her and the baby. There are places. We'll deal with you later."

"What about school?" Cecilia asked.

"I want to take care of Charmaigne and Abby," Kix insisted.

"You got to take care of yourself first," Tyler said quietly. "Can't help someone else until you get yourself squared away."

"I've helped," Kix said, and his voice cracked. He sounded tired. "Ever since Abby was born, I've helped. I've had to do everything. I even had to show Charmaigne how to love Abby."

"Could she take care of her without you?" Cecilia asked.

"No. Yes. Okay, I guess," Kix said.

"Can she take care of herself? "

"Of course."

"Does she have a problem with drugs?"

"No!" Kix said firmly. "We don't do drugs." Cecilia looked at Jack, to see if she should believe him. Before, when Kix had mentioned Charmaigne and drugs, he'd been lying about her being his wife. Should she believe him now? Jack shrugged. Kix's blue eyes were clear.

"Where do you think she is? Would she go to a shelter? Does she have any friends?"

"She didn't have many friends, and besides, she'd never go back to Normal."

"Then where is she?"

"Like you said, she's taking care of herself," Kix said stubbornly. "You know, it's not Abby's fault."

"And it's not Charmaigne's fault, either," Tyler finally interrupted, "or yours. And not Cecilia's if she doesn't want to keep Abby."

"I don't understand!" Kix cried at Cecilia. "Why wouldn't you? You live alone. You have tons of money. You don't do anything else with your life. Why not take care of a kid who can't take care of itself, who shouldn't have even been born?"

Wounded by Kix's assessment of her life, Cecilia took a shallow breath, which didn't satisfy her need for air, then another and another, finally holding it to avoid hyperventilating. How ungrateful could this kid be? After everything she'd done so far, he wanted more? She was a complete stranger to him. There was no reason she should be responsible for his sister's baby, his father's sin.

"She's not the one on trial, here," Jack said.

"No one is on trial," Tyler said, firmly enough that Jack sat back on the couch, as if to let him take over.

Kix paced the room, almost frantic. Cecilia wanted to help, she really did, but every time she considered actually adopting Abby, Tyler brought her back to reality.

"Not everyone is meant to be a parent, Kix. You know that. Look at your own father, for god's sake," Tyler said.

"Mrs. M wouldn't . . . ."

"Of course not. But consider this. She's not a Mrs. She's almost forty. She doesn't have the physical stamina she used to."

Cecilia winced, but Tyler blustered on. "The child wouldn't have a father. Wouldn't have brothers and sisters. Cecilia's profession requires her to work nights, to be willing to go out of town for weeks at a time on a moment's notice. If she'd wanted to be a mother, she would've done so by now. But she didn't. It's not her calling."

It seemed wrong that the men were discussing a matter that concerned most the three women involved, but since she couldn't say with conviction that Tyler was wrong, she took a sip of her wine, letting Kix know that she was considering his proposal even as she was allowing herself to be saved from it.

"She's a singer," Jack said.

She couldn't believe Jack, who she hardly knew, was entering the fray. "Not you, too," she cried. "You've never even heard me sing."

"Oh, but I have," Jack said brightly.

"You saw *Rumplestilt's Kin*?" she said, putting her hand over her heart, which was rumbling like a kettledrum.

"Too high-brow for me," Jack scoffed. "No, I think it was—," he cleared his throat, "'Daylight come and me wan' go home.'"

"That's our subway song, man," Kix said. "We—"

"Please shut up, Kix," Cecilia said in frustration, locking her gaze on Jack, and searching her memory for the kind-looking lawyer-type in the subway that first day.

"It sounded professional to me," Jack said. "I think they're right. It's your calling."

"I don't know what makes you all so certain of my 'calling,'" she said.

"Let's put it this way, honey," Tyler said. "We know what your calling isn't." The men laughed, hurting Cecilia's feelings, and switched their concerns back to Jack's plan.

"Normal, it is," Jack said.

"I don't know where Charmaigne is," Kix said, "and if I did, I wouldn't take her to Normal and make her sit in the same room with my father—even a courtroom. I'll go to Normal if that's what you want. I'll bring Abby. They can take Abby's DNA if they have to, but keep Charmaigne out of it. Let her start over someplace. She's tougher than she looks. She'll make it if she's given a chance."

They all looked at Jack, who studied the ceiling and then the floor. "Let's start with Normal, and we'll see what happens from there. Charmaigne—if she's guilty—might be out of our hands." Kix looked troubled, but Abby let out a sharp cry.

"I think we need another bottle," Jack said, emptying the last of the one he'd brought.

"So do I," Kix said, picking up Abby. "It's okay, sweetie pie. It's okay."

eighteen

Jack and Kix were on their way to Normal, Tyler was giving a class, and Cecilia had no good excuse for canceling her session with Dr. Richardson, so she showed up for her usual appointment. Sometimes she went to Richardson just to avoid Tyler's wrath, benign though it was; but today, with all the turmoil about the baby and what was going to happen to Kix, she found herself anxious to talk to the old man.

"So when you get home, the baby won't be there?" Dr. Richardson asked after she'd summarized the events since she'd seen him last.

"Right."

"So, your time playing mother is over." He tilted his head, as if that were a question.

"I wasn't playing mother," she said.

"No interest in that," he said. He was certainly chatty—for him—today.

She sighed. "I'm not very good at it," she said lightly. "I told you about the food, and the diapers. The panic every time the kid pooped."

"Charmaigne? Was she good at it?"

Cecilia paused. "I didn't see her alone that much with the baby. Kix, yes. Kix is great with the kid. Charmaigne, I don't know. I don't know that she had a very good role model—it doesn't seem that her mother protected her."

"Is that what mothers do?" Dr. Richardson asked.

"I don't know what mothers do," she said, not wanting to waste her time with Dr. Richardson going down paths that she felt had nothing to do with her and the reasons she'd agreed to come to therapy at all.

"The problem I want to talk about is singing. Tyler keeps saying that my 'calling' is singing, but I'm not singing. According to Kix, I'm doing nothing with my life." She looked at Richardson sideways. "I'm actually terrified to audition." She'd not used the word *terrified* with him before, even though she'd told him about the ghost and the time she couldn't even bring herself to show up. He seemed, as always, unmoved.

"How can Tyler know I'm meant to sing? Why shouldn't I just adopt Abby and be a mother, like normal women? I could learn to be a mother. Why can't I do both? Lots—some—other women do. Why not do both? Do something. Why am I doing nothing?" It had irked her that Kix had said she wasn't doing anything with her life, but she couldn't say he was altogether wrong.

Dr. Richardson nodded and then asked, as directly as he'd ever asked about anything, "Tell me about the last time you sang."

"The last time?" Cecilia asked. "I didn't sing publicly after *Rumplestilt's Kin*. I don't know if I told you, but the reviews were grossly unfair. The *Tribune* hated the show and apparently had a beef with the producers over something else, and they hated me for singing the lead. It was on the front page of the arts section, too. I know a lot of people get over bad reviews, but I couldn't."

"Why not?" Dr. Richardson asked gently. "Why this one review of all the reviews you've ever had?"

She thought for a minute. "I think because it crushed her."

"Who?"

She sniffed. "My mother."

"How do you know it crushed her?"

"She wasn't the same after that."

"How so?"

Cecilia blew out an exasperated sigh. "She didn't seem to care whether I sang or not. It was like I'd failed so badly that she was done trying."

"But how do you know it was the review?"

"She never mentioned it. Never said the *Tribune* was wrong or biased or that she thought my performance was good enough. She just went into this, like, denial that it ever happened. She didn't fight it or tell me, like she always did, how I could do it better. As if I couldn't do it better; that I'd failed and that was that. I was so afraid of having that happen again. I knew she couldn't bear it."

"You couldn't bear to disappoint her?"

"I guess you could say that. Embarrass her, let her down."

"Did she still love you?"

"I suppose."

"You don't know?"

Cecilia folded her arms across her chest. "She wasn't the 'I-love-you' type."

"That's hard, isn't it? She was your coach and your critic, but she didn't say she loved you?"

"I know she was proud of me. She always wanted me to do well and to always improve and do my best." She recrossed her legs at the knees. "Until that last show."

"Did you ever do your very best for her?"

Cecilia stared at the bronze ship's clock on the wall behind Dr. Richardson. There were three other clocks in the room, one modern one without numbers on the wall behind her and two smaller ones on the end tables, available for Dr. Richardson's subtle but precise timing of her sessions. She had twenty minutes yet to go. That was a lot of time to fill, and she didn't like the direction things were going. "Probably not," she said cavalierly. "There was no pleasing the old woman."

Dr. Richardson sat quietly. After a while he said, "No pleasing her."

"It used to infuriate me." She tried to smile as if that was all in the past, but she felt a palpitation in her chest. She fiddled with the hand-painted wooden beads of her casual necklace.

"This is sort of ridiculous, isn't it, when people like Charmaigne have mothers who . . ." Kix had said that their mother loved them, but that she couldn't help them.

"We're not talking about Charmaigne's mother," Dr. Richardson said sternly. "We're talking about yours."

She rolled her lower lip out. "It used to be I just didn't want to risk the bad reviews, but part of me thought, well, when she dies, it will only be me, and I'll be my own judge. But then I was worse than she was, and I got so afraid." Her throat ached, and she wiped tears from her face. He sat perfectly still, not moving even to offer her a tissue from the box on the end table next to his chair. He didn't try to stop her tears, and she let them come. She cried for her mother, for her fear, for her unspent love.

After five minutes, Dr. Richardson handed her a tissue. "It's a lot, isn't it?"

The sound of his voice, sympathetic and understanding, renewed her tears. He did understand her! He knew what it was like!

"I've often wondered, when you talked about your mother, how often you agreed with her and how often you thought she was wrong."

"She was almost always right," Cecilia said, irritated. Here she'd thought he'd understood. It wasn't her mother's criticism she minded, it was . . . She didn't want to finish her thought, but it was way ahead of her. "It wasn't the criticism. I'm probably as much of a perfectionist as she was, when it comes to the music. It was that all those mistakes that prevented her from loving me."

"How do you know she didn't love you?"

"You know when someone loves you."

"You know when *you feel loved.*"

"Right. She didn't make me feel loved."

"You took all her criticism to heart, personally, rather than, say, professionally."

"Yes. Of course. I was a child."

"Yes, you were a child. Then."

She felt the word *then* hang between them, implying a future that could be different. She'd been a child, then, and even when she became a "professional," she'd still been her mother's child. As a child, even as an adult child, she hadn't felt loved, but what if her mother had in fact loved her? Could it be that her mother's unvarnished commitment to the truth, her dedication to cataloguing human imperfection, was just the way her mother treated everything, from a restaurant meal to her housekeeper's windows to her daughter's singing? Was it possible that the critiques were part of her mother's enjoyment? That they didn't diminish the experience for her but enhanced it? That she so admired the effort toward perfection that she wished perfection for her daughter, who she felt to be so close to that ideal? Had her father known these things? Was it possible that her mother had loved her, in her own way, and had critiqued her only because she loved her that much? The thought brought new but different tears to Cecilia's eyes.

That was then.

This is now. It was possible that the ghost in the audience would disappear. It was possible that Cecilia would call out to Francine in the back row and say she would not sing for her critique, but she would sing. It was possible that the next time, she would sing for herself, not the audience; to her own, still perfectionist, standards, not the critics'; for her own joy, not her mother's. For the music. She could tell Tyler what he had been telling her: Having named the ghost, she could embrace it and let it go.

Feeling an unfamiliar optimism about her future, Cecilia walked an hour north from Dr. Richardson's office to a trendy bistro recently opened by a friend of Tyler's to meet him for dinner.

"I wonder what's going on down there," Tyler said, opening the black leatherette menu.

"Jack didn't tell you his plan?"

"Sometimes I think he makes it up as he goes along," Tyler said.

"He better be good on his feet," Cecilia said. Her mood flattened.

Tyler put the menu down and steadied his gaze. "He won't be bringing Abby back," he said.

"You were supposed to remind me to call the piano tuner."

"Call the piano tuner. He'll probably leave Abby with Mrs. Gordon."

She shook her head as if dodging a fly. "I know," she said, then lowered her face toward the restaurant's offerings. Back in Dr. Richardson's office, she hadn't said, but some part of her envisioned, though hazily, a new "now" that had it all, both Abby and a career. "How's their Caesar?"

"Horrible," he said. "They use rat droppings instead of anchovies."

"No anchovies," she said.

"You're not listening to me," he said.

She closed the menu and looked around for their waiter.

"I think the plan was for Jack to get the prosecutor to arrest Professor Gordon, move Mrs. Gordon into a shelter, and leave Abby in her care."

"Her care," Cecilia scoffed. She threw open her cloth napkin and arranged it on her lap, meticulously smoothing out the creases. "The woman allowed her husband to rape her daughter. She has no right to that baby."

" At least she's related."

"That means nothing. Being related is an accident of fate. In this case, a bad accident. The woman doesn't know how to love a baby."

"You don't know that," Tyler said, sounding tired. "No one knows what really went on in that house. You don't know what issues the woman had, whether she'd been abused herself, or the good professor beat the hell out of her, or what. People love other people but might not have the strength to save them, from themselves or others. You just don't know."

Cecilia stared at her hands in her lap. For the second time that day she was being told that she didn't know what went on in someone else's head, and this time she felt defeated. Her job as an actress was to know, and she'd always thought herself empathetic and insightful. She thought she understood other people's motivations—understood theirs better than she did her own. She'd thought she'd known what her mother was feeling, and maybe, as Dr. Richardson suggested, she'd been wrong, but she certainly knew what Mrs. Gordon should have done with respect to protecting Charmaigne.

"The Caesar is good, but they have this other salad, the Oriental chicken salad, that's really the best," Tyler said. "Chicken and mandarins and cashews and chow mein noodles, easy on the dressing. . . ."

"Got it," she said.

"You're gonna be okay," Tyler said.

"Telling me or asking me?" she said.

"Both?" he laughed. "You just came from Richardson, right?"

"Yes. Can't you tell by my good mood and clarity of thought?"

He held up both hands in a gesture of surrender. "Been there, done that. Honey, you're doing great, even if it doesn't feel that way. Next week, with all of this behind us, we'll start again, in earnest. I'll have you working within a month!"

"Promise?" she said and noted his surprise that she would assent so quickly.

"I do," he said.

After lunch, Cecilia wandered home, window-shopping and stopping for a few errands along the way. She got there just in time for the late afternoon TV news. There were shocking developments in the Illinois State shooting. Professor Gordon had been arrested. The station had sent a reporter to Normal, and the reporter interviewed the prosecutor, who told her about the letter that he'd just seen that very day. The prosecutor said there was other corroborating evidence but wouldn't specify what it was. The reporter said Mrs. Gordon was in protective custody along with the baby, but that the whereabouts of the abused minor daughter and her brother were unknown. Cecilia sat on the edge of the bed and studied the TV. Tyler was right. Abby would not be coming back to her. The reporter ended her story, promising to keep viewers apprised of developments, and the anchor moved on to a story about the economy.

She lay back on the bed and stared at the ceiling, reaching her arms above her in a stretch she felt all the way to the small of her back. When she brought her hands down, she felt lighter, the tension released. It occurred to her that Abby, and Kix, for that matter, had been distractions. They'd been in her life for a little while, but they weren't meant to be permanent. Like the story of the day, they were transients. She had other things to do. It was time to start doing them.

She took a deep breath. If those kids had had the courage to go through what they'd gone through, to make hard decisions, even wrong decisions, and keep going, keep trying, certainly, Cecilia Morrison, in her "lap of luxury" could sing a few bars onstage, couldn't she? And wouldn't that be the answer to the hole that had been eating at her soul?

That night Jack called to say they were back, that what she'd heard on TV was pretty close to true, and that Kix would spend the night at his place and in the morning would move to a special shelter in the city for youth, which would allow him to get his GED and get his life on track. He said he'd fill her in another time on all the nitty-gritty.

"What about Charmaigne? Are they going to arrest her?"

"They don't have any hard evidence. Nothing. No one saw anything, let alone a girl, or a baby stashed someplace or anything at all that might connect her. I think the prosecutor isn't too interested in bringing a case against a victim when it's not open-and-shut."

"So you think maybe she didn't do it?"

"Not my call."

"So Kix may have?"

"Again. Not my call. But he's not a fugitive right now, if you are going to see him again. I'm sure he'll call you," Jack said. "He thinks you're pretty special."

"I'm sure," she said.

"You are," Jack said simply, and they hung up. Her hand was still on the receiver when it rang again, startling her.

"That was fast."

"Yes."

"Thank you for telling them," the voice said.

"Charmaigne?"

"Yes."

"Are you okay?"

"I'm fine. I'm glad they arrested him. I hope they jail him for life."

"It sounds as if that will happen," she said. "But what about you?"

"I'll be okay," Charmaigne said. "I'll be okay. Don't worry. I'm going up to Ann Arbor, and then, when I can, I'll call my mom, and I'll stay in touch with Abby. I'll be a good sister to her." Cecilia wondered if she should tell her that Jack thought she was off the hook but thought better of it. It wasn't "her call," and Charmaigne, if guilty, had been careful so far. Chances were the Normal police weren't going to follow up their investigation, and certainly not out of state.

"Good, Charmaigne, good." She didn't know what else to say. She felt a little odd condoning someone who'd taken a shot at another person in a crowded classroom. Reckless. Dangerous. Revengeful. Totally understandable. Perhaps she didn't understand Mrs. Gordon or her own mother, but she understood Charmaigne. She understood good turned bad, expectations turned disappointments, love turned destructive. She understood.

nineteen

J ack's a pretty good lawyer, man. I wasn't so sure, you know, back at
the jail house that night, that he was all that slick. I kind of felt like
he was letting me stew there, to learn my lesson. I understand where
he was coming from, but he was way off. I've seen a lot more of life in
the past year than he has, ever. I didn't need to see any more of how bad
things could be. He thinks he knows? He doesn't even do much criminal
work, and by the time they get to him, if they get to him, I'm pretty
sure everything is simple and sanitized—legal charges and forms and
evidence tags. From my point of view, life's a lot messier than that. Some
of the people that night, scratching themselves nonstop and praying to
lightbulbs, man, they were really scary 'cause they were just boiling.
With my father, it used to be an explosion and then it was over, all calm
and smooth. I didn't need to stew to learn about how someone good can
turn bad. I didn't need a lawyer teaching me about life. Don't get me
wrong, I was happy to get out of there, and if having a fancy lawyer
there helped me, I'm grateful, man.

But this trip to Normal. He really showed his best stuff. He was way
cool, man. We drove down there in his Beemer—the big one—and he
rented a car seat for Abby and she slept in the back—all two-and-a-half
hours, like an angel. On the way down, he called a law school classmate
who was a prosecutor there, and then he called our father and said he
was a lawyer and that he had information about who had shot at him,

and that he wanted to meet. What could the old man say? He said he'd meet him at the prosecutor's office.

When we got there, he had me and Abby wait in the car. He told the prosecutor our story, and apparently our old man was just real calm, and Jack said he even dabbed his eyes, crying about not knowing where he'd gone wrong—that Charmaigne was a slut and I was a druggie. Man, I don't know where he gets that. There were drugs in my high school, sure, but I don't know, they never appealed to me. I took some heat from my buddies for that, too, like I was scared or something. Anyway, the prosecutor asked what proof Jack had, and then Jack showed them the letter. Still, I guess, the old man didn't crack. He kept ridiculing Jack, saying to the prosecutor, who was he going to believe, a tenured professor at a highly respected state university or two no-good runaway kids? Jack said his friend, a little slow to refocus from the shooting to the incest, kept looking at him like maybe he thought my father had a point. Jack said he'd been a bit of a grandstander in law school, volunteering answers and engaging in ridiculous debates with the professors, and his friend the prosecutor remembered that about him and was kind of taking my father's side, questioning how to prove it was Charmaigne, or even anyone else, if there were no eyewitnesses. Jack admitted it was only a theory, that Charmaigne couldn't testify against herself, and that she'd only said that I didn't do it, but that the prosecutor was missing the point. Jack said flat out that the attempted murder wasn't the issue at all, but that he could produce physical evidence and direct testimony regarding the Professor's vile crime against his oldest daughter, and he buzzed me on the cell phone and then I went up to the state's attorney's office with Abby in my arms, and you should have seen the look on the old man's face. He turned purple—really!!—in front of my eyes, and I thought he was going to stroke out! He wound up to come after me, and, as I turned away to protect Abby, he kicked my backside and this big deputy who'd been stationed outside the state's attorney's office burst through the closed door—must've been some secret signal from the prosecutor—and contained—that's the word Jack used—contained—my father.

The prosecutor had some technician come in and swab Abby for DNA, and they had my father's from a glass of water he'd been drinking and whatever stuff they can get on you even when you're doing nothing but sitting there, and they put my father in cuffs and the burly cop led him outside and the prosecutor went out in the hall with them and then came back in and asked me if I was okay and asked Jack where the mother was, and he said he honestly didn't know but thought that he should be able to get a conviction without her testimony, and that I'd be available at any time. I'd been shielding Abby, and soothing her after all the commotion, and when I looked up they were both looking at me as if I'd missed something, which I had. All they wanted me to say was that yes I'd testify and that if I heard from Charmaigne I'd ask her to, also. But the trouble is, I don't know where Charmaigne is, and she doesn't answer her cell. She'll contact me when she's ready. She probably thinks I'm mad at her for dumping Abby at Cecilia's, but I'm not. I understand. Being free of Abby—even though she loves her, I think—gives Charmaigne a chance to go to school and grow up to be somebody. That's what she's always wanted. She's not lazy. That's not why she left Abby with Cecilia. I was kind of surprised Cecilia didn't want Abby. I thought a kid would take her mind off of whatever makes her so unhappy, but even I could see Abby would be the same strain on Cecilia as it was on Charmaigne.

Anyway, then I thought we were done. But this is when I found out how really good Jack is. He didn't treat this as just a law case. He'd thought ahead to what the result would be on the lives of people—us, my mother, my brothers, and baby sister. He arranged with his buddy for the sheriff to provide security to my mom's house for twenty-four hours so that we could get her and the kids out of there, which was news to me. Jack said that my dad could possibly post bail within hours, and the prosecutor said they'd delay it as long as they could, but that we should do what we needed to do as soon as we could. He'd also arranged for a place for my mom and the kids to go to, a place for battered women, until they put my dad away and she could go back to our house. There, he said, they'd help her get an order of protection and a divorce and a financial advisor to help her figure out how to support my two younger brothers, who are like twelve and eight, and my three-year-old sister.

So, we had to go to our house, and she was there with the baby, my other two brothers not yet home from school. She cried when she saw me. Where have you been? Where have you been? *And she kept looking for Charmaigne.* Where is she? *She couldn't understand that I didn't know. I kept saying she was okay, that I knew she was safe. It was too hard to explain how I knew that—but we've been living together and supporting each other for almost a year, so I know she's a survivor, but there was no time to explain myself. She's safe. She's okay.*

My mom bawled for about ten minutes, and Jack just let her. Didn't try to stop her or nothing, even though we were in a rush. Finally, Jack said that my mom and the baby were in danger, and that we needed to pack up her stuff and stuff for the kids and get out of there right away. He gave her the brief story of why her husband had been shot at and why he'd been arrested, and you know what, she didn't seem surprised. All of a sudden, my mother was all efficient and energetic—I'd never seen her like that—it was almost like she was packing for a trip to Europe or something. Man, she was organized in like twenty minutes, in two huge suitcases, as if she'd been planning this her entire life.

We picked up the boys, and they were way happy to see me, and I lied to them—for their own good—and told them I'd been in school in Chicago and studying music and that they could come up and see me sometime and I'd take them to the ball games. We drove across town to a nondescript old neighborhood, with what looked like ancient two-story apartments. There were no signs or nothing to say where we were, but apparently this was the shelter Jack had arranged for my mom. Who knew there were so many abused women in a college town like Normal?

We settled my mom and the boys into the little furnished apartment they gave her, and the boys played with my baby sister. Jack said we would be leaving soon, and just the way my father'd turned purple, my Mom turned white. "Let me hold her," *she said, and I gave her Abby. You should've seen how she looked—almost as young as Charmaigne, no kidding—and you could just see that she loved that baby, no matter*

what. She was crying again. So was I. I felt like she wanted to say some-
thing to me, like to say she was sorry for not saving Charmaigne and me
from our dad, but she kept biting her lips and catching her breath and
the words just couldn't come out, like it wasn't that simple, and I know
it isn't.

Jack kept looking at me, and pointing to his watch. "We gotta go,"
he said finally. I got up and reached for Abby, but my mother looked
surprised.

"Abby will stay here," Jack said, and my mother put her hand on the
baby's chest.

"No," I said. I felt frantic. "I've raised her. I'm her da-da."

"I'll take good care of her," my mother said.

And then I lost it. "You didn't take care of us!" I said. "None of this
would've happened if you'd taken care of us!"

My mother looked as if I'd stabbed her. Her hair was graying and
wiry and I could see her skin was dry and taut and her eyes looked sore
with tiny red lines; her pupils were huge, as if she were dead. She couldn't
defend herself.

Jack intervened. "No recriminations, Kix." Big word, recrimina-
tions. Is that what he calls the truth? "Everyone here is doing the best
they can under very bad circumstances."

"But I promised. . . ."

"You're a good boy," my mother said. "You always were." Her voice
cracked, and she rocked back and forth in her chair. I felt—okay, this is
kind of weird—like she was comforting me, and I was sorry for what I'd
said. She added, "You did a good thing for Charmaigne and for . . ." She
stopped, her finger on the baby's chest, I guess because she didn't know
Abby's name.

"Abby," I said for her, and my mother smiled. I wanted to keep Abby
for myself, but watching my mother cradle Abby, well, I gave in. I could
see how, with all this stuff going on, and Jack trying to talk Cecilia into
calling Social Services, and Tyler reminding her all the time that Abby
was cute but music was her "calling," well, it probably was best for Abby
to be with my mother. Her home—even in a shelter—was a better

place than any foster home, because we were, for better or worse, her family, and, now that my father was removed, Abby would be safe with my mother, who would love her as she loved all her children. And if my mother kept Abby, she would have an older sister, and two more older brothers to spoil her, in addition to Charmaigne, if she came back, and me, her da-da. There was the possibility that Charmaigne would find her way home, and I would find my way, too, wherever that might lead.

I gave my mom my cell phone number, and Cecilia's number, too, and the number I had for Charmaigne, although she never answered it, and I bet by now she's sold it. Jack gave her his card, and I hugged everybody and we left her apartment together, me just a little nervous that my father had found out where we were and was lurking in the shadows. Jack assured me the place was protected by security and while it was unlikely my father would know where it was, even if he did, he'd be arrested if he came close.

You know, my mom didn't ask me to stay. I could've, I guess. Maybe that would've helped her with the babies and the boys. But I think my mom kind of understood that I'd been gone too long to go home and live under her roof, in her house. I was an adult now, and I think she knew that. I didn't need her to try to parent me any more, and, well, frankly, I was done parenting her.

Jack took me back to his place, and the next day introduced me to a "transitional living" center that's supposed to help me get back on my feet. Not sure it's really for me, but I can rest here a while, and if Jack says to do it, I suppose I should give it a whirl. I'm feeling pretty lucky, over all, to have run into Cecilia. She'd say "conned," but I think she was willing.

twenty

Dr. Richardson closed the door after Cecilia five minutes later than usual, forgiving himself, just this once, for his breach of technique. Clients always presented the important stuff at the end, in a rush, so as to prevent, perhaps, too deep a dive into the subterranean chasms of the "material." It was always so. Today, he'd let Cecilia run a little over because she'd let down her guard. She'd named her ghost, and soon, he knew, she would again tell him she was "fine." This time, there was a good possibility she would be right.

He was, in his own way, happy for Cecilia. There were a lot of side issues about the boy and the baby and Charmaigne and the amateur shooting in Normal, but he was quite sure those distractions would resolve themselves and Cecilia would return to singing. He personally would be pleased to hear her sing again—not in *Rumplestilt's Kin*, of course—it was a terrible show—but in something suited to her, something that would showcase the sweetness of her voice, and its range. He pictured her onstage and beamed, then caught himself. Sometimes, when a therapist had success with a creative person, they could take a disproportionate amount of credit for the talent they'd unlocked from a psychic purgatory. He reminded himself not to take too much pleasure in Cecilia's success.

However, when his daughter called for their weekly chat, Cecilia was still on his mind, and he indulged himself. "The songstress had a major breakthrough," he told Maddie. "Any day now, she'll be back onstage, Broadway-bound. Who says talking therapy doesn't work?"

"You've got ten sessions," Maddie laughed, referring to the limitations of many insurance programs.

"It took a little longer," Haverill said sheepishly.

"Let me guess," Maddie said.

"Fifty-fifty," Haverill encouraged.

"It's the mother."

"Surprise!" he joked, then turned serious. "You know, people are so different in how they express love and how they receive it. It's not always clear how the transmission gets muddled between the one and the other. Cecilia was so fragile, she thought if her mother criticized something, she didn't love her. Apparently the mother thought the love was assumed and that the criticism was helping."

"Right. Like we all want to be told how we can be better," Maddie scoffed.

"When you're a parent," Haverill started to say.

"Don't, Daddy," Maddie said.

The sound of the word *Daddy* lodged in his heart and he quickly retreated. "I'm sorry. I just mean . . ."

There was a sigh on the line.

"I don't know what I mean."

"Right. It sounds like Cecilia is a perfectionist just like her mother, who probably did have some narcissistic issues regarding her precocious daughter, and Cecilia probably did feel that she had to be perfect to be perfectly and unconditionally loved. But it sounds like she might be able to get past that. To separate her theater work from her person. That is, if she wants to do theater. Good work, Dr. Richardson." For a second, Haverill was taken aback by his daughter's conditional, "if she wants to do theater." It sounded to him like maybe Maddie wasn't convinced that he'd helped Cecilia to unlock a talent she actually wanted to use, but his daughter continued, "So, how's the marble?"

"Don't, Maddie," he mimicked her.

"Right," Maddie said and they hung up.

His next appointment failed to show, so he picked up his sketch pad and made his way to the plaza, stopping for a coffee. He felt somehow different than before. He bought a skim latté at a first floor shop and let it cool as he did quick pencil sketches of everything he saw in front of him: containers of drying geraniums and decorative grasses, an abstract sculpture of rusted auto parts, a young woman sitting at a table to his right and chatting on her cell phone, a crumpled cigarette box on the ground, a potted boxwood. None of them perfect or inspired, but all fluid, eye to hand, processed through an instantaneous filter of his own talent and perception and mood. When his wristwatch beeped that it was time for his next appointment, he closed his pad, satisfied that he had made a beginning. Cecilia had named her ghost, and for a short hour he had held his own demons at bay.

That night he warmed himself a plate of a chicken Vesuvio he'd frozen a week ago and poured himself a glass of a hearty burgundy. He was feeling upbeat and hopeful for the first time in what seemed like a long, long time, not counting the brief interlude when he'd thought Maddie was getting married. He rinsed his plate, swallowed the last of the wine, and went upstairs to his studio. He'd changed into his artist's clothes: comfortably worn jeans, a brown, long-sleeved T-shirt, and a once-starched old white dress shirt.

He unwound the canvas roll that contained his tools and chose the smallest pick. Positioning the instrument over the closest corner, he raised the hammer. He closed his eyes in a tight squint and started down, at the last moment checking his swing. So close!

So close. He dropped his tools in a clatter and retreated to his leather chair. He poured a scotch, took a sip, and stared at the workbench. The block of marble loomed. Off-white, like an ancient glacier on a dark gray day. Impenetrable. Over the past few months, he'd waited, and finally, Cecilia had talked. The marble hadn't. He thought he'd had patience, had waited for the right moment to point the chisel, but what, really, was he waiting for? The marble wouldn't speak for itself; it had potential but no volition. It would never reveal itself unless he acted. He studied the amber color of the scotch in his glass. He was the one who was hiding. He was the one who had yet to reveal himself.

His daughter's words haunted him. Was it possible that Cecilia, so very gifted, still didn't have the passion she needed to derive satisfaction from her work? Did Cecilia have a passion for her theatrical career? For music? For mothering? For any of it? Was her primary satisfaction still pleasing her mother? Had pleasing her mother obscured Cecilia's ability to find her own passion? Was passion essential? She had more than adequate talent for her given profession. What harm would there be in doing something she was so very good at, even if she didn't have that elusive "passion" for it? Wouldn't that be better than doing "nothing" with your life?

Sculpting was not a passion for him, was it? It was more of a pastime, something he liked to do, might even be good at? So what did it matter if he sculpted or not? Or if he was good at it or not? By not sculpting, what harm was he doing himself? He could hear his daughter presenting his case over the phone, as she used to do when she was young and a patient baffled her.

"Recently widowed client has suspended interest in his hobbies. Has seemingly moved on with everything else. Functions at a fairly high and normal level. Does not appear depressed or overly anxious."

Since he didn't know his daughter's clients, there was little he could say, except to point her to a deeper level of inquiry. What does the hobby entail? What does it represent to the client? The dying skydiver with nothing left to risk; the stamp collector with no future to collect for; the painter whose reality has been forever altered.

For years, the client, the therapist, had lived his life slowly, but always in flux. Clients like Cecilia changing at a glacial pace, nearly imperceptibly, week to week, leaving his office still unfinished. No wonder Rosalyn's death had jolted him so. Every small death— every time a client moved on—had not been so final. It was part of the therapeutic process. When his own parents had died, he'd understood those events as part of his own life's journey; he'd had many possibilities still ahead. Rosalyn's death, however, was like his own. Not just the loneliness of it, but the end of possibility. To make one cut in the marble was to foreclose others; to begin was to end.

The therapist for whom everything was in process, afraid of the end of the process, of being judged by a permanent legacy, of his own mortality. The sculptor, as afraid of permanence as of his own transience.

He thought about Cecilia's quest for her mother's love, her fear of situations where she might again displease the one she sought most in the world to please. That was then. This was now. Cecilia had seen that her future could be different. What did he see?

twenty-one

With Charmaigne and Kix at least temporarily out of her life, Cecilia had time to get on to doing other things. The first morning without Abby, she squandered the morning with the newspaper in her kitchen, while the piano tuner plinked away in the living room. She was glad he was doing it the old-fashioned way, with tuning forks and his own ear, repeating and repeating, a key and a pitch, a key and a pitch, until he got it right. Every so often he hit a middle E, and it reminded her of Abby's playful coos, and she saw a sunny but nostalgic yellow.

She'd been lucky that when she'd called the tuner yesterday afternoon, he'd treated her call like an emergency. Today the elderly gentleman who had appeared at her door at nine thirty confessed that he'd had a cancellation of another appointment—usually his waiting list was two to three weeks.

"Where's your baby?" he'd asked, and for a moment she was flustered. "Grand, is it?" he continued, and she led him to the living room.

"She's a beaut!" the man said. He struck a few chords and addressed the raised lid. "A bit cranky this morning, but we'll get you fixed up," he said.

"Thanks for coming," Cecilia said, recovering herself, and retreated to let him work in peace.

In the afternoon, she took a run along the lake and rested on the rocks at Montrose Harbor. She'd run more than three miles, farther than she'd intended. There would be three back, but it was a lovely day, and she had nothing better to do. In fact, she said to herself defiantly, what could be better? It was healthy, the lakeshore was beautiful, and running cleared the mind. It was too late for this year, but maybe next year she'd train for the Chicago Marathon. Maybe next year, to celebrate her fortieth year. She'd show them! Whoever "them" were. All of them! That would be something. That would be doing something.

For the next two weeks, she passed the time running and singing. Tyler coached her for a few sessions, and then one day, the Marathon goal being so far off, she checked the Equity website for auditions, and there were, remarkably, calls for a couple of parts that she could play.

She called Tyler, excited. "Good news and bad news," she said. "It's a world premiere, at the Goodman," she said. The Goodman was a nationally known regional theater, one of the largest legitimate theaters in Chicago. "That's the 'good' part! Bad news is, we know my record with world premieres!" She was surprised that she could laugh about *Rumplestilt's Kin*.

"Go for it," Tyler commanded.

She showed up at the audition with two prepared songs, "Stars and the Moon" from *Songs for a New World*, and again "What I Did for Love" from *A Chorus Line*. There were a couple of women in the theater lobby when she arrived. One, in a black leotard and short blue silk skirt, was limbering up as if, in fact, getting ready for the Chicago Marathon and clearing her head with a chimpanzee-like screech, "*EEEAAAWWW!*" One stretched on the floor in an exaggerated child's pose; a few feet away, another spoke to the wall, "IknowIknowIknow." A young man stood apart, flubbing his lips and sounding just like a neighing horse. Cecilia clasped her hands behind her back and raised them, stretching her back muscles and her shoulders, discreetly massaged her face and neck with her palms, and ran a few arpeggios at less than full voice.

She could feel her neck burning red, probably blotchy, and she arranged her scarf higher around her throat, determined to beat off a residual case of nerves. When a young man with a clipboard called her name, she was ready. She flew through her first song as if in a daze, and the director had her sing her second, all the way through, a good sign.

"Can you hang around a while?" the director asked.

"Sure thing," she said.

On her way out, the young man gave her some sheet music. "Give us about half an hour," he said.

She sat on the floor next to a couple other actors waiting for their turns and studied the music. They were obviously considering her for the role that sang this duet. It was a beautiful piece, the female parts squarely within her range, well below any break her mother—if alive—would be able to detect. She let herself imagine getting the part, getting a standing ovation, grabbing the reviewer's attention for a special call-out. Finally, she had arrived at the right place. She pictured a dressing room full of red roses and baby's breath and smelled the sweetness of success. Then, without warning, all that imagined success evaporated. Her mother would not be there to enjoy it. Her eyes watered. Finally, she heard Dr. Richardson's voice: This is not for your mother. This is for you.

When the young man called her back to the theater, there were two other men and another woman. The director paired them up, and Cecilia was paired with a brown-haired man about her age. Sight-reading the sheet music they'd been given, he sang, she sang, and they sang together. Then the other couple sang a different song, and then the four were asked to sing together. The director nodded at the two people with him and said, "That's it, folks. We've got four weeks until opening. Cast meeting Monday at nine. George here has the schedule and the contracts. Welcome aboard. Stay healthy!"

Just like that, no angst, no ghosts, no apologies, she had a job. She had something to do! Astounded at the relative ease of her success, she nonetheless felt all of the satisfaction of setting a goal and accomplishing it, the way she'd used to feel telling her mother she'd gotten a part.

She called Tyler as soon as she'd signed her contract and collected the script and libretto. She offered to take him to dinner to celebrate, but he had a date and had to take a rain check. "Actually, you're my third offer for the night," he said coyly. "I had to turn Jack down, too. Why don't you call him?"

"Because I wanted to thank you," she said. "Jack didn't do this."

"But he's done a lot," Tyler said. "Take Jack. Thank me another time."

Since he'd given her an opening line, she called Jack and was a little surprised when a woman answered, "Jack O'Malley's office." Of course, it was still the work day, and despite all the time he had, in fact, given to Kix and then to Charmaigne and Abby, he did have an office and presumably some paying clients.

Jack picked up the line enthusiastically. "Cecilia!"

"Tyler said I should call you," she started, and Jack interrupted her, "Now what?" He sounded panicked rather than annoyed.

"I got cast in *Subway*—it's a new musical at the Goodman—and I . . ."

"Congratulations! Oh, Cecilia," he sounded genuinely happy. "Please, let me take you to dinner to celebrate!"

She laughed. "That's why I was calling you," she said.

"Oh, I get it. Tyler couldn't go to dinner so he said to ask me? I'm second choice? Well, in that case, what the hell, I've been called worse. Yes! I accept." He named one of the most expensive new restaurants in town.

"We probably can't get in there," she said. Tyler would've named such a place for sure, taking full advantage of both the celebratory occasion and her wealth, but she thought Jack, who in the end would probably reach over and pick up the tab after all, would pick someplace more modest—less of a "date" or "special" type of a place.

"I've got connections," he said. "I'll swing by and get you, say seven thirty. Dinner at eight?"

"That's the line," she said. For the second time that day, doing something that invited rejection—in this case, making a date with an attractive, eligible man—seemed easy.

"Don't be late," he said.

She fussed more than usual, getting ready for dinner. A cocktail dress, which might be appropriate on a Saturday night at this place, seemed way too much for a dinner on a weeknight, when she'd asked the man—how old-fashioned of her, and it wasn't a date, really, just friends—so she tried on three separate black pieces: skirt and white silk blouse, slacks and light pink pullover, a sleeveless silk scoop-necked sheath with a covered belt and a silver flower buckle. Upscale casual or elegant? Could go either way. What kind of women did Jack date, anyway? Why did she care? It wasn't really a date, was it? How long had it been, as Tyler had said months ago, since she'd had a "real" date? So much had happened, and not happened. She'd been so distracted by Kix and Charmaigne and their troubles, and her own bumpy road back to the stage, she hadn't thought of dating. This was not a date.

Ali buzzed her at precisely seven thirty to say that Mr. O'Malley was on his way up. She'd been ready for half an hour, pacing her apartment in her sheath so as not to wrinkle it, her heels set by the door. She'd envisioned meeting him downstairs but now rushed to step into her shoes and check her lipstick in the guest bathroom. When he knocked, she counted to ten, not wanting to appear too anxious, and then opened it with a casual flair, assuming a sophisticated and urban air.

He stood in the door frame, taking her in. He wore a dark business suit and looked freshly shaven. "Wow," he said, as much to himself as to her.

She immediately worried that she'd overdressed. "Too much?" she asked, the sophistication gone.

Jack worked his eyebrows up and down in a suggestive parody.

"Too much dress? As in covering too much? Sounds like a leading question to me!"

"That's . . ."

"Not to worry. I'm a Loyola boy," he smiled, sweeping his arm toward the hall. "Shall we?"

They made small talk in the cab, discussing the restaurant, which was the current rave of the food critics. Jack had been there several times, not hinting whether he'd been with a client or a woman, but Cecilia hadn't been there at all. She liked nice restaurants when they were quiet and you could hear your partner, but she wasn't all that taken with oddball food combinations, plated food sculptures, and high prices. It would be interesting this once, but she expected to be hungry after. She was kind of happy she was with Jack, who might actually pay for this experiment—after all, he chose the place—rather than Tyler, who'd run up her bill with once-in-a-lifetime abandon.

A uniformed doorman met them at the curb and held the door to the old brownstone on the near North Side. From the outside, you'd hardly know it was a place of business. The only commercial sign was in discreet beige lettering on the brown canvas awning over the entranceway. Inside, the first floor dining room was old-fashioned, dark wood wainscoting topped by dull gold, cream-flocked wallpaper in a fleur-de-lis pattern. There was a fireplace at one end, with a heavy mantle graced by Lalique vases. Each of the dozen tables, mostly for two, a couple for four, was dressed in crisp white linen and had its own silver candlestick and two small vases of clipped roses in the faintest pink. Cecilia quickly surveyed the room and saw that she and Jack were dressed just right. Two young women, each no more than twenty-five, she was sure, stood out in backless dresses, one in silver sequins and one in a flimsy, flaming red. In each case, their dates looked old enough to be their fathers. Older women, including many of the ones her age, wore jacketed dresses of various kinds, mostly black, many bearing the insignia of her mother's favorite designers. As they were escorted to their corner table in the back, Cecilia tightened the muscles of her sculpted upper arms, grateful for all the running and exercising of the past few weeks.

Jack stood while the maitre d' held the chair for Cecilia, then sat. With no apparent signal from Jack, the waiter delivered a bottle of champagne, and the wine steward came by their table to tell them about the vineyard, the grapes, and the year but, Cecilia noted, not the price.

"To a rising star," Jack said, holding his flute to her.

"To . . . ," she started to answer, then realized how relatively little she knew about Jack, despite the time they'd spent together.

He must've read her mind. "How about, 'your greatest fan'?"

She laughed. "So, fill in the blanks. Tell me about yourself."

"I thought you'd never ask!" he joked. "Not much to tell, actually. Chicago boy. Catholic schools. Double-Domer. Mom and Dad moved to Florida. Three brothers, scattered. All married, dozens of kids among them."

"And your law practice?"

Jack smiled widely, looking to the waiter to refresh his champagne. "You're a tough one, Ms. Morrison. Law practice. Yes. Solo. Won a few really big ones early on. Don't know how, really. Conned two juries into hundred-million-dollar awards against a pharma company, and now I come and go as I please, taking on the clients and causes that interest me. Like your friend Kix." His face sagged a bit. "Aren't you missing the obvious question?"

Confused, she cocked her head slightly to the side, then reached for her glass. He studied her, his hazel eyes almost pleading with her to ask the right question.

"Why did you help Kix?" she asked meekly.

"The first time? Because Tyler asked me to. Been friends since high school. He's given me some interesting clients over the years, mostly paying." He waited. "Now you're supposed to ask me about the second time."

"The second time?" she asked dutifully.

"For you, sweetheart," he said and made a show of studying the menu card. After half a minute, he put the card aside, obviously a man used to quick decisions. "So the obvious question is . . ."

She didn't like being made to feel stupid. Who did he think he was, anyway? Just a lawyer having dinner in one of the city's finest restaurants with a woman . . . . She finally got it. "So, Mr. Wonderful, what's a catch like you doing single?"

"Bravo!" he cheered. "You know, I ask myself that all the time. In the early years, I was working really hard, had those couple of cases that consumed me. Made me, but nearly broke me at the same time. A high price for a high reward." He sounded almost wistful. "So, what am I doing single?" He tipped his glass in her direction. "Waiting." The waiter appeared, saving her from having to respond.

She fixed her gaze on the menu, trying to sneak a deep breath. What a day! A part, and now, a man? Where had he been all this time? What was going on? Was something going on? Did she want something to go on? She fiddled with the silver flower on her belt.

"Why don't you order for both of us?" she suggested. "Then you could taste mine and I . . ."

"Ms. Morrison! In an establishment of this caliber?" His voice was formal and obviously false. He winked. "We'll have to be discreet." He ordered the pâtés maison and the roasted quail to start, the asparagus soup with shrimp and the duck consommé, and the rack of lamb and the veal tenderloin. The waiter left and the wine steward suggested a pinot noir that he remembered Jack liked and that was available by the glass.

After ordering, they settled into a friendly banter about their professions. Jack was full of questions. How did she stand auditions? Didn't it ever get boring doing the same show, singing the same song over and over?

"How many times do you think Mick Jagger has sung 'Satisfaction'?" he laughed. "I don't know that I could do it. At least the Grateful Dead used to improvise." Jack had a collection of bootleg tapes of Dead concerts—now CDs. His goal, like a stamp collector's, was to have one from every concert; then he might go for duplicate recordings of the same concert.

"One recording of 'Truckin' would be sufficient," she ventured.

"Not your thing?" he asked.

"Not my favorite thing," she had to admit.

"That's cool," he said, laughing at himself for his adolescent-speak. "It's not a deal breaker."

Then she laughed, more nervous than amused. "What deal?" she asked.

He paused, considering, then reached across the table and lightly touched her hand. "You're still paying for dinner," he said and ordered the chocolate soufflé for dessert, which, the waiter said, would take an extra twenty-five minutes to prepare. She imagined it would cost an additional twenty-five dollars as well.

"We have all the time in the world," he said and ordered a cognac to go with his espresso. She was certain now he was going to pick up the tab.

"You know," she ventured, "they say each performance is different. That's what supposedly keeps us going. But I gotta tell you," she said, grimacing, "sometimes I have to say I do get bored. And then it's work. Like any other."

"To hear Tyler tell it, each time is a sacred experience. What I like about you, Ms. Morrison," he raised his cognac, "is your honesty."

Blushing the color of her wine, she said. "Careful. Honesty's a confusing trait in an actor."

"Aw, yes, the world of pretend and pretense. I know something about that world myself, Cecilia. Remember, I practice law."

When the waiter brought the check, he left it slightly to Jack's side of the table. He picked it up, as she knew he would, and studied it quickly, and then handed it to her.

"I believe you offered," he said. "It seems to be in order."

Surprised, and trying not to be disappointed at what she thought were his mixed signals, she took the leather folder from him. She glanced at the bottom line, pursed her lips, and reached for her credit card. When she met his eyes, trying to appear neither flustered by his stance nor shocked by the amount, he was smiling at her.

"And worth every penny. I'm so glad Tyler couldn't make it."

"I'll only have pennies left," she said, in exaggerated self-pity.

"Now, now. That's not honest," he said. "You're a working girl now."

"A week's salary for a meal?" She felt some satisfaction that this was her earned income, not a handout from her brothers. "This is probably not even an hour of your time."

"You can't play starving artist with me," Jack said. "Unless, of course, you're willing to have me support you in your old age." He put his hand at the small of her back as they left the table. "I'll save up."

They decided to walk the mile or so to Cecilia's apartment. It was a Friday night in the heart of the city, and the streets were busy, although she couldn't imagine why quite so many people were out. "Wonder if our buddy Kix is busking tonight," she said.

"I dunno. I recommended him to a halfway house, where they have pretty strict rules."

"Like a curfew?" she asked. "He's eighteen. Does curfew even apply?"

Jack shrugged. "House rules are probably different."

"I can't imagine him being so confined. You never told me the full story about how it all went."

"Way too long a story, but I'll fill you in sometime. The point is, he's a sharp kid. I was very impressed when we went down to Normal together. He has a lot of wisdom beyond his years—street smarts. A little confinement won't hurt him. With the right guidance, he'll definitely make it."

"I hope so," she said. "Despite everything, I really liked him."

"But I'm age appropriate," he smiled, at the door to her apartment building, and she gave him a jab in the arm. With a nod through the revolving glass door to the doorman, he whispered in her ear, "Let's do this again, sometime. My treat."

"I'll pick the restaurant," she said gamely.

"Can't do better than what we just did," he beamed. "Thank you." He was right there; the dinner tab had been the most expensive for two she'd ever picked up. Jack gave the revolving door a push, and as he turned to hail a cab, she waved good night.

"Age-appropriate," she mumbled to herself, and when the doors to the elevator shut she put her face an inch from them and said, in her best warming-up voice, "IknowIknowIknow."

She was one of the last to arrive at the theater for the ten o'clock cast meeting. It was held in a rehearsal room, where a bunch of school desks had been arranged in a circle. She took an empty one next to a woman she recognized as one of the leading ladies, and they introduced each other. Cecilia looked around the circle. It was a large cast, as new musicals went, at least, musicals that weren't spectacles like *Wicked* or *Les Mis*. The four actors who'd last sung for the director carried the show, but there were half a dozen other parts, including a young singer who plays his guitar in the subway. She hadn't kept up with the new male talent on the scene, and so she had no idea who the director might have cast for such a role. She'd read that part of the script with interest and had thought of Kix. She hadn't seen him since he'd come back from Normal. Jack said he was settling into a place and busy with his GED.

The leading man, Aaron, was in his forties, six feet tall, a high school basketball player of some local fame who went to college on a sports scholarship but was smitten by the desire to act and learned to sing and dance instead of shoot free throws. He was a regular on the Chicago musical stage, one of the rare few who could actually make a living acting, he was in such demand. The other leading lady—in the story the two women, one played by Cecilia, vied for Aaron's attention—was also, at thirty-five, a veteran. Donna had nondescript good looks, wide eyes, and high cheekbones, and that allowed the makeup artists to paint her in any number of ways, from blond bombshell—her role here—to mad hag. Cecilia had admired her work and was looking forward to reviving their friendship. Donna sat sideways in the school desk, knees crossed, her elbow relaxed on the desktop. Cecilia tried to mold herself to her confidence but bumped the top of the desk and her bottle of water toppled. As Aaron picked it up and handed it to her, she felt as gawky as she had as a gangly eleven-year-old too tall for the leading man. She faked a smile and mumbled a quick thank-you.

The director, a balding man with a gray moustache and goatee, counted noses and said, "We're missing one. Yes. The street musician. The kid."

As if on cue, a young man, dressed in clean jeans and a long-sleeved white shirt, burst in, apologizing to the room. "Sorry. I didn't leave enough time for the train. I promise it won't happen again."

"Fine, kid. Okay. We were just going to introduce ourselves."

Without hesitation, he said, "Kix Gordon." He took his place in the circle of chairs in the rehearsal room and looked around eagerly. "Cecilia!" He fist-bumped in her direction. "Yes!"

She felt the others in the cast turn to her, and, shocked, she smiled a curious, distant smile, a hodgepodge of emotions. When she'd last seen him, he'd been a likely suspect in an attempted murder case. He'd returned, not exactly exonerated, but not of primary interest, either. The question of his guilt not nearly as important to the authorities as his father's. The kid was awfully damn lucky.

How had he gotten cast? No one had told her he'd even auditioned for the part. What made him think—what made the producers think—he could perform as a professional? She'd clawed her way back through practice and determination and, yes, her therapy with Dr. Richardson, and he just waltzes in? Was Kix up to the likes of Aaron and Donna? She knew he wasn't on her level, assuming she herself could work her way back up to what she considered her own level. Did the director know what he was doing at all, or had he merely lowered his standards? She began to doubt herself. Did the director have a thing for street urchins and sentimental has-beens?

. They'd been at it a full hour and a half, introducing themselves, discussing the director's vision, the playwright's intentions, and the nitty-gritty of getting the show ready in four weeks for a highly critical and paying audience, when they finally took a break. Immediately, Kix ran up to Cecilia and threw his arms around her. Stiffly, she stood there, enduring his hug. She remembered he'd bet against her, and that resentment resurfaced. It took her a few moments to raise her own arm and pat his back, trying to find that balance between genuine familiarity and introductory handshake. "Good to see you, Kix," she said, her voice low and controlled.

"This is the cool-est thing!" Kix pumped his fists.

"How did you . . . ?" she started.

"Tyler called Jack, who called me where I'm staying, this place near Greektown, and I came and auditioned with all these real slick dudes, and I just played myself and next thing I know, I'm a star!" He grinned his best street smile, the slight gap between his front teeth endearing.

"Well, that was easy!" she said, a little edge sharpening her words, although Kix didn't seem to notice. "So, Tyler put you up to this."

"Didn't he tell you?"

"No. Jack told me—" she looked around to make sure she was out of earshot, but most of the cast had gone out to the hall and were on their cell phones, "—that you were at a halfway house, but he didn't say anything about this."

"I asked Tyler not to. I wanted you and Jack to be surprised. You two dating yet?"

"No!" She shook her head, bothered by his familiarity. Her personal life was none of his business. "Why would you say that?" she whispered.

"Because you should," Kix said. Then he repeated the line Jack had quoted him as saying, "You're quite a catch."

Despite herself, she threw her head back and let out a belly laugh. "You've got all the lines, Kix. You've got 'em all." She felt a little softening. For better or worse, they did have a relationship, and the kid, not just lucky, was awfully damn charming.

He raised his shoulders and lifted his hands. "What can I say? I'm a quick study."

"Have you heard from Charmaigne?"

He hesitated. It wasn't like him not to have a ready answer. "Right after Jack and I got back, we talked." She nodded. That was the last time for her also. "I'm sure she's okay. She'd call if she weren't. Listen," he said, "what you guys did—what Jack did— man, that saved us. I loved Abby, of course, but that was no life for a baby. These past couple weeks, I've seen that. Don't get me wrong, I miss her and all, but it's almost like a . . ." He looked toward the door, as if hoping the break was over.

"Relief," she said for him. "Don't be ashamed to say you feel some relief. Of course you do. You were doing the best you could, but it was way too hard. For everyone."

"Yeah," he said quietly. "The person it's hardest on now is my Mom. Another baby."

"She's probably happy—if I can use that word—to be able to help like that, to do right by Charmaigne, so that Charmaigne can get over what happened, and lead her own life."

"I don't know if Charmaigne knows what she wants to do with her life," Kix said, which struck Cecilia as the kind of comment a parent, not a brother, would make. She pictured the mustard couch in Dr. Richardson's office.

The director marched back into the rehearsal room, clapping his hands to gather his cast around him, like a bunch of kindergarteners, and Cecilia raised her right shoulder in a shrug. "But who does?" she said.

The first week and a half of rehearsals went quickly. They had costume fittings right away, before anyone had learned any of their lines, and then long days of choreography, scene blocking, and singing. Every night Cecilia tried to check in with Tyler, who wanted to be kept apprised of her progress and of Kix's, but he was also involved with a new love, and sometimes she just left a message.

During the days, there were long stretches of downtime, when Cecilia could study her lines or relax with a crossword or Sudoku puzzle. For Kix, there was no relaxation. He was studying for his GED, and if Kix shared the same downtime, he would sit with Cecilia in the theater or backstage or in the rehearsal hall, a hefty study guide open on his lap.

Just about every ten minutes, Kix would say, "I know this stuff," and she would say, 'I'm sure you do," and point her index finger back at the book.

"You think I'm too cocky, don't you, Cee?" he asked one day as they sat in the hallway outside the rehearsal room. Since everyone in the cast called her Cee, Kix had replaced "Miss M," which she'd once thought of as sweet, with the new nickname. It jarred but she was getting used to it, both as a name and its coming from Kix.

"I do," she said, and his face fell. Such a fine line, she thought, between cocky and confident. Her own mother had kept her in a nervous limbo, always on the brink of greatness, teetering on a professional precipice. Quickly, she sided with Kix's natural con. "But if you don't believe in you, who will?"

"Especially in this business," he said, sounding like an old pro, and returned his attention to the book. He was studying a physics unit and, with the book nestled between his knees, he was colliding his index fingers, studying impact or displacement or some such. He made a little popping sound with his mouth with each crash, which, even though she was fairly certain he hadn't taken the shot at Professor Gordon, Cecilia found mildly alarming.

"Cee?"

She pointed to the book.

"I've got this. What I need help with—" he scooted closer to her in the hall, "—I need help with my songs."

"That's what the musical director is for," she said.

"Mike is great, he really is," Kix said, "but sometimes I think he thinks I know what I'm doing, and, you know, I don't. I don't have training like you or Tyler. He tells me things and I don't really know what he means. He says I'm swallowing my sounds, so I do something, and he says it's better, but I know I could do better if I knew what to do, if you know what I mean."

"IknowIknowIknow," she laughed. "Swallowing means you're singing from the back of your head, not the front." She demonstrated a thin G from the back of her throat and contrasted it with a resonant G from the front. "When the voice is up front," she pointed to her upper cheeks, "it's not 'covered,' as they say. Try it."

He tried it, the initial difference being soft vs. loud. She demonstrated again. He tried again. Back and forth, they threw G's at each other, reminding her of the day they'd played Sonny and Cher in the subway. He did have a good voice, one that would only improve with training.

"Maybe Tyler could give you some time," she said.

"I can't ask him. He's done so much," Kix said.

"I guess that cuts me out, too," Cecilia said, indignant.

"Oh, no! Oh, jeez!" Kix scooted around to face her, his voice urgent and earnest. "You've done so much, too, Miss M. More, even! You introduced me to Tyler and Jack and you—you gave me sixty dollars, which they never would've done, in a million years! And you brought us home. I can't thank you enough. I can't. I only meant, you're a real singer, and I want to learn. . . ."

She shook her head in mild rebuke. The director had paid for a haircut for Kix's program picture, and while it wasn't particularly styled, it was trimmed in white circles around his ears, making him look innocent and needy in her eyes. She held his gaze and said, "Let's call him." When Tyler didn't answer, she left a message.

"How about if I take us to dinner, and then we can practice?" he asked. When she started to protest, he said, "I have do-re-mi now. Legit."

"Save your do-re-mi," she said. "Now, back to G-E-D."

The stage manager stuck her head out in the hall. "You're up, Cee," she said, and Cecilia got to her feet. "Beginning of Act Two."

Tyler called back to say he couldn't meet them that night, but Kix looked so disappointed that she said he could come over and she'd run his songs with him. He wanted to bring a pizza, but she told him no dairy products before singing. "Here I've been loading up on milk," he said. "They push it at the House, being healthy and all."

"Healthy, but not good for voices," she said. "Bring Chinese instead." She knew it would make him feel adult and equal, and, having received his rehearsal pay, he could probably afford it. She'd felt a little of that when Jack had let her pay, as if she were his equal in professional success.

"Pop?" he asked, placing two small white bags on her kitchen counter.

"I'll make tea," she offered. "'Throat-coat' tea," she said. "Some singers swear by it."

"See, I knew I needed to learn the tricks of the trade," he said, eager.

"You really have a nice place," he said, wandering out to the living room.

"You've been here before," she said.

"I knew it was nice, but I didn't know how nice until I went to some of my friends' apartments."

She brought plates and utensils to the dining table and opened the cartons.

He was sitting at the piano. "A couple of the younger people in the show have invited me over," he said, by way of explanation. "Listen to this!"

He pounded out the opening trills of "Rhapsody in Blue." "Aaron is teaching me," he said. "I can't believe the guy looks like a basketball star and does all this artsy-fartsy stuff, singing and dancing. He says I have natural talent. What do you think?"

"I think you do, Kix," she said, releasing a sigh. The kid had talent and energy and also, it appeared, the desire. "Come, let's eat, and then we can work on your talents, plural."

He'd brought fried rice and chicken with cashews, and he ate about three-quarters of it. When they finished, she looked in the bags for her fortune cookie.

"Don't believe in 'em," he said. "All they ever tell you is what you want to hear." She frowned, a little disappointed not to have a written predictor of their coming success. Of course, she thought, that was what she wanted to hear. "Have almond instead," he said, and she grabbed one and held it up to him like a glass of champagne.

"To your debut," she said.

Kix cleared the table, rinsed the dishes, and pulled out his guitar. In the show, he was to accompany himself, but there would be a second guitar backing him. He played a few chords and launched into the opening lines of the first of his two numbers.

"Stop!" she cried. "Never sing without warming up. You could hurt your voice. Professionals warm up."

He put his guitar aside, and she ran him through twenty minutes of warm-ups, showing him first how to massage his face and neck, open and close his jaw in exaggerated yawns, stretch his arms over his head and behind his back to open his chest. "Wake up, voice!" she sing-songed, Mother Goose–style, making fun of herself and their contortions. Then she ran him through scales, working on pushing his notes forward, what she called, "freeing his voice." He had good range, an octave either way from middle C, and in the course of an hour Cecilia heard a subtle, but to her ear substantial, improvement in his tone. It was always easier, she thought, to hear other people's improvement than your own.

"That's enough for today," she said around nine.

"We didn't sing my songs!" Kix protested.

"That's what Mike is for," she said. "I'll help you with your singing. But the performance—how he wants it done—that's Mike's business."

Kix looked at her quizzically.

"Mike will tell you how he wants the songs shaped, the phrasings, the volume, and tempo and all of that. You know, to fit the character you're playing."

"Got it," Kix said. "Sometimes I forget I'm not just playing me."

"Right," she said. She could appreciate how difficult that might be for a beginner. For herself, her own persona was sufficiently different from her role—a gregarious, comedic party-girl type—that she had more trouble getting into the character than getting out. She had three up-tempo numbers that she shared with various cast members, and a power ballad with the leading man, the poignant climax of the show where the comedy turned serious.

Kix paused at the door. "Thank you," he said, and she waved him off. Kix was an eager student. It had been kind of fun to watch him try to follow her directions and to get results. "No, really. Thank you," he repeated.

For the next week, Kix and Cecilia worked every night, not on his numbers, but on his singing. Jack invited himself over one night, bringing a bottle of wine, but didn't open it when Cecilia said she didn't drink alcohol during shows. He offered to go get ice cream, and Kix winked at Cecilia and then piped up that he was avoiding dairy for the same reason.

"I thought the theater was supposed to be fun!" Jack complained, but good-naturedly. He sat on the couch and listened intently, despite his professed lack of musical training.

"Might learn something for the courtroom," he'd said when Cecilia'd said he might be bored.

It wasn't even eight thirty when Kix yawned in exaggerated weariness and said he was too tired to go on.

"More than anything, a singer needs sleep," Cecilia said.

"Do you think I'm a singer now?" he asked, his eyes soft with what might have been tears.

"You're in good voice," she said.

"So I'm a singer?"

"A singer sings," Jack said, as if applying the law of a case.

Kix let loose an arpeggio, holding on the fourth note until he was totally out of air.

"That's it," she said. "You're a singer as long as you're singing."

"Are you coming to opening night?" Kix asked Jack.

Jack looked at Cecilia, as if he'd been waiting for her invitation but was grateful to have his. "Wouldn't miss it," he said.

"That would be great!" Kix said. "I'd love for my mom to see it, but . . ."

"I think she has her hands full," Jack said.

"Have you talked to her?" Kix asked.

"Just once. What about you. Have you called your mother?"

"Just to tell her I was okay, and Charmaigne was okay."

"I hope you said you loved her," Jack said steadily, as if that was the key piece of evidence, not to be left out. What good advice, Cecilia thought. How unusual for a man of his age to give it.

"Yeah," Kix said hurriedly. "I'm pretty sure I did."

"Pretty sure isn't good enough," Jack said. "Call her tonight. Tell her. And tell Charmaigne to call her." From his commanding tone, Cecilia concluded that Jack knew from personal experience the importance of his mandate.

"Yes, sir," Kix said, and his tone was not sarcastic, but sincere. "I hear you."

When Kix left, Jack turned to Cecilia. "Is it true about the wine?"

"That's the deal," she said. "Open it. I'll have tea."

"I'm invited to stay?" he asked.

"For tea," she said, and he smiled a toothy grin.

"Tea for two," he sang. He was off-key, but she didn't care. Jack O'Malley was the kind of person who wouldn't hesitate to say, "I love you," and she felt an unmistakable twinge of anticipation.

twenty-two

Tech week was exhausting, and Cecilia saw Kix only at rehearsals and Jack not at all. The choreographer was changing his mind more than Cecilia thought professional. Some of the actors were whining about their costumes or their mikes, the authors and composers were tinkering with lines and notes, and tensions were generally higher than usual. It was, after all, a world premiere. What critic worth his or her salt would rave uncritically, when given the chance—in fact, the mandate—to dissect and analyze, appraise and condemn? Backstage, some of the less experienced actors speculated on what the critics would say. The four leads tried to ignore their constant worry, but the pervasive fretfulness on set was infectious. Every night Cecilia felt the apprehension as a stiffness in her shoulders that no amount of self-massage could alleviate. Only Kix, who arguably had the most at stake, next to the author/composer, seemed unfazed by the nervous tensions of the week. Before and after rehearsals, he opened his case on the street corner outside the theater and played his part for real, until the germophobic director, worried about keeping his cast well and in good voice, saw him and immediately put a stop to it.

On the day of the first dress rehearsal, the pressure of the week's accumulated anxiety erupted inside Cecilia like a geyser. She'd thought she was doing so well, working with Kix, rehearsing her own parts, calming her fellow actors during breaks, but she woke up with a stress blister on her upper lip and a tremor in her hands. She felt flushed from the neck up, red, and splotchy. Stage fright! She knew the symptoms. She'd had them when she was young, they'd subsided during the successes of her brief career, and they'd returned after *Rumplestilt's Kin*. She hadn't had any of these during rehearsal, nearly convinced that her talking to Dr. Richardson had possibly made a difference, even if not the initial difference she'd been looking for. She could see how admitting her terror to him, and her feelings about her mother, had in fact freed her. So why was she in this distress? Could she recover by opening night? Panicked, she called Tyler. He tried to reassure her with his litany of all the greats, from Sir Laurence Olivier to Barbra Streisand, who were said to have had severe stage fright.

"So we're all sick! Have Barbra come sing my role," she said, desperate.

"I thought you said the music director loved your work," Tyler tried.

"They say these things to encourage us," she said stubbornly.

"Not in the big leagues, my friend. No false praise, no kid gloves. Mike calls 'em as he sees 'em and you know it."

"All of a sudden, I'm so nervous. I'm hot, I'm flushed. I don't know what to do with myself."

"Stop whining, will ya?" The anger and frustration in his voice stopped her short.

She took a deep breath.

"That's better," he said.

"I'm sorry," she said. "Will you come tonight and tell me what you really, really think?"

"Will you believe me?" he asked.

"Yes," she promised. "You're the only one I can trust."

"Go for a run," he said. "I'll see you tonight."

"Marvelous, dahling," he reported in a flamboyant greeting when she met him in the theater lobby after they were let go for that

night. Her symptoms had not exactly subsided but at least had settled into only a mild roil. She'd felt them, but Tyler insisted they
would not be detectable by the audience, even an audience of critics. Later, sitting across the table from her at a coffee shop, Tyler
assured her that the stress blister had been completely camou-
flaged by the extra street makeup she'd plastered on it and would
be totally invisible, even from the front row.

"I guess I'll survive," she said. "You think a girl would get over it
by now."

"You'd think!" he agreed.

"What I don't get is how cool Kix is. You know, some of the
people in this cast are . . . I mean, they're no slouches. He's making
a helluva debut."

"Sometimes ignorance is bliss," Tyler agreed. "He has, quite literally, nothing to lose. No one has any expectations for him. No past
glory to live up to."

"Or to overcome."

Tyler nodded. "So he doesn't know what he doesn't know. He's
never forgotten a lyric, or watched his scene partner skip four
pages of essential dialogue or opened the paper to a bad review."

"He has no idea what he's missing!" she tried to laugh, but they
both knew that the memory of *Rumplestilt's Kin* loomed. "I hadn't
thought of it that way."

"He sounded good."

"Mike, the music director, told him in front of everyone that he
was amazing."

"Is he?"

"He does sound better each day," she said.

"Then he has you to thank for that," Tyler said.

"That's what he told Mike, which was sweet of him." She thought
for a minute and then, shy in front of her coach, said, "I actually do
think I helped. I just tried to do for him what you've done for me."

"Each one, teach one," Tyler said, and she rolled her eyes at him.

The afternoon of the Preview opening, Cecilia was restless and fidgety. It wasn't that she was imagining a disaster necessarily, but she was having trouble imagining the performance at all. What she'd told Dr. Richardson at her sessions during the rehearsals was that she was feeling confident, doing what she knew how to do, and that it felt good to have experience and to pass it on. With the exception of her minor breakdown on the day of the dress rehearsal, what she'd said was true. If it hadn't been for Tyler's encouragement, she probably would've thanked the good doctor and quit again, but Tyler thought she should give herself the luxury of Dr. Richardson's support—she'd scoffed at the word—during what he called her "comeback."

She wondered if the pressure was finally going to get to Kix. It would have to hit him soon. How could it not? This was a big break for him. Huge. It was bigger than asking a stranger for sixty bucks, and a failure here would mean much more than merely needing to find another mark. She dialed his cell phone.

"Cee!" he answered. "I'm telling you, I can't wait for tonight! A real audience!"

"You've done real audiences before," she reminded him, a bit of a reversal of the conversation they'd had not all that long ago, when she'd sung with him at Water Tower.

"As you say, this time the audience pays first," he laughed. "And this is my Chicago stage debut!"

"There's no reason to be nervous, Kix," she said, aware she sounded maternal. "You've worked hard, and you sound great."

There was a pause, and she realized that he'd not said the word *nervous*. He'd said he "couldn't wait." She was the one who had been paralyzed with fear for years, fleeing from auditions and seeing ghosts in the back row. Kix wasn't nervous! Probably wouldn't be! He'd steadied his hand any number of times to slip a loose bill from a drunk's wallet, and he'd stared Cecilia herself into her purse for sixty bucks. The boy had nerves of steel, honed perhaps not by success so much as by necessity. To run the con, you had to believe in yourself, and it helped if your survival depended on it. Was acting on a stage any different? Just a well-orchestrated and elaborate con.

"You're not nervous, are you, Cee?" The concern in his voice touched her. "'Cause if you are, I could come over. I could give you a massage or something."

The kid had solid instincts. She could almost feel him kneading her shoulders and back.

"That's a great idea, Kix. There's a new walk-in massage place here in the neighborhood. I should give it a try. That's exactly what I'll do. I'm not nervous," she lied, "but at my age, all that choreography is taking its toll."

"Yeah, I didn't think you'd be nervous, exactly, being a professional and all. But you haven't done it in a while, and I know when I haven't picked—well, you know—but see, that's when I'm out of practice. We've been practicing. Now we get to do it for real. And, in all honesty, Cee, what I think, you are the very best in the show. You really know what you're doing out there."

They arranged to meet for tea an hour before the call, and then Cee went to the massage place in her neighborhood, where you didn't need an appointment. She was assigned a small man who bowed slightly and spoke with an accent. He appeared to her to be Thai, and when he asked, "What you do today?" she blurted out that she was singing in an opening night at the Goodman, and only later realized that he could've been asking her only what kind of massage she wanted. The menu listed a dozen different kinds, including Reiki, stone, oil, traditional Thai, aromatherapy.

"We sing," he said and led her to a dimly lit room, a candle in one corner and a beautiful array of brass bowls on a small table opposite. She'd heard of the Tibetan Singing Bowls, but she'd never actually heard one.

"Fifth chakra, throat," he said, picking up a bowl and striking it, the bowl vibrating with a perfect G. "Fourth chakra, heart," he said, picking up another bowl and striking F. She stared at him, not

239

knowing how she was supposed to react. "Perhaps it is the third chakra," he said knowingly and struck a third bowl, a fine E.

"Third?" she asked.

"Manipura," he said. "Where the butterflies are."

She smiled weakly. She'd studied the mechanics of singing, not the mysticism of it. She changed from her jogging clothes into the loose gown the masseur gave her and sat on the edge of the table. The man played a few of the bowls, mixing a variety of sounds and notes, and urging her to relax. Then he settled on one bowl, the E bowl, and walked around her, so that the sound came from all the points of a circle of which she was the center. Then he played in front of her, the bowl not far from her solar plexus. She'd come for a massage and was at first inclined to tell the man to cut the hocus-pocus, but her breathing became slow, and she felt the tension draining from her body. Although she was sitting, she was nearly asleep when she noticed that the sound had faded away, and he asked her to lie on the table. He then began the body work of the massage, and she felt herself melting under the combination of his alternating pressure and light touch. She was in a trance, when he broke the silence by again playing the singing bowl. He left her then, "Stay as long as you like," he said. "We have released all negative energy. You are in balance and you are safe. Namaste."

She knew enough to mumble "Namaste," wishing the man the peace he had indeed brought to her. It took a while before she was ready to take a hot shower, dress, wrap a lightweight white-and-gold scarf around her throat, and head to the coffee shop near the theater to meet Kix.

When she walked in, he jumped up and starting waving at her, even though the place was neither big nor particularly crowded. It was after five, and most people who would be meeting friends would be meeting in bars, not coffee shops. Although she wasn't hungry, she knew Kix always was, and so she bought a boxed turkey croissant sandwich and joined him at the table.

"Thanks!" he said. "They were having grilled cheese sandwiches for lunch at the Home," he said, "but I just had a jelly sandwich and an apple," he said. "Here, this is for you." He reached down by the chair and held out a yellow rose wrapped in stiff clear plastic, with a yellow bow. "Yellow, the color of the energy of the Third Chakra, where your self-esteem resides," he said. "Wearing yellow boosts self-confidence."

"That's on the GED?" she asked, intrigued that he would be aware of something as esoteric as chakras, which she'd just experienced for the first time that day, and that he would pick out her troubled solar plexus for this attention.

"No, there's an Indian kid at the Home. Ran away when he came out. He's been telling me all sorts of stuff."

"How sweet of you, Kix," she said, leaning over to give him a peck on the cheek. He immediately blushed, and she quickly moved on. "I just came from a massage, with singing bowls."

"*OMMM*," he hummed.

"Something like that," she said, and they settled into their respective silences.

At the theater, they joined Mike around the piano for warm-ups, then parted ways. When she got to the women's dressing room, the younger women were huddled around a huge vase of red roses, interspersed with baby's breath. They were the expensive kind of red roses, on straight two-foot stems, and there were at least two dozen of them. One of the young women was lifting the white card that hung from the raffia bow around the neck of the clear vase. "For Cee!" she cried, and it took Cecilia a second to recognize the women were looking at her. "Who are they from?" they asked, almost in unison.

"I can't imagine," Cecilia said.

"They've got to be from your boyfriend," Donna said.

"Don't have one," she said, hoping she didn't sound defensive.

"If they were mine, they'd be from my parents," one of the girls said. "But they're out of the country," she said, excusing them.

Aware she was being studied, Cecilia opened the little white envelope, and lost her breath when she read, "I love you. Jack."

twenty-three

From the wings, Cecilia heard a rise in applause as Kix made his bow to the audience, and then Aaron, the other leading lady, and she entered stage left as a threesome and parted the rest of the cast for their curtain call.

While it wasn't, strictly speaking, opening night, it was the first performance before a paying audience of a musical never before performed on any stage, anywhere, and the audience rose to its feet in appreciation. A stagehand brought spring bouquets to each of the three leads, and Cecilia waved to the audience as if in a parade. She felt giddy—for the authors, of course, and for the production and the rest of the cast, but mostly, and especially, for herself. She'd performed well, and she'd enjoyed it. She searched the audience for Jack but through the lights couldn't see past the first few rows. When the curtain closed, she stayed onstage hugging and cheering the triumphant cast members the way a championship team congratulates itself after a big game. As soon as she'd hugged everyone but Kix—he was constantly surrounded by cast and crew congratulating him on his debut—she hurried back to the dressing room to change for the after-show party. The author and composer, a team who'd been together for sixteen years, had invited the cast, the band, and the crew to a modern hotel near the theater for drinks. Jack would be there.

She took a little extra time to wash her face and reapply her makeup and dressed quickly in black jeans with a sterling silver belt and a black T-shirt. She anchored a colorful silk scarf around her shoulders with a gaudy beaded pin that had belonged to her grandmother and was about to step out to the lobby when she was swept off her feet.

"Yes!!!!" Kix cried, swinging her around.

"Put me down!" she cried. She'd had no idea he was so strong, but he was clearly pumped up.

He put her down, panting. "Wow! That was the best, Cee! The best!!!"

"You were great, Kix," she agreed, for the moment totally caught up in his excitement.

"You were the best, Cee!" Kix said. "You're the one! You deserve . . . everything!!"

He hugged her again, and she felt a bittersweet joy, like at the end of a race: the exhilaration, the spent effort, the pain, the replay, the crash. The end and the beginning, both. The opening night before The Opening Night. Her emotions whirled inside her. She reached for his cheek. "You're full of lipstick!" she said.

He rubbed at it furiously. "Thanks. I'll take care of it," he said and dashed off. "I'll meet you in the lobby," he called back over his shoulder.

She made her way there, but at first she didn't see Jack, only Tyler and his new friend, Henry. They were talking with her two brothers, who'd come with their wives to show support on her first night back.

"Beautiful, darling," Tyler said.

She sucked in a breath, for the first time feeling that familiar queasiness, waiting for the other critical shoe to drop. "Okay?" she asked tentatively, some of the backstage excitement slipping into her old insecurity.

Tyler looked at her. "Marvelous." He furrowed his brow as if to emphasize that his was a serious assessment.

"Really?"

"Don't beg, darling. It doesn't become you."

"You were terrific," her brothers said, almost in unison, and Henry agreed with a showy bow. Just then, Jack walked up to them, his arms outstretched toward Cecilia.

Words escaped her, and she looked up at him, shaking her head. He wiggled his fingers. "Come here."

"I've never seen roses like those," she said.

"I've never heard singing like yours," he answered, and she threw her arms around his neck. When she broke away, he held his arm around her waist. Her brothers beamed.

"About time, you two," Tyler said. "Shall we?"

The brothers begged off the party, pleading work early the next day, but the rest of them found the party in a room off the main bar at the hotel. There were probably sixty people there, including all the spouses and friends, and Tyler and Henry offered to bring drinks to a table Jack claimed for them. Tyler and Henry returned with a red wine for Jack and a club soda for Cecilia. Kix joined them and, without fanfare, Tyler handed him a half-glass of champagne, which he accepted, raising his glass in toast, but then he spotted the carving table in the far corner, where a chef in a white hat sliced a sirloin roast for sandwiches, and another tossed fettuccini to order with add-ins of shrimp, chicken, ham, baby peas, and mushrooms. "Food," Kix said, abandoning the champagne.

"We'll go with you," Tyler said, nudging Henry. "A star needs an entourage."

When they were out of earshot, Jack said, "I think he is. The kid has something special. I'm no expert, but onstage, he's got a lot of charisma."

"I think you know something about charisma," she said.

"Daniels," he said, naming the florist that had delivered the roses. "And you, my friend, were superb."

She sighed. "Boy, I'm so glad it's over."

"Technically," he said, "it hasn't started."

"For me it has. I'm back on the horse." She cleared her throat. "I think I gave a pretty good performance."

"Great."

"Pretty good," she said. "In some ways, if it weren't for Kix, it would be my show. I mean, it's that kind of part."

"He's got the personality for it, that's for sure. But also the voice. And he has you to thank for that, I think."

"And Mike, and Tyler, and the guy who got him out of jail. Kind of a group project," she laughed.

He took her chin in his hand. "You were wonderful," he said. "Wonderful." He gave her a light kiss on the lips.

She glanced around, hoping neither Tyler nor Kix saw. "Ja-ack," she whispered.

"Don't worry," he said, chuckling. "I'm the slow and methodical type."

Jack drove everyone home, dropping Cecilia last. She was both surprised and disappointed when he stopped in front of her building and ran around to open the door. When he offered his hand, she took it, and he gave her a tender peck on the cheek, reminding her of a teenage boy. He waved good night and promised to call the next day.

The roses opened gradually over the next five days, and Jack called every afternoon, before she left for the theater. He bought a ticket for each performance and sat in different rows. Under the lights, she couldn't see him, but she knew he was there, and she knew that he would be, as long as she wanted him to be.

After five preview performances, the theater was dark for two nights, and then the real Opening Night, to be marked by the producer's opening party. Despite cancelling her appointment with Dr. Richardson, another Thai massage and a meditation with the singing bowls kept her nerves in check. Although she'd thought the show had opened strong, she felt that it jelled during previews and was optimistic that the reviews would be positive. Rather than dreading Opening Night, she found herself looking forward to it. Although it was probably assumed between them, she specifically asked Jack to the party and then realized she had nothing appropriate to wear. She called Donna, the other leading lady, and they spent the day before shopping.

"Remember the roses!" Donna said. "Jack will love this!" Her friend hardly knew Jack, but she caused Cecilia to face the truth: she was buying a new dress for the evening with Jack, not for the critics or producers or other must-meet mavens who would be at the party. The dress was a maize yellow satin, knee-length, and scoop-necked, with long sleeves and a low back. It was belted with a yellow satin flower with a center of small gold balls.

"Not too much of a diva?" she asked Donna.

"Not on you," Donna said generously. "Besides, that's our business. People want their stars to look like stars."

Although, strictly speaking, she didn't need to, Cecilia studied the price tag.

"I don't care how much it is," Donna said, although Cecilia knew Donna would indeed care if it were her money. "If you have to sing on the street to buy it, buy it. It's you!"

Cecilia's heart skipped a beat when Donna mentioned singing on the street, and then she realized it was a fun story, not an embarrassing one. Singing on the street was the kind of thing Donna wouldn't hesitate to do to advance her career. She'd gotten her start as a flying monkey and a Dorothy understudy at an amusement park in Kansas.

"Been there, done that," Cecilia said, wondering how much she should tell her friend.

"I'll get Kix and we'll all pitch in," Donna suggested.

"Okay, okay. I'll buy the dress," she laughed. They stopped for a cup of tea at a café and Cecilia told her about singing with Kix in the subway.

"I wondered how you two got so chummy," she said. "He's special, don't you think?"

Cecilia agreed that he was. He even knew about yellow.

247

Being theater people, most of the cast could convince themselves that opening night was the first performance of *Subway*, and so there was heightened excitement backstage before the curtain. Two of the girls were angry at their boyfriends for not sending flowers, one stood nervously shaking herself out like a swimmer before a race, and another energized her manipura with boat and warrior poses.

Cecilia felt oddly detached from it all. They'd done the show five times already for live audiences. She knew what she could do, and she would do it. Only if she thought past the final curtain did she get a few of the familiar butterflies in her solar plexus, and those she welcomed: Jack! She was looking forward to the party and was only slightly disappointed that he hadn't replaced the sagging red roses with a fresh bouquet. Sometimes her expectations were way out of whack. She hadn't expected the first one. Why on earth would she expect a second? As to the performance in front of her, it felt more a chore than a challenge. She hadn't seen Dr. Richardson in two weeks. Tomorrow, she would have to ask him what he thought that meant. Ever since she'd said she thought her mother didn't love her, he'd been more willing, she thought, to speak up.

Because the author and composer had a following, the official opening night of their new musical was sold out, and the cast, energized by positive expectations, were at the top of their form. Cecilia could tell by the thunder of the applause that the audience loved the show. When Kix bent on one knee, hands spread toward an open guitar case, the crowd rose to its feet, and there was no lift in the applause for her own bow, the crowd simply couldn't make more noise. There was no doubt in her mind: Kix was a star. Like a parent at a law school graduation, she marveled at how the boy had become a man. She would never know for certain everything that had brought him to this point, and she would never be a hundred-percent certain of his innocence, but she was never a hundred-percent certain about anything, including her own performances and her own talent. She could, she decided, live with that small uncertainty; at the moment, the only thing of which she was certain was Jack.

The producers were, of course, ecstatic, and the party was noisy. Tyler, Henry, and Jack had gone over, as soon as the applause stopped, to grab a good table. Kix escorted Cecilia. He'd worn a nice shirt to the author's party the week before; today, he sported a tweedy gray sports jacket, black silk shirt, and cuffed gray wool slacks. He wore a pair of expensive loafers, shined, and his red-blond hair was nicely combed. "Wow," she exclaimed. "You look great."

"Donna pointed me toward the best resale shop," he boasted. "You wouldn't believe the stuff that was there."

"Did Donna go with you?" she asked, as much jealous as embarrassed that it hadn't occurred to her to take Kix shopping. He always seemed to be so self-sufficient.

"She offered, but you know me, I like to do my own thing."

"You did well," she said.

Jack was waiting near the door when they arrived, holding a presentation bouquet of yellow roses, buds down, in his right hand. "I see a theme," he said, presenting his offering to her.

"Good color!" Kix said.

"Beautiful!" he said.

"I meant the flowers. They go good with the dress," Kix said.

"I meant the girl, Kix. Get lost," he said and winked.

"Happy to," Kix said, skipping off toward the buffet.

"I think he's in it only for the food," Cecilia said after him.

"You were wonderful," Jack said. "Again." He took her arm and guided her toward the bar, against the wall in the middle of the room. They were stopped along the way half a dozen times for Cecilia to accept the greetings of guests she didn't know, guests of other cast members, no doubt, obligated to like the show. But their praise sounded sincere. "Loved your performance" rather than, "Congratulations," and while she didn't feel the thrill she'd felt at the after-party for *Rumplestilt's Kin*, she thought it was because she knew that this wasn't the audience that mattered. She'd been burned once, and badly, but when Matt James, the critic for the *Chicago Tribune*, stopped her to say he nearly cried during her climactic duet, she knew this was going to be different. Jack stood by her side, his hand at her elbow, ready to escort her like a queen to her next loyal subject. Unlike her mother, who would've felt compelled to add her own opinion—"all those lessons I gave her finally paid off! I'm so proud of her!"—Jack didn't interrupt, and he didn't take his eyes off her, the woman of the hour.

At the bar, she ordered club soda and he a scotch on the rocks. They headed toward the far corner of the room, where Tyler had saved a high cocktail table with a candle in a globe in its center. As they approached, she saw Tyler and Henry sitting farther from each other than normal, and a salt-and-pepper-haired woman in a navy suit. She had a giant glass of 7-Up or club soda in front of her. When it dawned on her who she must be, Cecilia looked up at Jack.

"How did you manage that?" she said.

"Connections," he said.

"Does he know?" Cecilia asked.

"I didn't want to worry him," Jack said. "It just seemed like the right thing to do. Although it interferes a little with my other hopes for tonight," he said, slipping his hand under the low cut back of her dress and giving her a tickle. She saw Tyler watching them, and she waved to cover up what otherwise might have been a squeal. He winked at her. "But I trust we have the rest of our lives, and this is a special night for Kix."

"And for his mom," Cecilia said, for the first time missing her mother. "Mine always loved opening nights," she said.

"And for his mom," Jack agreed, just as they approached the table. "The last time she saw him, he was fresh from the encounter with the father. It wasn't a pretty sight." As soon as they got to the table, Tyler was on his feet to adore her and the dress. Henry studied Jack appreciatively, and Kix's mother covered her mouth and nose with her hands, as if she might cry.

"Tyler told me everything you did for Kix and Charmaigne," Pamela Gordon said. "I don't think I can ever thank you enough."

"He's a very special kid," Cecilia said. "Have you seen him yet?"

"Not yet," Tyler answered for her. "Henry and I are going to circulate for a while, and Jack's going to bring him over."

Cecilia sat next to Kix's mother, who, despite her wide-set eyes, looked so absolutely ordinary that Cecilia couldn't imagine picking her out of a host of women at the faculty club. *There's Pamela Gordon. Did you hear the professor beats her and molests his own children? Why does she stay with that brute? Why doesn't she do something?* Cecilia studied the woman. She was ordinary, yes, but if you looked closely enough at her blue eyes, you could see a sort of startled fear, a deep remorse.

The men left, leaving Cecilia with Mrs. Gordon. "I can't thank you enough," the woman began again, and Cecilia felt uncomfortable.

"Did you know he had so much talent?" Cecilia asked.

"No, no. It's not something that he ever expressed an interest in at school," she said. "But my mother sang in the church choir and had a little career before she had me." She giggled nervously, like an embarrassed girl. "I guess I sort of spoiled it for her. In those days, she couldn't pursue her passion, as she called it, with babies to take care of." Her face darkened. "You saw Charmaigne?" she asked.

"Lovely girl," Cecilia said, "but I haven't seen her since she left Abby with me. I imagine you have your hands full."

"I do love babies," Mrs. Gordon said and looked around anxiously. Cecilia spotted Jack and Kix before she did.

"There," Cecilia pointed, and Mrs. Gordon got to her feet. She started crying, one hand over her mouth, one hand holding her stomach, as if she'd been stabbed. Kix broke with Jack and stopped. He looked down, then raised his chin and met his mother's eyes. Shoulders back, he walked slowly toward her, Cecilia unable to read his thoughts. Was he pleased to see his mother? Embarrassed by her? Worried about what she thought of his performance? Angry? Cecilia held her breath and was relieved when Kix fell into his mother's arms, his head on her shoulder, purple- red in the face, eyes squeezed tightly shut, crying.

Jack signaled to Cecilia, and they left the two of them alone. Cecilia imagined what her mother might say to her on this occasion, but before she could fully play it out, Jack started talking with Donna and her boyfriend, and then the producers, a husband and wife team, launched into short speeches welcoming everyone and thanking the cast and crew for their hard work. They again introduced the cast, who raised their hands and waved to the crowd to receive another round of applause. When the producer-wife introduced Kix, the crowd broke into hoots and hollers. Cecilia couldn't see over their heads, but Jack reported that Pamela was beaming, and that Kix had both hands in the air like a basketball star, high-fiving whoever was standing near him. "I'm going to drive Pamela down to Normal tonight," he said.

"Full service!" Cecilia said. "That's pretty amazing. Want me to come with you?" They'd not been alone all night. At least on the ride home, they'd be together, just the two of them. It seemed to her a "wifely" thing to do.

"You and Kix need to stay here, get some sleep, read the reviews in the morning." It sounded like a husbandlike response, along the lines of, "If you watch the kids during the game, I'll take them to the park now."

"Actually, I do have an appointment in the morning," she said. "Aren't you coming back tonight?"

"That's the plan," he said. He draped his arm around her shoulder. "But even if I come back tomorrow, you'll wait for me, won't you?"

She nodded. Whether she'd ever admitted it out loud or not, she'd been waiting a long time for someone like Jack.

Cecilia counted sheep, visualized a sandy island beach, counted backward from a hundred, hummed "*Ommmmm*," but couldn't escape the excitement of the evening or the anticipation of the morning. When she finally fell asleep, it was as if into a deep black hole, and she woke up with a start. It was after nine! The *Chicago Tribune* had been at her door for hours, its unread review like the sound of a tree falling in the forest with no one to hear. She shoved aside the invading "what-ifs?" and dashed to her door, where she quickly retrieved the paper and dropped the first two sections in her front hall, opening the arts section on her way to the kitchen. The review was in the bottom left, under the headline, "New Musical Births a New Star." The critic who'd praised her performance just last night was crazy about Kix. Loved his "naturalness" onstage, his "energy," his "charisma," and his "sweet but powerful" voice. "Only 18, Kix Gordon makes his debut at a level many seasoned actors never achieve," Matt James wrote. He picked on a couple of phrasings he thought could be improved but otherwise did not find fault with what he called an "auspicious beginning." He said nice things, too, about Donna and the leading man, and, finally, a note for her. "It's great to see and hear Cecilia Morrison back on the Chicago stage," he wrote, without saying it had been nearly ten years, and, more important, without saying or speculating as to why. "She has prodigious range and tone and knows how to show off her substantial talent to best advantage."

Satisfied, Cecilia made coffee and reread, more slowly this time, the review. Tyler called.

"Sorry to call so late," he bubbled. "We slept late, and I just read Matt's review. Fantastic, honey! He loves you!"

"I wouldn't go that far, Ty," she said. "I think he said essentially that I was well trained."

"Of course you were!" Tyler agreed. "Trained you myself!"

"Apparently my training shows," she said, a little testily.

"Only you, darling, could find something to complain about in that review. It's very positive. Period. It's far better than getting reamed, or worse yet, ignored. He's got a job to do, so he takes tiny little digs that only someone like you could possibly interpret. And what about Kix!"

"He's in love with him!" she said.

"Fabulous. A good review from Matt James the first time out. Makes him very employable in this town."

"What did you think of his mother?" she asked. They'd had so little time one-on-one, she wasn't sure she'd gotten a good feel for the woman.

"Very tender," Tyler said in his lower, more serious voice. "Like a lost puppy. You can see how she used to be a regular person, trained as a special ed teacher, I think, but then got beaten down."

"She said that?"

"Not about being beaten down. That's my take. She said she was proud of Kix for striking out on his own at such a young age, and being so capable. She said, and I'll quote, because it was so striking, 'Me, I just lost my courage.' She said she didn't know when or how it happened, and I didn't push her. About then, I think you guys came over."

"Jack took her home," she said.

"Jack is a helluva guy," Tyler said. "You're very lucky. Do me a favor, though, honey, and don't blow it."

"How could I blow it?" she said, giving up any pretense of denying that there was something between them.

"You could get all depressed and poor-me, no-time-for-men-too-good-for-mortals."

"Me?" She thought his depiction of her both mean and wrong.

"The old you. The dark days are over," he said evangelically.

"I've never been too good for mortals!" she said. "I was trained— you, you're part of my training, don't forget—to be as perfect as possible. That wasn't my goal. It was . . ." She trailed off. She'd told Dr. Richardson she'd come to a new understanding of her mother, and she didn't want to take that back. Yes, her mother was a perfectionist, and, she had to admit, she herself was, too.

"Then welcome to the imperfect, but well-trained, human race," he said.

Dr. Richardson opened the door with what Cecilia thought was a contained smile. She assumed he read the papers, and that he'd read her reviews.

"Well, the good news is," she said, before she'd even settled on the couch, "we had a wonderful run of previews, a grand opening night, and we got a great review from the *Tribune*."

"Great," he said back to her.

"It is great, especially for Kix." She told him about all the accolades Kix was getting.

"How does that feel?" he asked.

"You mean am I jealous?" she asked.

Dr. Richardson shrugged. "Jealous?" he echoed. "How so?"

"I didn't say I was."

Dr. Richardson nodded.

"It's natural that when someone makes their debut, they get special notice," she said. "I'm definitely not jealous. I don't know why you'd say that."

"Just to be clear, Cecilia, I didn't use the word. You did."

She played the conversation back in her head. He was right. "Well, I'm not, and I wouldn't be. The point is, frankly, that was the best part for me. I loved coaching him."

"Then what about your own performance?" Dr. Richardson said. "How was that?"

"Good. I felt good," she said. "I had a case of nerves, and I went for a massage but ended up with a Thai guy who was into chakras and opening up by solar plexus, and, I know it's crazy stuff, but I felt better. The butterflies went away and I was just fine. If anything, it was a bit of a letdown. By the time we got to what was billed as opening night, we'd done the show five times, and it was kind of old hat."

"Old hat? Not a thrill?"

"Yeah," she said, with a grimace. "I hate to say it, but for me, it was no big sense of accomplishment. For a moment there, I missed my mother. She always got a thrill. She would've liked this. But for me, the real thrill, honestly, was in watching Kix."

"His accomplishment, not your own?"

"The best times were just singing together in my living room. He came over every night for about a week and a half, and I gave him a crash course on how to sing."

"You know how to sing," he said.

"I do. And," she laughed, "thanks to my mother, I know how to criticize."

"Putting perfectionism to good use?"

"There's a difference between destructive criticism and encouragement," she said, and he waited for her to say more. "Are you saying that I'm a better coach than a performer?"

Dr. Richardson looked around, as if to see if there was someone else in the room. "Did I say that?" he asked.

"I liked coaching," she said. "That's what . . . ," she hesitated, drawing out her thought, "I like to do."

"Is that your calling?" Dr. Richardson asked.

She caught her breath. "Wouldn't that be something?" she said. "After all this time, it turns out that I want to be my mother?"

"A version of your mother," Dr. Richardson said kindly. "In my business, we call it wanting to be yourself."

twenty-four

Wow. It was a total kick, man, being up there, singing for an audience like that, playing my part. I can't tell you how real I felt. How right. Cee, she taught me so much, and all the people in the cast, they treated me like a real professional, and I have to admit, getting that review was the icing on the cake. I hope I get to do this for the rest of my life. Although I did promise Jack that I would get the GED. I'll take the test next week, on Monday or Tuesday, and then Tyler says I should go to Columbia College here and get some formal training and some more experience, and I think I'll take his advice. These guys have been right so far. Might as well give it a go.

It was great to see my mom. She's not mad at us about putting my father away. He's not in jail yet, but he might as well be. I was afraid she would be mad. The newspapers in Normal went nuts, she said, and she's such a private person, she wouldn't even tell her pastor when my father hit her, for fear of embarrassing him. But she seemed relieved, even though she now has two babies and not much help. I told her that if she moved someplace away from Normal, maybe Charmaigne would come back and help her. Charmaigne would never go back to Normal, but if my mom moved, like to Chicago, I could help, too. I told her Jack has connections and Cee has money, and they both have big hearts, but she told me she has friends in Normal, and, thanks to Jack, support there, and the boys are doing fine, and that I shouldn't worry, and that I should call home every week. And I should tell Charmaigne she loves her.

Charmaigne called this morning. She didn't go to Ann Arbor, but she might. She's in Evanston now, hanging around Northwestern and waitressing at two different places. She didn't say where. She said she'd come to the show sometime, if I could get her a free ticket and she could get an afternoon off. She says she misses Abby. She surprised me by saying that she might go back to Normal, might even try to go to college there instead of Ann Arbor, but she wouldn't do anything until our father had been put away for good.

She's pretty cynical about my mom, which I totally get, but I don't know how to help her get over that. I don't know how you get over everything she's been through. Myself, I just got unbelievably lucky. I told her that if my career—what a word for singing!—continues, I'll be able to take care of her like I used to, so she won't have to waitress. As soon as I pass the GED, I'll coach her, although I think she's smarter than me, and then, whatever she wants to do, I'll help her. Even if I have to sing in a real subway again, I'd do it. I feel like I'm just warming up.

twenty-five

Therapy was always most interesting to him when it led someplace he hadn't suspected. Haverill Richardson watched from the window where six months ago he'd seen Chicago's newest star bum a light from his newest client. Today, they shared a stage, and what he'd thought were his client's aspirations had, by her account, become instead the kid's. He opened the *Chicago Tribune* and reread the review. Therapeutically speaking, he shouldn't have read the article before the session. He should've heard her side of it first, if she'd wanted to tell him, but he had been anxious for her success, and while he'd not attended the previews or opening night, he'd read the review with delight. He'd noted, however, the disproportionate amount of attention showered on the boy, given that his was a minor (although significant) role compared to Cecilia's and the other two mentioned in the critic's piece.

So, his client had conquered her fears and earned rave reviews. What could be a more meaningful or successful therapeutic outcome than that? Reconciliation with her mother's brand of love had been a meaningful, if predictable, result of all that talking, but how exciting, from his point of view, that Cecilia'd gone deeper, had discovered that what she was trained to do and was so very good at doing wasn't her heart's desire. She liked to teach, to coach, more than she liked to do. For so long, all of her nurturing qualities had lain dormant for reasons so convoluted that their first unraveling—it's the mother!—had seemed to be a sufficient revelation. But there had been more.

The phone rang, and Haverill smiled at it victoriously.

"Hello," he said, upbeat. It was, dependably, wonderfully, his daughter, and she, too, sounded upbeat.

"Congratulations!" she said. "Do I understand that you had something to do with that new musical at the Goodman? I take it your lady is the one with the training to deliver the song?"

"I never told you her name," he said, a little defensively, given that she was complimenting him. "How did you . . . ?"

"Read it online this morning. Everybody got praised, so I'm just guessing that yours is the one with the talent but perhaps not the passion."

"You got that from the review?" he asked.

"No. I got all that from how you described her. The more I thought about it, I thought that a person who really has a passion for the stage doesn't hole themselves up that long because of one lousy review. Even performers like Streisand, when they had their spells of stage fright, went into the studio. Your lady just didn't seem to want it enough."

"I thought it was the mother."

"Yeah, so did I, and I think that's probably part of it," Maddie agreed. "But getting so involved with those kids? Not having kids of her own? When I read that review, I just thought gee, I bet she feels terrific for having discovered that talent."

"Spoken as someone—don't yell at me—who doesn't have kids?"

"Yes," she said, and she didn't sound at all irritated. "I have clients all day long. Cecilia had nothing, until the kid, Kix, came along. I get all the opportunity to nurture that a person could possibly need. At least for now."

"How's the barge guy?"

"He's hanging in there. He's a real possibility," she said, laughing. "You might get to be a granddad yet." He decided not to take the bait. They hung up, and he realized she hadn't bugged him, either, about the marble. Sometimes, he thought, you didn't know who changed more, the client or the therapist, the storyteller or the listener.

He was reminded of a story a professor of his had told to the graduate students when they received their degrees. The gist of it was that when a person comes to you and tells you your story, your sins are forgiven, you are yourself healed. He had, until now, thought of this in prosaic terms: an alcoholic's story, which tempered his own taste for scotch and fine red wines; a client's black-and-white way of looking at the world, which forced him to see grays; another's stony silence, jarring him out of his own isolationist tendencies to an open and treasured relationship with his daughter. How he'd learned from his injured clients the importance of saying, "I love you."

That evening, he headed up the stairs with a renewed energy and determination. He felt entitled, finally, to this time to play. He had not, as he'd thought, deterred Roslyn from her creative career. It wasn't his fault that she'd chosen not to act when Maddie was born. It wasn't his fault that she'd put it off too long. Had acting been her priority then, had it been the passion that she later professed to have, then she would've done it. She would've found a way. She would've asked him, and he would've helped. It's true that he could've bugged her about it more, needled her into auditioning more and giving it a real try—he could've been more like Francine Morrison—but he hadn't, and he wasn't even sure he should have. Francine Morrison had pushed, and Cecilia had tried, and they'd both succeeded for some period of time, but when the going got tough, Francine had backed off, had seen, no doubt, that her daughter didn't have the fire in the belly her career required. Roslyn, too, had been good at it, damn good, but she didn't have the fire either. She'd been instead a wonderful mother, a wonderful wife.

There was a lot of freedom in knowing the difference between what you were good at doing and what you needed to do for your own soul. Whether Kix became a star or not, Cecilia had found what it was she wanted to do with her talent, and no review could take that away from her.

He picked up his cell phone and dialed Maddie's number. When she answered, he said, "There's something I want you to hear."

He put the phone down near the marble, and *tap-tap-tapped* at a corner until a piece broke away and he saw a vein in the marble he hadn't known was there.

When he picked up the phone again, she asked, "What's it going to be?"

He was amused at the answer that came to him. "It's going to be itself."

Acknowledgments

T his is my seventh novel, and the second to be published. I am excited for *Warming Up* to be on the debut list of She Writes Press, and I am grateful for their commitment to women's character-based fiction. Of all my works, I am particularly fond of this one because I've learned a lot from these characters about hope, faith, and love. Hope, in pursuing my own dreams of being a writer and a published author, and the difference between those two ambitions. Faith, in the taking pen to paper and chisel to marble and trusting the process enough to follow it where it leads. And love, of course, the essential ingredient in any creative effort and offered so generously by my fellow writers, my friends, my agent, and my family.

I would particularly like to thank Enid Powell and the members of her workshop, who heard and/or read every word of *Warming Up*, in draft and in revision, particularly Leilani Garrett, Deborah Hymanson, Scottie Kersta-Wilson, Carma Lynn Park, Ben Polk, Pam Spence, Eric Sutherlin, Randall Van Vynckt, and Elyssa Winslow. I am also grateful to Fred Shafer for teaching me how to write a novel, and the members of his workshop who did not read this novel, but who, over the years, have taught me so much about other manuscripts, including Lois Barliant, Sue Gilbert, Bill Kennedy, Julie Weary, and Anthony Roesch. Author! Author! writer, editor, and all-around raconteur Anne Mini has been a true writing friend ever since we met at Words & Music in New Orleans.

My weekly writing workout with poet Lucia Blinn helps immensely to keep me going, and I am also inspired by the creative successes of my family: my father, LeRoi E. Hutchings, who holds seventy chemical engineering patents but also designs furniture and mousetraps; my actress-sister, Donna Steele, and the theater she founded twelve years ago, Steel Beam Theatre in St. Charles, Illinois; and of course, my late mother, librarian Mary Jo Hutchings, who told the best bedtime stories, taught me how to spell, loved reading, and was nothing like Francine Morrison. My childhood friend, Barbara Lachenmaier Spangenberg, has, since the publication of my first book, *Courting Kathleen Hannigan*, read every new work with unfettered enthusiasm.

Barbara Scott's early interest in my manuscript inspired me, and Marjie Rynearson's draft of a screenplay based on *Warming Up* honed the story's edges. I was very pleased when the judges named *Warming Up* a Short List Finalist for the William Wisdom–William Faulkner Prize for an Unpublished Novel, 2011, and am grateful to the Pirates Alley Faulkner Society for providing such opportunities to writers.

As always, Dr. Robert Rynearson provided a useful check on the psychology of my characters. The Night Ministry introduced me to the harsh realities children face on the street, and I am happy that 10 percent of the sales of this book will go to supporting their mission among the homeless in Chicago.

My thanks to author-advocate and literary change agent, April Eberhardt, April Eberhardt Literary, for believing in me as a writer and for introducing me to She Writes Press, and to Chris Haralambidis, who supports so many of my creative projects with his generous photography. Thanks also to Shari Stauch, Shark Marketing, who has given me the marketing tools to tell people about Cecilia Morrison, Kix, Charmaigne, and baby Abby Gordon, and about Dr. Haverill Richardson, Jack O'Malley, and Tyler, the kind of supportive friends every creative person needs.

My deepest gratitude goes to my Haverill, my Jack, my Tyler, and my love, William R. Reed.

About the Author

Mary Hutchings Reed has always wanted to be a writer and remembers fondly a toy printing press with handset type on which she wrote her first poem. Now a novelist and playwright, in addition to practicing advertising, entertainment, and media law with Winston & Strawn, Chicago, her fiction has appeared in *ARS Medica, The Ligourian,* and *The Tampa Review. Warming Up* is her seventh novel and the second to find its way to print. Her first, *Courting Kathleen Hannigan,* was published in 2007, and her musical, *Fairways,* has been produced three times in the Chicago area, including its 2006 premiere at Steel Beam Theatre, St. Charles, Illinois.

Mary lives with her husband, Bill, in Chicago, where she was named "2012 Lawyer of the Year" in Advertising Law by Best Lawyers. She is a graduate of Brown University with a combined bachelor's degree in public policy making and a master's degree in economics. She earned her J.D. from Yale Law School. She is represented by April Eberhardt of April Eberhardt Literary of San Francisco.

Mary is pleased to donate 10 percent of the proceeds from the sale of *Warming Up* to The Night Ministry, which serves the homeless in Chicago, an organization she strongly supports. Visit Mary at maryhutchingsreed.com.